TOBIT'S DOG

Michael Nicholas Richard

TOBIT'S DOG

IGNATIUS PRESS   SAN FRANCISCO

Cover photograph by Milo Persic
With the assistance of Neil Westmoreland and James Bryant of Walkertown, NC

Cover design by Milo Persic

ISBN 978-1-58617-909-0
Library of Congress Control Number 2013920838
Printed in the United States of America ∞

One

A flood of scent unfolded around Okra. He wanted to follow the interwoven ribbons of odor in a compulsive exploration. There was the smell of food, the smell of other creatures, and the smell of the intriguing unknown.

In his mind they had as much depth, length, and variation as the sight of smoky tendrils rising from the smoldering piles of rubbish would have in a human mind. Some wove through the landscape, some of them roiled in place, and some of them spread low and wide like a mist.

He wanted to roll in them. He wanted to find that promise of food. He wanted to give in to this delight of the senses.

He did not. There was the master to consider. Okra glanced at the master. He knew the master did not want him wandering in this alluring place. Okra did not understand why this might be. It frustrated him. It made him quiver with restless yearning.

Finally he just sighed and reluctantly moved away from the sensory promise, closer to the master. Okra was often torn between what he wanted and what the master wanted. While Okra certainly feared the anger of the master, he was pulled more by some innate desire to please the master. Fear he could work around, but this desire to please the master was even more relentless than the compulsion of the senses.

Also, there were the treats.

The dog trotted up to the man and tilted his head inquisitively. A slight smile was returned to him, and just as importantly the hand went into the pocket of the overalls.

"That's a good boy", said the man as he pulled out a small piece of beef jerky and gave it to the dog. "I know this place is like a paradise to you, but it isn't. Not at all; there are dangers all around here, even snakes. Stay with me."

Tobit considered the dog as it considered him. Old folk called this sort of dog an Indian dog. They claimed the animals had been here and about for longer than white men or black men. Many of them were feral or half feral. Even when attached to a man or his family they could be anxious, hardheaded, and easily distracted.

He had found Okra as one of four puppies in a burlap sack along the banks of Ridge Creek. Someone had put the puppies in a sack with a brick and tossed it over the edge of the bank. Coursing between two low ridges, the creek had steeper banks than most creeks in the area, and to the great fortune of the puppies, the sack had snagged on the root of a tree. Only the brick was submerged in the water.

Tobit could not imagine why the culprit had just left them there; perhaps whoever it was simply did not think it worth the effort to climb down the bank and complete the job. The second stroke of luck for the puppies was that Tobit, hearing their plaintive squeals, climbed down the bank and rescued them before a rising tide finished what their erstwhile executioner had not.

Okra was the most contemplative of these puppies, and he was more intent on being with Tobit than the others. He had a very faint melanistic mask, beginning slightly black around his nose and long, dark whiskers, then fading quickly to a pale tan mixed with white. His body was mostly a golden tan, long legged, with a tightly curled tail, and with a rump seeming slightly higher than his shoulders, which was something Tobit noticed as common with what he called jumpy dogs. It was, however, the ears that were first noticed—long, tall, and erect ears.

After those extraordinary ears, the eyes were his most distinctive trait. They were so dark as to be nearly black, but with dark brown fur marking a thin line around them, almost the way a woman might apply makeup. Tobit had thought of them as "Egyptian" eyes because of the resemblance to the stylized eyes of ancient Egyptian art.

Those eyes were why Okra ended up staying with Tobit, who was not at all sure what he was going to do with these puppies. Times were difficult, but he could not bring himself to complete the grim task another had failed to do. A solution presented itself when, through a peculiar string of coincidences, a white professor from the Agricultural and Mechanical College in Raleigh turned up with an interest in the dogs.

The man explained that he was intrigued by the phenomenon of feral dogs across the world, and the way they seemed to be of similar size, build, and coloration. He brought pictures of dingoes, Canaan dogs, and pariah dogs from other parts of the world.

He also showed Tobit photos of the kennels and runs where the dogs would be kept, and made assurances that they would be well kept and suffer no harm, as he was most interested in their personalities and their nature. As it turned out, he was least interested in Okra of the four because he was larger and had those peculiar eyes. The professor suspected that maybe Okra had a different father than the others, as sometimes happened with dogs. He doubted that Okra was of as primal stock as his siblings.

This worked for Tobit. Those eyes that set Okra apart from the other puppies were what attracted Tobit to him. Tobit himself was known for his own extraordinary eyes, and he felt an immediate kinship to the dog. So the other three went off with the rich, white professor and Okra stayed with the poor, black, jobless man.

Tobit smiled and looked down as Okra sniffed his master's fingers with a pointy wet nose to make certain no more treats were forthcoming. That black nose, those dark eyes, and those tall ears all seemed focused tightly upon wherever the dog's interest might rest at any given time.

Tobit chuckled to himself. Okra was not a big dog, maybe forty pounds or so, but he was tough. Not fearless, he could be quite uncertain and nervous, but there was always a point beyond which he would not be pushed.

He winked at the dog, "Enough of all that now. Just stay close by. I've got to get on with some work."

Tobit turned his gaze now to the dump around them. This was the source of Okra's fascination. Tobit found it less intriguing, especially on a hot day such as this. The smell of rotting food and stale ash permeated the air. He had dabbed some Mentholatum Ointment between his nostrils to offset the stench until he was acclimated. He had work to do.

A large chest of drawers had caught his attention. First it had to be dragged up and over less promising garbage. He removed the drawers first, stacking them near the cart where his mule, Joe-boy, stood patiently waiting. Then he heaved the chest itself up and over.

With that bit of exertion done, Tobit stood up and removed his straw hat so that he could wipe away the sweat from his brow with a broad handkerchief. As he replaced the hat and stuffed the handkerchief back into his pocket, he heard from behind him a series of clipped snaps.

"That's a good boy", he chuckled, as he watched Okra leaping and snapping at the flies attracted to the stoic mule. It was entertainment for the dog and relief for Joe-boy.

"Make yourself useful."

He returned his attention to the dresser. It would need refinishing, to be sure. One of the squat legs was missing. A few of the drawers had loose joints, but all in all it was a good find, and something within his ability to repair.

Tobit straightened up from his inspection and surveyed the hellish scene around him. The county had only recently burned and bulldozed the garbage heap. There were still small coils of smoke wisping up from the ash. Pickings were always slim following a burn.

The dresser was a good find because there was naught else to be found today, he thought. The dresser meant the short trip from his home had not been a waste.

He moved the stack of drawers onto the mule cart, and then hefted the dresser up behind them on its back so that it would not tip over. Then he clambered up onto the wooden bench and patted it. Okra sprang onto the seat beside Tobit, and his focus of nose, eyes, and ears burned forward as Joe-boy responded to a light slap of the reins and began pulling them homeward.

The graveled road curved through an expanse of second-growth pine before intersecting a cracked and worn asphalt road. The older, tar-bound macadam shone in patches beneath the neglected asphalt surface. Once this had been one of the main roads winding through the county, but the building of a bridge over Rush-Knott Creek had rendered this loop of the road redundant.

The cart and its load creaked as the wheels rolled through the rutted end of the gravel road and up onto the raised pavement. As man, mule, and dog turned their gaze southward along the road, Tobit sighed at the sight of a white car rolling toward them through the heat shimmering off the pavement.

The pot-light on top of the car flashed red. Lord, that man loved to play with those lights, thought Tobit. Tobit knew what was next, and he heard the truncated wail of the siren. Okra tilted his head quizzically at the sound of it.

Tobit coaxed Joe-boy to a halt. The curve of Okra's tail thumped against the back of the wooden seat until Tobit's shush told him they would not be dismounting. The white car coasted with a slight squeal of brakes until it came to a stop, and the pale, sweat-glistened, white face of the driver was opposite Tobit.

"Toby."

"Sheriff", replied Tobit, with a polite tip of two fingers to the brim of his hat. The young sheriff's patronizing greeting grated, but Tobit's expression remained unreadable. The sheriff's grandfather, Judge Oliver, would have at least used a man's proper name, even if he was a black man. The judge would have included a "mister" if the man was significantly older than himself. No "Toby" for the judge. "Mister Tobit" was what it would have been.

"What you got back there?" asked young sheriff Oliver.

"Just an ol' chest-o-drawer I found at the dump. Looks like I can fix it up for selling. Reckon times are improving that folk can throw away something that's not beyond use."

Oliver nodded amiably enough, though his eyes remained cold, dark, and calculating. "I'm right glad you've found a way to make a living, Toby. Had you played straight with me it wouldn't have come to this."

Tobit sighed and shifted his gaze to the nearby shallow ditch so as not to betray his anger. He gathered himself to look back at the sheriff, even as he brushed one of his large, worn hands along Okra's back to ease some of the tension the dog had picked up from his master's brief moment of irritation. Okra did not care much for the sheriff to begin with.

"Now, Sheriff, I have always played straight with you, sir. I can't let on to things I know nothing about."

Oliver's gaze hardened even more, and the pleasant façade faded. "Toby, I know your pappy and you got into some trouble o'er in Lawson County."

"Yessir, I reckon we did", Tobit sighed. They had been over this many times. "Seems trouble can find a man no matter what he has done, or not done. I told you before that neither my father nor I have ever dealt with the 'shine. Sheriff Quinn and that old police chief in Harper Bay had other reasons for disliking my father. Reasons I guess we both know, but 'shining wasn't one of them."

A look of exasperation passed over the sheriff's face as his fingers toyed at the brim of the hat sitting on the seat next to him. He gazed back up at Tobit, trying to look officious, but to Tobit he looked like a flatulent toad.

9

"Toby, whatever may be the truth about that, you are likely to hear things. All you colored people are tight."

How many times was this man going to work "Toby" into this conversation? thought Tobit, who kept his composure and shook his head ruefully.

"Not so tight as white folk might think. If they know you don't hold with something, they aren't likely to speak of it to you no matter the color of your skin."

The round, sweaty, pasty face formed a frustrated frown as the car was put into gear before the sheriff spoke again. "I reckon you had it nice, Toby, back in my grandpa's day. Ain't got to be the way it is now, but that's up to you. I plan on running all the 'shiners out of this county. I reckon you best remember that it was being uppity that got your pappy run out of Harper Bay. You should take care you don't make the same mistake."

With that the sheriff's car roared off with a crunch of loose gravel beneath its tires. Tobit steadied Joe-boy before urging him on with a slight pop of the reigns. He cast a quick glance over his shoulder at the sheriff's car rounding the bend in the road behind him.

Tobit snorted to himself. Driving the 'shiners out of the county? More like making sure they paid him to operate in these parts. It was a dangerous game that young man played. The small-time 'shiners were one thing, but the fingers of big-city gangsters were stretching into these backwoods counties.

While Tobit was lost in his thoughts, Joe-boy turned by habit into the long lane home. The crunch of the oyster shells Tobit used to gravel the drive brought him out of his musings. Chickens that were looking for bits of crushed-shell calcium protested with indignant clucks as the uncaring mule plodded through their scattering flock.

On the right side of the lane Tobit's beehives sheltered in the filtered shade of long, lean pines. On the left side was a small field where he grew strawberries, with a boundary of blueberry shrubs near the edge of his property.

His home was a white, two-story frame structure. It was beginning to need painting, but that would have to wait, given his money problems. It had been built by freed slaves, from whose heirs Tobit had bought it.

As Joe-boy made his way to the unpainted barn, Tobit mused on his own mother having been born into slavery, though she never claimed any memory of it. His father had been born a freeman, as had his grand-father. Neither had been born in the Americas.

His grandfather had been born somewhere in North Africa. There were conflicting stories involving the Tell Atlas mountains, or, con-versely, Tunisia. What was more certain was that his family had origi-nated in those mountains and then moved somewhere near Tunis.

The old man claimed that they were from a holdout clan of Chris-tian Berbers. Given the time frame, midnineteenth century, this seemed unlikely to Tobit, and there had been some insinuation that his grand-father had adopted this story to justify having assisted the French in their conquests in North Africa. Still, his name, Augustine, hinted at some tradition related to the lost Christianity of the Maghreb.

Augustine had become a runner for the French forces, and hence the surname Messager. At some point Augustine saved the life of a young captain, Tobiel Saint-Sauveur, who belonged to a wealthy and influ-ential French family. He became semiofficially attached to this young, rising officer and served him across the far-flung Second French Empire.

During that service Augustine wed the daughter of an Ethiopian mer-chant. They followed the French officer to Martinique, where Tobit's father, Tobiel, was born, named in honor of the officer. It was there that the officer died as the result of a duel with the offended brother of one dalliance or another.

Saint-Sauveur's will stipulated that a generous cash payment be made to Augustine, and the family honored it. With this bequest, Augustine set his eye on the opportunities in the growing American nation. He settled in New Orleans because he thought his knowledge of French would serve him well. He also made his legal name Augustine Freeman Messager, and that of his son Tobiel Freeman Messager.

The family thrived in New Orleans. Tobiel eventually moved to the coast of the Carolinas to expand the family business, and it was there that Tobit was born and baptized, Tobit Freeman Messager.

Tobit laughed to himself. All his life other colored folk had been irritated by his middle name. They thought it snobbish and an aspersion on their own slave descent. In truth, while Augustine's Berber ancestry made him overly proud of his free status, his wife had been colored, and Tobit's own mother had been born in slavery, so Tobit felt their irrita-tion to be as snobbish as what they imagined from the Messagers—none of which kept him from naming his own son Tobias Freeman Messager.

As Tobit climbed from the cart to unload the dresser, Okra leapt down to hunt for mice or rats. He was often a timid dog around people, and unsettled by loud noises, but he was bold with rodents. He followed a scent into the cornfields that bordered Tobit's property.

Tobit had dreamed of one day buying the fields on either side of his own place. He once had seven acres altogether, enough for his bees, his berries, some fruit trees, and a large garden. A half acre was mostly useless swampy woodland that descended toward Rush-Knott Creek. There were thirty acres of land on either side that he had long planned to purchase and make a proper farm.

Now that no longer seemed possible, and his jaw set tight as he thought about it. He led Joe-boy into the paddock, offering him an apple in payment for his work. It was the crash of '29 and that boy-sheriff who had disrupted the dream. The money was gone now, and he had even had to sell two acres along the north boundary so that he could pay off the overall mortgage.

All he had was four acres, including the swampy land, a cow, and the mule. Even making the taxes was growing difficult. The assessors were harder on Negroes than they were on white folk, and the Lord help you if a white man with powerful friends had set his sight on your property.

Tobit often did not sleep well as his mind pondered the possibility of losing this place. He knew he was better off than many folk; at least he had enough property for some level of self-sufficiency. Still, it haunted him.

He sighed. Once he had envisioned buying those acres so that he would have enough land to lease out when he was too old to tend it himself. That would have let his wife, Anna, and him stay on this place and not be a burden to their son, Tobias.

Tobit shook his head as he checked the wooden handles he had lathed and was curing. When they were dry enough he would do the final sanding. He sometimes found spades, rakes, and such that people had thrown away simply because the handles had broken. He would turn new handles, with a foot-powered lathe he and Tobias had cobbled together, and sell the repaired tools, when he could. Between the unspoken threats of the sheriff and the resentment of many of his own folk, Tobit could not count on anything resembling a fair price.

The resentment rose from his former position as a purchasing agent for Judge Oliver, combined with his having moved into the county from the city, if Harper Bay counted as a city. It was not that the judge was an unfair man; it was just that any kind of bartering sets up at least a trace of an adversarial relationship. It was worse among his fellow Negroes when a white man would be the most significant beneficiary. At the same time they harbored resentment for colored folk who might be building wealth, as if it were a betrayal of their race to do so.

Then there was also Tobit's religion. Colored folk in this part of the country had only a little less suspicion of Catholics than did the white Protestants. They appreciated the schools opened by missionary orders, but remained imbued with fundamental distrust of papists. In Tobit's case, they thought him standoffish and somehow outside of the community formed by the color of their skin.

As he shuffled about inside the barn musing on these things he saw Anna going from the house to the garden. The basket in one hand and the short-handled metal claw in the other indicated that she was going to dig up some potatoes.

Her life had become hard, but still she moved with a smooth grace. He could detect the barest beginning of a stoop, but thought it as much the weight on her mind as the physical wear of the world. When Tobit had been dismissed by Sheriff Oliver as the purchasing agent for Oliver Trade and Produce, Anna had taken to cleaning the houses of well-to-do white folk.

Cleaning houses, clothes, even cooking, whatever she could do— Tobit had thought since first he had met her that he would protect her from such a grinding life. Proud fool, he admonished himself these days.

She was younger than he by more than a few years. The only daughter of a proud and selfish man whose wife had died when Anna was a young girl, she had taken care of her father at the expense of any real life beyond that.

Tobit was in his thirty-seventh year and she in her nineteenth when they had met. He was working for the Olivers, and Anna's father, Walter Wheeler, was farming fifty acres of tobacco. Walter and Anna lived in a house that Wheeler had built by connecting two shotgun bungalows. It was a large but rambling affair, a rabbit run of many small rooms. Wheeler was pleased with its size, even if it was beyond inefficient.

As Tobit and Wheeler haggled over the purchase price of the leaf the older man was too sick to harvest, they sat in the largest of the many rooms. This one acted as a parlor, though you had to pass through two smaller, nearly useless rooms to access it. Wheeler rang a bell sitting on the table between them, and Anna had appeared with a pitcher of lemonade and a half dozen small cheese sandwiches.

She seemed older than her years, but only in bearing. She was dark-skinned, with a round face and hair pulled into a flat bun on the back of her head. Other than being a bit tall and shapely, nothing really stood out about her until she lifted her eyes to look at the man doing business with her father.

"Toby, this is my daughter, Anna", Wheeler had introduced in his raspy, consumptive voice.

It was then that she looked up from the floor and the largest, warmest, and most velvety brown eyes that ever Tobit Freeman Messenger had seen smote him through his heart.

He shook his head, coming out of the past and into the grim present. Poor Anna; he could not help but think she deserved more. He glanced down, just outside of the barn door. The yellow dog was looking at him with contemplative curiosity.

"Well, Okra," he chuckled, "ain't much I can do about this situation, it seems to me. But, I can go and help the woman dig up some taters."

Anna was tired, but there was still supper to get. At least the workweek was over and she could try to revive her strength and spirit over the weekend. She saw Tobit closing the barn door and heading over toward the garden. That strange yellow dog, seeming to have figured out where the master was going, was trotting ahead of him.

Tobit just plods nowadays, she decided. Tobit's footsteps had become slower and heavier the past few years. His arms hung loose and heavy-handed as he mechanically lifted one foot and then another. She had questions for the good Lord about this: why this good man should be so put upon.

She shook her head to herself. Tobit was so much better a man than ever had been her father. She knew it was not her place to judge, but she could not help feeling that way.

Tobit's name was known to her when first her father had introduced them. She was surprised by Tobit's appearance. Walter Wheeler had been a black man who loathed most everyone of his own race, though he would never have admitted as such. When he talked of Tobit he often made much of the younger man's "French-Ayrab" ancestry. Anna had thought for sure Tobit would be what folk called a high yellow.

The man whose gaze met hers was fairly tall, lean but with big bones, and had moderately dark skin. Other than perhaps rather more leanness to his face, he seemed as much like any other Negro as not—except the eyes, which were dark and extraordinary for anyone of any race, with long dark lashes, dark irises, and dark skin as if someone had drawn a fine line around them with ink. Berber eyes, she would decide upon looking at such people in a picture book.

She had expected Tobit to be haughty and proud, based on what folk sometimes said about him—this Tobit *Freeman* Messager, this man who worked so high-handedly for the rich, white Olivers. What she found was a man with a quiet, confident pride, and a natural gentleness. He could, at times, be terse, even short-tempered, especially with folk he found suspect. He could also be so stubborn as to make old Joe-boy look solicitous. Nobody was perfect, but most important in Anna's mind, he was very unlike her possessive, domineering father.

He was nearly eighteen years older than Anna, but she had always found the young men of her age to be unappealingly clumsy, immature, and self-centered—not so with this man.

Fate had finally been kind to her. Her often tyrannical father was dying of consumption. That was why Tobit had arranged, for a flat fee, that Oliver Trade and Produce would harvest the Wheeler tobacco and take it to auction. It guaranteed Wheeler a profit, and with only a minor gamble Oliver Trade and Produce should see a larger profit.

The inevitability of his pending death had removed something of Walter Wheeler's selfishness. It did him no harm now to let his daughter go, and he thought Tobit a fine man. The great fortune for Anna was one of sheer chance: Tobit was a Roman Catholic, and so was her father.

Or, so he had been once, since he had not entered a church of any kind since burying his wife. Despite this he remained inordinately proud of his religion. She guessed this was because it set him apart from other Negroes in Chatqua County. He for sure was fond of being set apart.

Anna liked to think, too, that there was some element of repentance in the old man's approval of the marriage. So it was that Walter Wheeler went one more time as a living man into a church, for his daughter's wedding. It was a small affair, since nobody much cared for Wheeler, and few knew his daughter other than as the tall, shapely girl who was burdened with taking care of her ailing and ornery parent. Added to that was the fact that they had to travel nearly fifty miles to the Catholic church in little Washington because Tobit did not dare to step foot in Harper Bay. Among the few folk who would deign to step foot in a Catholic church, even fewer would travel so far to do so.

She smiled then, thinking about those early years as she set the basket on the ground and knelt carefully so that only her light canvas apron touched the soil. Her father had moved in with them only a few months after the wedding. He was fading fast, though, and died within a year. She had found him easier to love and forgive as he died. Dying had softened him.

With his death her brother had come back to the county. He was a man much like their father and that was why the two had so often butted heads. The son finally left for a job in Raleigh and had hardly spoken to either of them after that. He rushed home after Walter's death, and he made much noise about inheritance.

There was no will, so rather than engage in a bitter, expensive legal battle, Anna and Tobit had acquiesced to most of Elias Wheeler's demands. In the end, Anna inherited less than a third of the estate. Still, it had helped Tobit in the purchase of this place and gave her a feeling of equality in the possession of it.

Her reminiscing was interrupted when the yellow dog came bounding into the garden, nosing curiously where she was digging potatoes. Anna shooed him away, and he retreated just barely beyond the bounds of disapproval. In a moment Tobit appeared opposite the row from her and dropped creakily to his knees and began brushing aside the loosed soil in search of potatoes.

"You'll wear out the knees of your overalls", Anna fussed.

Tobit nodded slowly, deliberately. "Reckon so. Don't recall having ever had a pair of overalls I didn't eventually wear the knees out of 'em. Well, there was the pair I set afire once, but other than that I'd reckon I've killed the knees in all of 'em.

"Course, now, I've got me this clever woman and she saves each pair of overalls so as to use 'em to patch up the knees in the next pair."

"Well, if this woman is all so clever as that", admonished Anna, "she would have married a man who wouldn't wear out the knees so quickly, and that way save her a lot of work."

"I told her many a time she could have done better", replied Tobit, with a sly smile. Then the smile faded into a somber wistfulness. "I guess that is truer now than ever it has been."

"Hush, don't be feeling sorry for yourself, and for sure don't be feeling sorry for me", said Anna. "You are the best thing to ever happen to me, if only because of that boy of ours."

Tobit tossed a handful of small potatoes in the basket as he thought of Tobias. "He is a clever young man, that's for sure. Though what any man or boy sees in those noisy motor contraptions is beyond me."

"I don't know", mused Anna. "It would be nice to have a car or a truck. We could get over to church in little Washington more often."

Tobit nodded as he tossed a larger potato into the basket with a shroud of dusty soil trailing behind it like a shadowy comet's tail. He and a few of the white Catholics in the county had built a little chapel just outside the county seat, Stonebridge, twenty years back. A priest from Harper Bay would come down to the county for Mass once a month. The little chapel had burnt to the ground one winter. It was so cold that water froze before it could be pumped or even tossed onto the flames.

Officially it was declared that a smoldering cinder from the wood stove that heated the building had ignited in the chimney and set the place ablaze. That was nonsense, because it would have had to have smoldered for nearly forty-eight hours. It was the Klan that had burnt that place.

Worst of all in the Klan's eyes, unlike Harper Bay, where there were separate churches, the white and colored Catholics actually went to the same services here in Chatqua County. Years later he heard that one of the Klansmen had pointed out that some of the coloreds from north of Harper Bay had been coming into the county to attend those services. Next thing you know, he had asserted, there'll be Jews building one of their Christless temples. It did not matter that there were fewer than thirty Catholics in the county, and only six of them were colored; the Klan hated Catholics near about as much as Jews and Negroes.

It made Tobit chuckle morbidly to think about where that would place a colored Catholic in Klan estimation.

Anna looked up at him. "What?"

"Nothing; I was just musing. Oh, I saw the boy-sheriff again today. I think maybe I should just build a still somewhere and then report it to him. Maybe that way he would let go this notion he has."

"He would only produce a new notion", said Anna. "I have never seen a man that so needs to hate. A lot of folk say his father should have been more firm with him."

"Not that", replied Tobit as he borrowed the claw to clear more soil. "If anything, his old man was much too hard on him. How Judge Oliver could have produced such a spoiled, mean-spirited, no good drunk as that boy's father is beyond me. No, I'd be more likely to think the son is hateful because he felt hated by his own, worthless father all those years.

"I only ever saw that man do one kind thing for that boy. Back when he was maybe seven or eight he bought him a little shotgun, a child's shotgun. Pretty little thing so finely made. Had it made over in Europe.

"Well, Chuck was just a little boy. The first time he fired that thing it knocked him down even though it was just a four-ten gauge, and the noise of it scared the young'un half to death. So little Chuck starts crying and his father starts calling him names and talks just ruthless to the boy."

The judge's son had died in Atlanta. Shot down in the street, the Harper Bay News had reported. Shot in a fight over a whore, said other folk around the county.

"The judge's daughter seems to have turned out all right", noted Anna. Melissa Oliver had become a school teacher and married a lawyer. They lived in Greenville and had produced a large family of seven children.

"Fine girl", said Tobit, remembering the cheerful, freckle-faced child with ginger hair and hazel eyes. "Sweet, kind little child she was. It's a wonder how things turn out, ain't it."

Anna got to her feet, brushing dirt from her canvas apron. "That's enough for the entire weekend and most of next week."

Tobit pried the basket from out of her hands. "I'll carry that up for you, clever girl."

"You are so kind, sir", laughed Anna.

"Well, if I didn't carry a lady's burden when I ought to, I reckon my mama would rise up out of her grave to cuff the back of my head. What's for dinner?"

"Fried potatoes, and scrambled eggs", replied Anna softly.

Tobit just nodded. Meat was scarce for them these days. "I hope that boy of yours gets home at least before his supper goes cold."

Tobias worked part-time for Crafty Forgeron, the owner of a motor repair shop and gasoline station. His given name was Francis Forgeron, but he went by either Frank or Crafty. His shop was called Crafty's Repair. He was indeed crafty with things mechanical.

Tobias was only twelve when he started working part-time at Crafty's. At first he had only done some sweeping and cleaning. Forgeron let him watch sometimes as cars were repaired and let him help with the handing over of tools and parts. Then one day, sometime after Tobias's fourteenth birthday, Crafty Forgeron had towed in a battered Model A Ford. "A Model A Tudor Deluxe", Tobias had reported to his father, who had no clue what that meant.

There was already a junked, plain Tudor sedan behind the shop, and Crafty told Tobias that he could, on his own time, begin the repair of the Deluxe by using the junker for parts. He said that in this way Tobias could learn how to repair cars, and at the end of it Crafty would have a car he could sell for a profit.

"That is, if you've got the incentive and desire to learn", Crafty had told the boy.

Tobit laughed now at the thought of it. The boy had both. He spent any spare moment he could working on that old car. At first that was quite a lot of time, though it became less and less so as Crafty began letting him work in the shop for pay. Nearly four years had passed, but the car was virtually complete.

Despite liking him, Tobit thought Forgeron a peculiar man. Tobit was more than a little unsure that Crafty's Repair was the sort of place Tobias should be working. Forgeron was a short, thin white man with bowed legs and cropped hair atop a large head. He wore cowboy boots, though he had never been west of the Mississippi River. He was known to associate with loose women of any race, though he was careful to conduct such goings-on outside of the county.

Crafty repeatedly had the notion that maybe somehow he and Tobit were related due to their French surnames. The Forgeron family was descended from French Huguenots who ended up in America by way of Wales. Tobit would point out that his own ancestry was Negro and Berber rather than French, and Forgeron would reply, "I reckon you're right." Then days, weeks, or months later he would bring up the notion again.

Despite his reckless ways with women, gambling, and drinking, Crafty Forgeron was a good-hearted man. He was essentially color blind when it came to race. Tobit worried about him because of that, but Forgeron had one brother who worked for the Justice Department in Washington and another for the North Carolina State Bureau of Investigation. It was unlikely that any organized Klan violence would fall upon Crafty.

Tobit figured that some memory of the persecution the family had faced in France was passed down through the generations, and it made the three brothers peculiarly sensitive to the tribulations of Negroes. As he washed his hands and face at the pump, Tobit smiled to think of Crafty talking about his important brothers.

"You see," said the little bowlegged man, "I'm the black sheep of my family! Reckon that's why I get along so well with the colored folk."

Once inside, Tobit began to clean and cut the potatoes for frying. These days Anna worked about as hard outside of the house as he did, so he did not feel it was appropriate that he should leave all the housework to her. Truth was, she actually earned more money now than he did.

After he had finished, Anna was about to shoo him from the kitchen when they heard the sound of Crafty Forgeron's truck trundling noisily up the drive. Tobit frowned; it was not unusual for Crafty to give Tobias a ride home, but only when he had kept him working late or the weather was bad. This was early and heightened a sense of concern.

The truck creaked to a halt with a wake of ground oyster-shell dust catching up and swirling past it. Tobias emerged from the truck, appearing healthy enough to the relief of his parents, who had stepped out onto the front porch of the house. Forgeron hopped down from the driver's side and followed the young man.

Tobias looked much like his father. So much so that folk were always commenting on how he was the spitting image of Tobit until one day, not one of his better days, Tobit had finally tersely replied, "He damned well better be."

"Daddy," called out the young man as he approached the porch, "Reverend Walker says he needs to speak with you and that he'll come by first thing in the morning."

Forgeron followed to the steps, nodding as Tobias spoke, and pulling his perpetually unlit pipe from his mouth, said, "I thought I'd tell you, Tobit, that he seemed out of sorts with worry. Very put out. So look here, if y'all need some help tomorrow, you let me know."

He had punctuated each statement with a jab of his pipe, Forgeron's habitual expression of earnestness. "You know you can count on me. You can trust me too."

Tobit nodded in reply. "I know that, Frank, and I thank you for it. Won't you come in for a bite of supper?"

"No, I reckon I better get back and finish up the brake job I was doin' when the preacher came by. But I thank you for the offer."

The Messagers waved a farewell as the truck bounced back down the drive. Tobit looked over to his son as the vehicle disappeared onto the road. "Did Gaston say what this was about?"

Tobit knew the reverend might be hesitant to talk about colored business in front of a white man, even Crafty. Tobias shook his head. "No, sir, but by the look on his face, it's bad. Real bad."

Two

Tobit was up and about earlier than usual. He was not sure what time Reverend Walker would arrive, and there were chores to do. He fed the chickens, collected eggs, milked the cow, gave Joe-boy his grain, and let him out into the corral. While he was busy with this, Anna had also risen and made biscuits for the day and scrambled some eggs for him.

Tobias helped him with some of the chores, and then they went inside to eat. The young man made his own breakfast of yesterday's cornbread crumbled into a glass of buttermilk. He then excused himself because he was going to Crafty's since they were behind on some of the work. Tobias was enthusiastic for Saturday work because Forgeron would pay him a little extra for it.

Tobit had just finished his own breakfast when he heard Okra barking. He and Anna walked out onto the porch. Tobit shushed the dog and waited as Walker drove slowly up the long drive and parked the car. A deliberate man, the reverend took time to collect himself, adjusting his tie before exiting the car, and buttoning his suit coat and putting his hat carefully on his head after.

"Gaston", said Tobit in greeting to his friend. Walker was one of his few acquaintances still openly friendly. Both men were outsiders in the county. The reverend was pastor at the only African Methodist Episcopal church within three counties. He was from Harlem originally and had been assigned here ten years ago when the church was founded as a missionary effort in a county where most of the Negro churches were Baptist of one sort or the other.

Gaston Walker was a short man and a little overweight in a soft-seeming way. He was round-shouldered and round-faced, with small round spectacles sitting low on a short, round nose. He had round, owl-like eyes that seemed even more somber than usual today. Everything about him was round, as if God had made him to offer no irritating edges. Yet, he was also a man with a steady, unwavering will.

He slowly nodded his head as he brought his fingertips to the brim of his hat and replied, "Tobit, Anna, I hope the morning finds you both well in the eyes of the Lord."

"Well enough, I suppose. You look grim today."

Again the reverend slowly nodded. Tobit gestured to the porch, then said, "Come on up, have a seat, and tell me what's on your mind."

Anna sat on the swing as both men settled into creaking rocking chairs sitting side by side. Walker removed his hat for a moment and out of habit wiped his forehead with a handkerchief, even though the heat of the day had not really begun. He was collecting himself, and let go a sigh before speaking.

"First, I want you to understand that I do not come here lightly. I know, of course, of your troubles. I want you to know that I will understand if you feel you must refuse me."

Tobit nodded. The reverend nodded back and, having replaced his handkerchief, folded his hands on his lap in a prayerlike aspect.

"You know Mabel Farmer, six children, and with her husband, Joss, dead going on three years now. I expect you know her oldest boy, James."

"I know of him", replied Tobit. "He's maybe fourteen years old, tall and thin. Shy, not much to say and soft-spoken when he does. Seems softer than has been good for him, and the other boys tease him right much."

"He has been hanged."

The word "what" had begun to form on Tobit's lips as both question and exclamation, but died unspoken. Anna's hand went to her mouth as if to catch her breath. Gaston Walker was gazing now down the long drive for a moment before turning his eyes back to his friends.

"Lynched", he sighed. "Little doubt of that."

"He was just a child", whispered Anna.

"Lynched? Why?" muttered Tobit. "Why lynch a soft-spoken child like that? It has been years since the Klan has lynched anyone around here simply for the terror of it."

"They made the *why* of it clear enough. If it was the Klan."

Tobit sat back, shaking his head. "Who else in all of God's green world would do such a thing?"

"If you will come with me to fetch down the boy's body, I think you'll see what motivated whoever did this", replied the reverend as both answer and request.

"Fetch the body? Reverend, tell us what is going on here", pleaded Anna.

"The boy has been hanging for three days. The sheriff was called, but nobody has gone to the scene. Widow Farmer is beside herself, with five other children to look after. Everyone is afraid to touch the body.

"Tobit, I can't just leave the boy there any longer. You're the only man I know of, other than Mason", said Walker, speaking of Mason Newberry, the church's groundskeeper. Gaston continued, "I know of nobody else who might help me. We have got to take him down for that poor woman. We have got to get him buried.

"I know the trouble it might bring down on us, and that you have trouble enough. So, I will understand if you choose not to be involved."

Tobit laid his head back against the top rail of the rocker and sighed before lowering it again with an expression on his face that was both stoic and resigned.

Anna bore it all with the stoicism particular to women. Whereas troubles were broken upon the hard-set features of a stoic man, with a stoic woman troubles were absorbed. Anna's eyes drew it all in before she spoke. "No mother should face such a thing alone."

"And no pastor should face such a thing alone", added Tobit. "I will go with you. I'll fetch a ladder, and harness up ol' Joe-boy."

"The child is about three miles down a dirt road just past Merchant Crossing", said Walker.

"The old logging road", Tobit said and nodded. "I've gone blueberry picking down that road. Look here, you take your car. I'll gather up some things and be along in just a minute."

"You're a good man, Tobit", offered Walker, as he rose solemnly from the rocking chair. He turned then toward Anna. "I am truly sorry to bring such troubles to your home, ma'am."

"It is a world of troubles, Reverend, all around us."

"It is indeed", said Walker as he slowly descended the porch steps and began walking to his car.

As Tobit turned to go to the barn, Anna called to him, "Should I go with you? The boy will need cleaning up before his mother sees him."

Tobit paused a moment before shaking his head. "I'll see to that. After three days in this weather, I'd rather you not."

He then went to the barn. He pulled the cart out, loading it with a ladder, some tools, a worn blanket, and an old canvas sheet. After harnessing Joe-boy, he walked over to Anna's flower garden and cut an armful of lavender, which he bundled and laid in the back of the cart.

As he was urging the mule toward the drive, Anna came out of the house and handed him a pint of the rose water that she distilled from her own roses. Okra was with her. He seemed to know he was not to accompany the master on this trip, but still he whined a bit until Anna reached down and scratched him lightly atop his head. The dog leaned against his mistress' leg and watched with disappointment as man and mule disappeared down the drive.

Joe-boy was strong, steady, and determined. Joe-boy was not fast. By the time Tobit arrived at Merchant Crossing, he saw Gaston's car pulled off to the side just before the logging road. He saw also that the reverend had gone by his church and enlisted the assistance of the grounds-keeper, Mason Newberry. The groundskeeper was older than Tobit, and while not at all tall, was a strapping, powerfully built man. He had never moved beyond the sixth grade but possessed a quiet wisdom.

When Joe-boy had drawn close, the reverend steered his car onto the logging road and proceeded slowly so as not to raise a great cloud of dust. On either side of them were acres of plantation pines still nearly a decade from harvesting. A few worn, often collapsed sheds were scattered along the way, the ruins of past harvesting.

Ahead of him, Tobit saw the car pull to the side of the road. He saw then one of the taller pines curved by the weight of a hanging body. As Joe-boy pulled up closer to the tree, Tobit could see two boys sitting nearby. He recognized Ephraim and Menasha, most often known simply as Eph and Nash, the twelve-year-old twins of Joss and Mabel Farmer.

Looking to the trees around the site, Tobit saw a few buzzards perched watchfully in the branches. The boys had a collection of stones and still-tight pinecones they were using to keep the birds off their brother. Near them lay an old, big-boned hound, probably to keep other creatures off of the twins.

Venturing a look into the pine, Tobit grimaced. The face of young James bore the signs of what had happened before he was found and his younger brothers had taken up their vigil. James was a light-skinned boy, and rumors of rape rose from the fact that both his parents and all his siblings were darker skinned. It spoke well of Joss that he took Mabel for his wife and treated James as one of his own until the end of his own life.

The corpse was naked save for torn underpants hanging more tattered than not around the fluid-swollen ankles. A short piece of weathered wood, probably pulled from one of the ruined sheds, was hung by strips of what Tobit guessed to be the remains of James' shirt. Someone had hastily carved crude letters into the surface of the wood: QUEER.

Gaston and Mason emerged from the car to meet Tobit. Mason gestured with his white-haired head toward the twins. "Revr'nd, you just goes on over there and takes care of them boys now. Toby and me, we can gets poor Jamie down from that tree."

Tobit nodded. "Those boys need you now more than James, Mason, or I do."

"I'll fetch your ladder", said Mason as he saw Tobit gathering up the canvas sheet and a hatchet. "But seeing how it be a rickety ol' thing, I reckon I'll hold it while you goes up."

At the foot of the tree Tobit could see the flies gathered on the dead boy's face, and crawling along the loosening skin of his torso. He reached into the pockets of his overalls and drew out the jar of Mentholatum, and after dabbing some around his nostrils offered it to Mason, who did the same. He then spread the canvas before going to break off a branch of nearby wax myrtle.

Mason held the ladder against the trunk of the tree. Tobit threw the old blanket over his shoulder and climbed toward the body with one hand also holding the myrtle and the hatchet hanging from a loop on his overalls. He could smell that the boy's bowels and bladder had been loosed upon death, but he paused not because of that, but because something was wrong with what he saw.

After only a moment he proceeded on and used the branch of wax myrtle to shoo off the flies. He also used it to brush away ants crawling along the rope and across the corpse. After that he tossed the branch to the ground and draped the blanket over the body. Then he cut the rope in two with a chop of the hatchet. He wedged his knee into the gap between rungs so that he could use one hand to guide the body. The moderately stiff corpse bent over his shoulder, and the fluid-swollen hands flopped heavily on his back.

Even as dead weight, the slightly built James was not much of a burden. When Tobit reached the ground, Mason helped him to lay the body on the sheet of canvas. There was still some rigor to the limbs, and the groundskeeper carefully massaged them until he could fold the arms over the chest. He then pulled what was left of the underwear to cover the mutilated genitals.

"I can clean him up, Toby."

Tobit shook his head. "Not just yet."

He knelt and placed his handkerchief over the insect- and vulture-ravaged face. Then he pointed at the neck. "See that?"

Though light-skinned in life, James' color had already begun to darken in death. Breathing shallowly to avoid the stench, Mason leaned over to inspect where Tobit had indicated. A frown deepened on the big man's face. "This here boy ain't been kill't by no hangin'."

Reverend Walker was approaching them. "What do you mean?"

Mason straightened and stood. "Toby is right. This here boy was dead 'fore he was hung."

"How do you figure?"

Still kneeling, Tobit pointed to the dead boy's neck. "I first noticed when I was going up the ladder. The rope wasn't even tied as a proper hangman's noose. It hadn't tightened enough to choke the child. Also, it was too far up, set just below the jaw. Now, look there, see that bruising? There is no hanging that makes that sort of bruising."

He extended his hand over the pattern of bruises. "That was made by hands much smaller than my own, but an adult's hands nonetheless. This boy was strangled to death, and then he was strung up in the tree."

"I don't think the Klan done this", muttered Mason.

"I don't know who did it", replied Tobit. "But I can tell you it wasn't typical of a lynching. They hadn't tied the boy's hands. He could have pulled aholt the trunk of the pine tree, freed himself, and climbed down.

"And look all along his sides, chest, stomach; this here boy was beat bad."

"Now, that would be like a lynchin'", Mason reminded him.

"True, but looking at the nature of some of those scratches and gashes on his body, I'm thinking he was killed and then dragged here and strung up, already a corpse."

Gaston was frowning, trying to take all this in as Tobit began pulling the blanket and the canvas over the body. "You take those boys home, Reverend. The sheriff might not come out here to investigate this, but I can take this boy to *him*."

27

"I'll come with you, Toby", growled Mason.

"I thank you for that offer", replied Tobit. "But you don't need the sheriff turning his ire on you. He's already about as ill with me as he can get. You two go on now."

"Well, I's gonna help you get Jamie into the cart", decided Mason.

As the reverend went to gather up the twins and their hound, Tobit splashed some of the rose water on the floor of the cart. Then he and Mason folded the canvas over the corpse and carefully lifted it into the cart. The scent of death caused Joe-boy to twitch his ears and shift his hooves in place, but gentle shushing from Tobit calmed him.

"If you're sure 'bout this—" began Mason, but Tobit cut him off with a nod, so the groundskeeper joined the reverend and the twins in the car. Once back on the pavement near Merchant Crossing, the car turned one way toward the Farmer house, and the mule turned the other way toward Stonebridge, the county seat.

It took three-quarters of an hour for Joe-boy to reach Stonebridge. The buzzards had followed them half that time before giving up or being distracted by the possibility of fresher carrion. It was nearing noon when Tobit urged the mule to a halt in the shade behind the county courthouse. He had positioned them so that the slight breeze would carry the smell of death away from the mule.

The sheriff's department and the county jail were situated behind and slightly to one side of the courthouse. As Tobit was walking over he saw a deputy coming from out of the department. He recognized Del Gaines, a tall, barrel-chested man with dark eyes and dark hair showing the first streaks of white.

Del was a decent enough man. He was the chief deputy, and many people thought he should have had the job of sheriff instead of Oliver, but Del had no taste for politics and had refused to run against the younger man in the election.

"Mister Toby", he greeted with a finger to his hat.

"Deputy", replied Tobit. "I don't see the sheriff's car. Is he nearby?"

Gaines chuckled cryptically. "Today's Saturday."

Tobit nodded; he should have thought of that. He drew in a breath before speaking again. "Deputy, I've got something you need to see. It won't be a pleasant sight. If you'll come over to the cart with me."

Gaines followed him. The deputy's face drew into a grimace. "God a'mighty, what's that smell?"

"It's a body. A boy, James Farmer, though I 'spect you don't know him."

"What are you doing with a body in the back of your cart?" asked the incredulous deputy. He had paused a moment, not entirely sure he wanted to continue toward the stench.

"The boy had been hanging from a tree for three days", was Tobit's grim reply. "The sheriff was called near the end of the first day, and again the mornin' of the second, but still the boy was hanging."

The deputy's eyes widened a moment, but then Tobit could see the man drawing a mask over his face. "Ain't no record of such a call, that I know of."

"I 'spect not", sighed Tobit as they reached the cart. He leaned over the side rail and loosened the canvas and pulled it back from over the body. He reached down and turned the wooden plank so the deputy could see what was carved into it.

"God a'mighty", Gaines repeated in a whisper before turning to look away.

"I don't think this boy was lynched, deputy", explained Tobit. "If you look at the bruising on his neck, it looks like he was killed and then strung up. And look at the rope; it wasn't a noose, not even a good slip knot. His hands weren't tied neither."

Gaines forced himself to look again for a moment. He nodded his head uncertainly before replying, "You might be right, Mister Toby. I'm gonna hafta call Chuck—Sheriff Oliver. You shouldn't have moved the body, Mister Toby."

"Three days", replied Tobit pointedly. "The boy has a mother, brothers, and a sister. Three days he was left hanging."

The chief deputy's lips pulled tight and he slowly nodded. "I'll call the sheriff and tell him he needs to get over here. Might take a spell to track him down."

Tobit glanced over at the jailhouse and offices. They were not the sort of places to make him comfortable. "If you don't mind, I'll wait out here. Is it okay if I get my mule some water from that spigot over yonder?"

The deputy nodded and then with long-legged strides hurried from the cart and back up the steps into the sheriff's department. Tobit replaced the canvas over the corpse and then took a small pail from under the seat of the cart and went to the spigot. As he filled the pail halfway up, he was beginning to reconsider the wisdom of what he was doing in bringing the body into Stonebridge, but he thought of the twins sitting in vigil near the tree, and he thought of their bereaved mother.

"What else could I do, Lord?" he asked into the air as he walked the bucket back over to the thirsty mule. "It just seems as if things keep piling up on me. Was I so arrogant that I needed so much humiliation? I know I have never been perfect, but I sure have tried to be a decent man. Lord, even though I can't get to the Sacrament every Sunday, I at least go to Reverend Walker's church to hear the Word preached."

He forced himself to be silent for a moment as Joe-boy drank from the pail. He was trying to listen—trying to hear something beyond his own complaints echoing back to him. Finally he sighed, "I reckon I don't thank you as I should. Don't near enough tell you how I'm thankful for my health, and for the blessings of Anna and Tobias.

"It's just, thinking 'bout that boy there, about his mamma, and thinking too 'bout poor ol' Joss. Now, he was a decent man. Hard workin' man. He took up that little Mabel who weren't but a bit of a girl. Joss raised that boy like his own. Weren't the boy's fault how he was fathered.

"I can't figure it. I know we have to accept that bad things happen, Lord. If we're to have a free will, some folk will do that which is not from you. Still, I just don't understand how a man like Joss dies, and a boy like James is murdered in his youth."

I've just got to be still and listen, thought Tobit. He went and sat beneath a spreading oak so that the trunk shielded him a bit from the windows of the courthouse and jailhouse. He reached into his pocket and pulled out a worn rosary. It had been his father's rosary.

He cupped it in his left hand. He needed the comfort of it, but in this county such praying was considered with suspicion, so it was best he keep it out of view as much as was possible. He began the familiar, calming prayers as he fingered the beads.

He prayed the Rosary once, and then began again. It did soothe him, but he still felt alone, and nothing seemed to come back to him from the silence. He was nearly through with a second praying of the beads when he heard Sheriff Oliver's car pulling into the graveled parking lot.

As Tobit slipped the rosary back into his pocket, he saw the chief deputy emerge from the building and meet Oliver halfway to the cart. The sheriff's pale face had gone red and angry.

"Toby, what in hell you been doing, boy?"

Tobit had risen and walked over to the cart before the two white men got there. "I've just done what someone had to do, Sheriff. It ain't right that a young boy like that should be left strung in a tree."

"You messed with a crime scene", growled Oliver.

"Reckon I did, sir", admitted Tobit. "But I ask you again, how can a boy be left like that? A boy with a momma and a family? You were called twice."

"Who the hell says such a thing?" snapped Oliver. "Tell me the name of the two liars and I'll put them in jail for obstructing an investigation."

"I ain't said it was more than one person", noted Tobit.

Oliver cut his eyes from Tobit to the canvas-shrouded body on the mule cart. Then he looked over to Gaines. "Del, get Doc Mack on the phone. Tell him we've got a body he's gonna have to look at."

"I've done that, Sheriff", replied the chief deputy.

Someone knows how to do their job, thought Tobit, but he maintained a stoic visage as he spoke, "You want me to take the body over to Doc Mack's office?"

"You?" sneered Oliver. "You stupid coon, that cart is a crime scene itself now. I'm impounding that cart."

"Sheriff," said the deputy, "Mister Toby is a good man"; his demeanor suggested that Oliver consider his words and actions carefully.

"He's a meddlin' fool", spat Oliver.

"Can I unhitch Joe-boy and take him home?" asked Tobit.

"Hell no. I'm arresting you for interfering with the scene of a crime, and interfering with an investigation."

"Sheriff?" repeated Gaines, puzzled at the sheriff's explosion of anger.

"You heard me, Del. Arrest him."

"Joe-boy", protested Tobit as the chief deputy reluctantly took him by the arm.

"Shut up or I'll pull out my revolver and put that damned mule out of its misery", replied the sheriff.

"I'll see he's taken care of", offered Gaines softly.

"Cuff this nigger, Gaines", ordered Oliver.

A protest died on the chief deputy's lips. He gently and loosely cuffed Tobit's hands behind his back, but spoke softly to him again. "You know ol' Ben Cobb; he's a trustee. I'll get him to take the mule to your farm."

31

"The mule is being impounded", growled the sheriff, though some of his anger ebbed away when Gaines turned slowly, methodically toward him with a demeanor that suggested things had gone just about far enough. "Have Ben put him in that old stable. Toby can pray that old heap of planks don't fall on his precious mule."

Almost Del Gaines said something, but his decency could not break the weight of duty. Instead he led the forlorn, head-bowed Tobit into the jailhouse.

The colored jail was in the half basement of the white jail. Only three feet of it was actually below ground, but in this coastal area it was enough to keep the place dank and mildewed. Set only inches below the ceiling—which was in fact the floor of the white jail cells above—were a few long, narrow, and barred horizontal windows. There were only three cells. Two were small, meant for trustees, and they each had two cots, a sink, and a chamber pot. The third cell was large, with a wooden ledge running the length of one wall to serve as a sleeping platform. There were no mattresses, only a few dirty, worn blankets. An elongated, two-handled galvanized tub served as a communal toilet.

Tobit sat on the wooden ledge, but leaned forward with head bowed so that neither his back nor head touched the mildewed brick wall. There were only two other men in the cell with him. They sat in the gloomy light from the window and played checkers on a grid they had scratched into the earthen floor, using small pebbles as makeshift pieces.

Ben Cobb came shuffling down the stairs into the corridor that ran between the large cell and the two smaller ones. He was in his forties, but looked much older. A hard drinker, hard gambler, and generally disagreeable sort who had figured out things went easier on him if he feigned resigned obedience to the white men who ran the jail.

He had once worked for the Olivers. Tobit had bailed him out of jail twice during that time, once for public drunkenness and another time for simple assault. When he was arrested a third time for drunkenness, Judge Oliver had fired him.

Cobb cast a glance over at Tobit. "We took that boy over to Doc, and I put that mule of your'n up in the old stables. I hope he don' mind snakes and spiders."

The trustee cackled at his own humor. The two checker players just shook their heads. Tobit nodded his own thank-you.

"Don't thanks me, nigga", snorted the trustee. "I just does what the man tells me do. You must be plumb crazy in the head to cut down that boy like that. Then all you coloreds in this county been spoilt by that Judge Oliver. Made you all uppity."

Cobb spit on the earthen floor. "This is the white man's world. That ol' judge, he makes you Geechees think y'all gots a chance, but that's jus' so he can makes some money. Ever axe yo'self why he treated you special, Toby? I tells you why, so he can gets you to squeeze some money out of the rest of the Geechees."

"The judge was a fair and honest man", replied Tobit.

"For a white man", said one of the checker players with no trace of sarcasm, while the other player nodded in silent confirmation.

"Maybe so, in a manner of speaking", considered Cobb. "But that makes him a rare man of any kind, and more so as a white man dealing with coloreds. But that spoilt you people. Me, I's from up 'round Durham, and I can tell you if the white man decides he's gonna string up some nigger, you best just be glad it's not you. They can hang 'im, burn 'im, drown 'im in the river, jus' long as it ain't my neck getting stretched."

Tobit said nothing. The trustee cackled again, "What be the matter, mister high and mighty Toby freed mans? You jus' another nigger now the judge dead. You lucky that big hoss of a deputy take a shine to you, or the sheriff woulda probably beat you to death for being so uppity."

"Nigga," said one of the players, glancing up at Cobb, "you say 'nigga' too much. Shut up so's I can concentrate before I lose to this here Geechee."

"Ain't none of us suppose t' be Geechees even from Georgia", snorted the opponent.

In the first-floor office, the big hoss of a deputy was looking ruefully at the paperwork he had just filled out. He should never have gone in that day. He had just wanted to get caught up on some work when the office was not so crowded. He figured it just proved there was no profit in doing the right thing.

He leaned back, pushing the chair onto two creaking legs as he looked out the window. It had to be Toby, as fine a colored feller as ever he'd known. Chuck would probably try to put the poor old man on a road gang. For reasons Del could hardly hope to guess, Chuck hated Toby. Well, Chuck hated dang near everybody.

He let down the chair and laid his huge hands on the desktop. He looked at Tobit's belongings set in a small grouping on the desk: a quarter, two dimes, and a nickel, and a pocket watch and "that string of beads". Regulations said he had to take anything metal so it could not be used as a weapon. It was hard to imagine someone being killed with a dime. Then again, regulations said a colored man could not even have his belt, lest he strangle a keeper. If a colored man's pants were loose, they would give him about six inches of twine so he could tie the final loops together.

Del's gaze fell on the crucifix attached to the beads. The graphic, tactile Catholic expression of the great sacrifice was unsettling to him. He liked his Jesus clean, triumphant, and very white. He hated that he had to take these beads from ol' Toby, but the crucifix was metal, possibly silver.

Turning his eyes from the bowed and suffering head of the Christ, he scraped the pile into an envelope. He placed the envelope into a desk drawer that he then locked. There was a cabinet for such possessions, but he knew that Toby would never have gotten his money or watch back if he put them there. Someone would probably have even taken the cross, since it looked to be silver. Mister Toby did not deserve that.

When Del was just a boy, his own daddy had run into some money problems. Cheated by the banker Johnson was the problem. When the Crash came and that old usurer had blown out his own brains, Del doubted even Johnson's own family grieved.

It was Toby who'd saved Garrett Gaines. Now, as an adult, Del knew what a risky business that had been for the colored man. Even in helping a white man, a Negro was taking an awful chance. Being obliged to a colored man was about as low as a white man could be, and the resentment could be a dark, dark thing.

Still, Tobit had remembered how hardworking and honest Garrett Gaines had always been. He mentioned that to the judge—talked about how Garrett had a knack for getting along with white folk, black folk, and even Yankees. He put the notion in the judge's head that Garrett Gaines would be a solid choice as the new bailiff. Garrett Gaines was hardworking, smart enough, calm, and a strapping man who could handle trouble if it came.

Garrett Gaines had borne no resentment. He held Toby in high esteem—told him often if there was ever anything he could do for him, to just ask, and told his son Del what a fine colored man was Toby Messager. Garrett had died before he could ever repay that debt.

Del looked at the phone hanging on the wall. He felt as if he should rage. He felt that he should stand up to Chuck Oliver about this Toby mess. That he could not bring himself to do so gnawed at him. I'm not the man my daddy was or wanted me to be, he thought, and I'm not even half the man Toby is.

He stood up, muttering under his breath, "I'm just a coward. There's not much I got the guts to do here, but I know one thing I *can* do. I know somebody who might help Toby. It being a Saturday night, most likely the old drunk ain't at home. It'll be God's will, I reckon, one way or t'other."

He strode purposefully to the phone.

Three

The shadows were stretching long when Reverend Walker's car came trundling up the oyster-shell drive. It had been a miserable, confusing day for Okra. He barked at the newcomer with more aggression than he usually would have, especially since he knew the reverend and his car, but it was his opinion that there had already been too many appearances by strangers.

Anna and Tobias came from out of the house and simultaneously shushed the dog. Okra hushed, but he fretted nonetheless. Word had filtered through the colored community concerning Tobit's arrest, and neighbors had come by to tell her and offer such meager assistance as they could. This parade of well-wishers had upended the dog's routine and he did not like it much.

The reverend brought his car to a halt. Anna could see that he had brought Mason Newberry with him. The nearly as wide as he was tall groundskeeper was carrying a stout piece of well-cured ash wood as they approached the house.

"I reckon you have heard", sighed Walker when he had reached the steps. Anna nodded. Walker looked upward as if seeking strength. "It's my fault. I brought this upon him. Upon you."

"No, no", said Anna, shaking her head. "If he'd not heard of the boy from you, he'd have heard from someone else and thought you less of a man for not having told him. And he chose to do what he did, and Tobit can be as hardheaded as that mule of his when it comes to doing what he thinks he's got to do."

"Thank you for those words, Anna", replied Walker. "Look here, Mister Newberry is going to stay here tonight. He'll sleep in the barn. He insists."

"That's right, Missus Anna", added Newberry. "If maybe them Klan fellas come here tonight, they'll find a heap o' trouble fallin' on them from the barn."

"That will just be the death of you", said Tobias. "You know if you hurt a cracker you'll end up like little Jamie. We've got my daddy's shotgun in the house; we can take care of 'em."

"Tobias," scolded Anna, "don't talk like that."

"Why not?" grumbled Tobias. "They're always callin' us niggers, so I call them crackers."

"Why not?" replied Anna. "Because, boy, you might be eighteen years on this earth, but I am *still* your mamma and I told you not to talk like that."

"The boy axes a good question", said Newberry. "But I'm old. My wife is done gone on to the Lord. I don't mind makin' the trip if it's for a good purpose. Toby Two, you keeps that gun in the house. If'n we got to, you can lay into 'em up front while I come wailing on 'em from the rear."

"Let us pray that it doesn't come to that", pleaded Reverend Walker. "You men keep your heads, like Missus Anna here is doing. Maybe just knowin' that y'all are not alone will be enough to keep any trouble from stirring up.

"I fear not so much the Klan as I do just young, stupid troublemakers, likely to be drunk on a Saturday night."

"Two strong men to guard the house will be a comfort", admitted Anna. Then she looked down at the still-fretting Okra. "And we'll have Tobit's shadow with us as well."

The three men laughed. The reverend said a prayer and then made his way back to his car and down the long drive. Anna sent Tobias in to fetch some bedding for Mason.

"Are you sure you won't sleep in the parlor, Mason? With Tobias here, there'd not be anything inappropriate about that."

"Oh no, ma'am", replied the groundskeeper. "I can sleep well as I need in the barn, and besides, I want t'be able to come at 'em from behind likes I said."

Tobias had just arrived with a thin cot mattress, pillow, sheet, and blanket when Okra went from worried fret to alert mode, but then he gave a recognition bark just about the time Crafty Forgeron's truck pulled into the driveway. The white man curved in front of the house and drove back down the drive about a quarter of the way and parked there.

He hopped from the truck, and his bowlegged gait carried him quickly to the porch. He pulled the unlit pipe from between his teeth and stuffed it in his shirt pocket while nodding and saying to all, "Miss Anna, Tobias, Mason. I heard about Tobit. I got a phone call from someone who would prefer to remain unknown. Tobit will be looked after about as much as we can hope while he's in that jail. I tried to get in to see 'im, but they wouldn't let me. I'll go again Monday and I'll get him out of that place. I'll do whatever it takes. This jus' ain't right. There so much jus' ain't right in this world. I can't let it all pass."

"Mister Forgeron, this could be trouble for you", Tobias reminded him.

"Young man, when have I ever been 'fraid of trouble?"

Knowing what he meant, Mason Newberry gave forth a deep belly laugh, earning him a wink from Crafty.

Forgeron then looked at the ash-wood club. "Ain't you got a gun, Mason?"

"Jus' an ol' shotgun, Mister Frank, but the Reverend Walker gave me a ride over here, and it don't do for a colored man to be riding with a gun in the car."

Forgeron nodded and reached behind his back and pulled a pistol out of the waist of his pants. "Take this revolver."

A pleased smile spread on Mason's face. "Well now, I gots to decide if I'll shoots 'em or beats 'em."

"Do both", shrugged Forgeron. "I recall that Tobit has a shotgun?"

"Yessir", replied Tobias. "We ain't got but three shells though."

"Well, I got another pistol in the truck, so if there are more of 'em than can get past ol' Mason and me, we're probably all done for anyways."

He turned then to Mason. "If it comes to it, you don't shoot until you see me go down. Least me being a white man, if some of 'em needs be laid out, there won't be none of that 'persons unknown to the jury' bull—uh, nonsense."

"Well, if you goes down, Mister Forgeron, there may be no avenging angel fallin' on 'em, but there'll be two hundred and twenty pounds of avenging nigger."

"Mason!"

"Sorry, Missus Anna; I forgets myself, sometimes."

"I'll keep watch in the cab of the truck", said Forgeron. "I ain't had a drop to drink, so it ain't likely I'll fall asleep, but maybe that Okra dog can stay out here with me jus' in case I doze."

38

"He knows you", replied Tobias. "Just call him to you and he'll be glad of the company. Good thing too that he had a flea dip jus' the other day."

"I hope I don't give 'im any fleas", worried Forgeron with a wink.

Francis George Forgeron settled himself behind the steering wheel of his truck, with his head resting against a folded blanket that in turn rested against the back window of the cab. A pistol he had found on a dead German back in the Great War lay upon his lap. It turned out that Okra preferred not to be in the cab, but rather to climb onto the roof of the cab so he could keep an eye out on house, barn, truck, and drive. Tactically sound, Forgeron had decided.

Sitting in the truck, wishing he had a drink, Forgeron considered why he was here. Tobit would have advised against it. Most colored folk, and damned near every white person, would have advised against it. "Don't get involved in things that aren't your business."

The colored folk often feared reprisal. Even if a white man treated them decently, they worried that other white people would think it might make them uppity, and the result would be an effort to put them in their place. White folk told him, "Coloreds just ain't worth the trouble."

So why was he here? He was here because Tobit Messager was one of the most decent men he knew of any color. He was here because of the family memory of persecution of Protestants in France. He was here because of things he had seen and done in the Great War. He was here because although he had lost almost all the faith he had ever had, he felt a need for atonement. In his mind he needed to atone not just for things he had done, but for the white race in general. He needed to show that "at least some of us ain't like that".

He remembered too the time he spent with the army in the Philippines putting down the native insurrections. He saw terrible things there. He did terrible things. He was young, and it bothered him some at the time, but there was such an us–against–them survival factor that he put it away in his mind.

Until France: in France he was killing people that looked like him, people with eyes like his. In France there were people that were trying to kill him that looked like him. It was a soul-wrenching revelation to realize that the carnage in the Philippines had not bothered him as much because his enemies had been *different*. It shamed him to this day.

His musing was interrupted by the noise of Okra's claws on the roof of the cab as the dog repositioned himself. He smiled. I'm here too, he thought, because Tobit is a friend, and that boy of his is the kind of son I would have wanted if I were to have had a son.

His smile faded, thinking he might have a son or a daughter out there in the world—if one of the women he had been with chose not to eliminate it. It happened sometimes with the prostitutes. He sighed and whispered to himself, "I'm here too so that I can atone for any child of mine that might not know their father, and for any child of mine that might not ever have lived because I jus' laid money on a table somewhere."

He half dozed thinking on that need for atonement. Tobit had told him once that it was the grace of God, told him that faith was like a rope made up of many strands.

"There's hope, desire, trust, what is knowable, what is intuition", explained Tobit when their casual conversation had turned more serious. "But the finest, most difficult-to-see strand of all is grace. It's also the strongest because it is of God. All the others may fray, but that strand will endure. We mayn't even recognize it for what it is, but it will endure. It's a shining, gossamer thing that just will not break. That's why bad folk can sometimes do remarkably good things, and Frank, you are not a bad man. You have been blinded to grace, but still you respond to it."

In the moonless dark, Forgeron heard Okra's low growl. He was not sure how long he had dozed when he heard the sound of a motor and the slight squeal of brakes. His eyes opened and saw headlights switch off and a vehicle coming down the road from the direction of the beehives.

The sound of a motor went silent, but he heard and then saw a truck coasting into the drive. He sat up. Okra barked, but Forgeron shushed him. He grasped the pistol in his lap and slowly, quietly opened the door. I want to shoot someone, he thought. I want to bring pain to those who would bring pain.

As his feet settled on the ground, the realization of what he was thinking settled upon him. Lord, I've seen enough of that. Just as he leaned back in the truck and flicked on the headlights, he heard Mason call his name from the direction of the barn.

40

The truck at the end of the drive immediately turned over its motor and began to back up with a grinding of gears. He could see three figures seated in the retreating cab, illuminated by his headlights. He strode in front of his own truck and with much posturing aimed his pistol.

With a crunch of gravel and a slight squeal of the tires, the intruding truck sped away down the road. Forgeron nodded to himself and stuck the pistol in the waistband of his pants. He heard Mason again. "Mister Forgeron."

He turned around to see the groundskeeper standing a few yards behind the truck, with the revolver tucked in his belt and the ash-wood cudgel in his hands. Forgeron raised his hand in reassurance. "We scared 'em off, I reckon, Mason."

"I reckons you scared 'em off", chuckled Newberry. "I reckons they done soil't they britches when they seen you drawin' bead on 'em."

Forgeron chuckled, "I wasn't gonna shoot at 'em, just wanted 'em to think about it."

"I reckons they *still* thinking about it. I think I recognize 'em, least ways two of 'em. Looked like them two Dunlin boys; don't know who the third boy was."

"It did look like their truck", agreed Forgeron as he went to stand beside Newberry.

"Jus' young'uns, really", said Mason. "No Klan, I reckon."

Forgeron looked up at the night sky. "Don't reckon we're likely to see any. Most likely those boys just lookin' for stupid mischief."

"I reckon, but they's already beat up one colored boy, Terrance Leach's boy, Isaiah. They was talkin' rude to his sister, and after he tells 'em to leave off her, they jump out of that truck and starts a'whooping on 'im. Then they saw some other colored boys comin' down the road, so they jumps back in the truck and drives off."

"But I can't say they was nearly so rough with Isaiah as poor Jamie gots it. Mostly they just push Isaiah around and swung on 'im a few times."

"Maybe", replied Forgeron, chewing the inside of his cheek. "But, who can know how bad it might have been if those other boys hadn't showed up?"

"No way to be sure, I reckon. Well, I'll get myself back to the barn", said Mason as he turned and shambled the way he had come.

As Forgeron opened the truck door and switched off the headlights, he felt Okra's pointy nose sniff at the top of his head. Before taking his place back in the cab, he reached up to rub the dog's muzzle. "You did good, boy."

Settled back in the truck, he relaxed. He was thinking now that it was too late in the night for any real Klan trouble. The click of nails on metal came from over his head as Okra resettled on the roof. That's a good watchdog, thought Forgeron, as drowsiness settled on him.

The drowsiness gave way to dozing, and the dozing to sleep, and the sleep to dreaming. He dreamed about Brenda Wiggles—not her real name, of course. She was a buxom prostitute with a tumble of blonde hair and the fullest lips he'd ever known on a white woman. He dreamed that she was kissing his cheek, and a familiar stirring began in him. He sighed, until it seemed that her lips became impossibly large, and then bristly.

The impossibility caused him to wake in confusion. He saw that it was the gray predawn; Okra was on the hood of the truck looking at him through the windshield with a wagging tail. Still he could feel lips muzzling on his cheek, and he cut his eyes toward the window of the truck.

The face and lips of a mule caused him to throw himself the other direction. "What the—"

A more full wakefulness passed over him. He managed a half chuckle at his own expense. "Joe-boy, is that you?"

"Well, 'course it's you or Okra would've been raisin' Cain, I reckon."

He rubbed his face to remove mule slobber and waken himself even more. Then he opened the door as the mule backed away some. He cast a suspicious glance at the animal. "You are supposed to be in jail."

Okra had climbed back onto the roof of the cab and was sniffing his head. Forgeron pushed his muzzle away. "All right, I've had enough smooching from animals. Come on, you stubborn ol' mule. Reckon you don't care a damned for what that worthless sheriff wants. Let's get you back to your barn."

Newberry met them three-quarters of the way. "Look at that! Reckon for sure ol' Joe-boy knows his way home. He done broke hisself out of jail!"

He ran his hands along Joe-boy's flanks as he inspected the mule. "He looks sound enough. Gots a few scratches on his haunch here. I'll see if they is any ointment in the barn."

"I reckon it's best not to think what he might have done to that shanty stall they put him in", chuckled Forgeron.

"He sure do seem to like you", laughed Mason as Joe-boy tried to muzzle a kiss to Frank again.

"Well, I reckon I sure do like mules", chuckled Frank. "I have since my time in the Philippines with the army. They slogged some badly needed supplies to us more than once, Mason. Their drivers were usually colored troops, tough-as-nails veterans of the Spanish-American War. They kept us alive, they surely did. Them and their mules."

Tobit opened his eyes. He was not sure where he was at first, until he saw the dingy ceiling of the jail. He heard Ben Cobb stomping down the steps, cussing for all he was worth. All through the night, Tobit had been bothered by dreams, the dreams of movements in the night, and a dread emotion that carried over into his waking.

Ben Cobb stamped to the cell bars, glaring at Tobit. "That mule of your'n done tored down the stable. Looks like he kicked out the side wall, then the other walls fell in and the roof collapsed."

"Is Joe-boy hurt?"

"How's I supposed t'know? Worthless mule is gone. I wish it kill't 'im", growled Cobb. "The sheriff likely t'kill 'im if he sees him."

"Over that ol' shed?" mused one of the checker players who had introduced himself as Sam Cord to Tobit. Sam was from the county. His opponent, Will Morse, was originally from Charlotte but had been living in the county for more than ten years. "They hardly never used it. Reckon the sheriff's gonna start arresting mules right regular now?"

Will Morse laughed and slapped his knee at that, but it only brought another glare from Cobb. "Yeah, you coons laugh it up. Ol' Toby ain' gonna be laughing, though. Not when the sheriff makes him pays for that shed."

"I'll lends him a nickel", said Morse, yawning. "That should just about cover it. Shoot, I'll give him the danged nickel just to have seen your face when you came down them steps!"

Cobb walked to the end of the corridor and pulled three metal shackles from off the wall, then tossed them into the large cell. "Shackle yo'selves up. See if you y'all thinks this is funny when you is cleaning up the mess that mule made. Ain't no rest on Sunday for a colored man in a white man's jail."

As they were shackling their own feet, Sam looked up to Tobit. "Colored don' get no breakfast, Mister Toby. No sir, we gets two meals. One 'tween breakfast and lunch, t'other same time as last night, jus' 'fore we goes to bed."

Then he and Morse went to the galvanized tub that served as a toilet. Sam winked at Tobit. "We've gots this today. Gonna take you some time to gets used to walkin' in them shackles. I don' wanna hafta cleans up if you cause this to spill."

"Don't worry yourself none, though", added Will. "You can have two turns once you've learned yourself how to walk right. You can help Sam 'cause I done beat him twice playin' checkers, so he owes me two toilet dumps."

"Shut your mouth and get moving", snapped Cobb.

With Tobit shuffling awkwardly behind them, the two men made their way cautiously up the steps. Once they were outside they went to a door made of planks that covered a cesspit where once an outhouse had stood. They emptied the contents of the tub, poured some water in it, and rocked the tub between them before emptying it again.

While they were taking care of that, Cobb took the axe handle he was carrying and prodded Tobit, "Get on over yonder to that shed. You can start picking up the ruination that damned mule has brought about."

The rusted tin roof had split in two as it collapsed. Tobit began prying at the half-rotten, tar-paper-covered timbers pinned beneath it. It was difficult because the dry-rotted tar paper still had enough strength to hold the pieces together. He had just decided to try and shift the roof when his two cell mates joined him.

"I thinks that be the idea", said Sam, nodding.

Together they dragged half the roof off the pile. Then they began pulling apart the timbers and clapboard. They made a pile for timber, a pile for clapboard, and a pile for the tar paper they were pulling off the wood.

"Don't sees no blood", noted Sam. "So I reckon your mule didn't get hurt much."

"Well, he's a fugitive now", said Will Morse. "When the sheriff gets ol' Longears he'll put him on the work gang. Might even take him to the gallows so's no other John-mule or Hinny gets no ideas."

"Joe-boy isn't a Johnnie", said Tobit as he ripped tar paper from off of clapboard.

"That's the problem", decided Sam. "You cain't leave the full equipment on no boy mule or he gets ornery."

44

"That's usually true", admitted Tobit as he shuffled over to toss the clapboard onto the appropriate pile. "But ol' Joe-boy behaves himself well enough. Smart mule too."

"He sho' figured out how to gets hisself out'n jail!" laughed Sam.

It took nearly two hours to pull apart and pile the ruin of the stable shed. They knew it was a pointless endeavor since it had been a worthless collection of rotten wood and paper even before Joe-boy had underscored the fact.

When they had finished, they were brought what passed for breakfast. Each of them received a cup of grits and one day-old biscuit. They had to scrape the grits up with their fingers. Then they rinsed out the cups, drank some water, and rinsed them again before surrendering them to Ben Cobb.

"Ain't no rest for y'all", said the trustee. He directed them to a ditch that edged the unpaved parking area. "Get that trash outta there."

They were given a single soft-tine rake. Two of them would pick up larger pieces of debris while the third raked up the finer bits. It was not back-breaking work, but it was tedious and clumsy because of the shackles on their legs.

Just a little after one o'clock they were given a break. To escape the heat, they shuffled into the shadow of the same oak that Tobit had shaded under the day before. While the two checker players bantered between themselves, Tobit watched a flock of sparrows flitting in the branches above him.

On the roadway in front of the courthouse a car backfired and the startled birds swept low, tight, and quickly out of the branches. The backfire caused Tobit to blink, and just as he reopened his eyes, bird droppings splattered across his face.

"My eyes", he muttered.

Ben Cobb laughed, "Them birds shat all over Toby's face!"

"My eyes."

"He's got bird droppings in his eyes", Will Morse pointed out before turning to the trustee. "Let me get some water so's he can wash them out."

Cobb shrugged but tossed a cup at Morse. The inmate shuffled quickly to the spigot and filled it with water. As he was hustling back he heard Sam saying, "Don't rubs yo' eyes, Mister Toby. Don't rubs 'em."

"Lean back", directed Morse. He poured a bit of water in each eye and brushed away the droppings. Then he poured more water. "Now blink and then lean forward so's the water can wash away."

When Tobit had done this he looked out toward the light beyond the shade and blinked his eyes. Then he held his hand in front of his face. "I can't see. Can't see nothing but gray. Can't hardly make out my own hand!"

"Bull", spat Cobb. He motioned for the other two to back away as he knelt in front of Tobit. He waved his hand back and forth, and then made as if to poke him in the eye. There was no reaction from Tobit.

"Lawd, he's done gone blind", Sam groaned. "Poor Mister Tobit's done been blinded."

"Blinded by bird droppings", chuckled Cobb.

"Shut up, nigger", snarled Morse as he shuffled back to Tobit's side. "He ain't done nothing to deserve this."

Cobb shifted the axe handle threateningly, but Morse just waved him off. "I ain' gonna hurt you, fool. You ain't nearly worth hanging for. We jus' need to get Mister Toby inside."

For a moment Cobb only glared, but then he sighed and rose. "All right, get him to his feet. Blinded by bird droppings, if that don' beat all. Looks like your good Lawd puttin' you in your place, Toby."

He cackled as Tobit's two cell mates led him back toward the jail.

In the dim light of the jail, Tobit could make out only the globs of gray where light filtered through the high, dirty windows. He sat on the wooden ledge, hunched over with his elbows on his knees and his head in his hands. The shackles had been removed and collected by Cobb.

"We gots to get him a doctor", fretted Sam. "We've washed his eyes out three times already."

"On a Sunday?" replied Cobb. "Don't be stupid. He'll be lucky to see a doctor come Monday. For sho' one thing, I ain't callin' the sheriff over this."

"That leash ever choke you?" asked Will Morse.

"Better a leash than a noose", retorted Cobb. "Look, I'll gets you some more rags and water. Jus' keeps a wet rag on them eyes. Might not cure him, but maybe it'll be a comfort to him."

"You is the soul of kindness", sighed Sam.

For the rest of the day and night Tobit lay stretched out on the ledge with his head resting on a pillow made of folded towels and with a cool, damp rag folded over his eyes. The night seemed one of the longest of his life. He drifted from the dark of wakefulness to dreams that remembered the light and then back to the dark.

When the welcomed oblivion between dark and dreams would come no more, he sat up on the ledge. He heard stirrings and called out softly, "What time is it?"

"It be 'bout nine o'clock, Mister Toby", reported Sam. "Will and me, we gotta get to work on that ditch we didn't finish yesterday, but Deputy Gaines is gone t'fetch the doc to takes a look at yo' eyes."

In his world of gray gloom, Tobit heard Cobb descending the stairway and passing the shackles through the bars. Nothing was said, but he heard the door to the cell moan as it opened then closed. He heard the shackled shuffle of the two inmates as they climbed the stairway. Then he was alone.

He had no way of telling how much time passed, but without the distraction of sight, he was so attuned to sound that he heard the door at the top of the steps open and the trod of feet—a large man, he reckoned, by the sound of the footfalls.

"Mister Toby," Del Gaines greeted him, "I'm gonna take you upstairs now so the doc can look you over. I've gotta put them shackles on you. I don't want to, you understand? But it's the regulations, and the sheriff would have my job if I didn't."

"I understand."

He heard the sound of shackles and then the cell door opening. He felt the shackles being placed around his ankles. A large hand settled around his bicep. "Come on, Mister Toby. I'll help you up them steps."

As they negotiated the steps, Gaines spoke again, "That Forgeron fellow has been by. He's trying to get you released. He's trackin' down a magistrate. He seems determined. Maybe he can get you home 'fore the day is done."

"That would be welcomed", said Tobit softly. "I ain't had a bath since Friday night. After workin' in the sun most of yesterday, I hope I ain't giving you too much offense."

"Reckon you got nothin' to apologize for", replied Gaines. "Nothing at all."

The smell of pine disinfectant filled Tobit's nostrils as he was led through the warren of corridors and small rooms. Finally a door opened and then he smelled Doc Mack. Cicero Virgil Macklin was an alcoholic. He was so far gone into alcoholism that his body bore a constant sickly sweet odor barely veiled at times by the scent of stale cigarette or cigar smoke.

He had more Negro patients than white patients these days. Many of the old folk of both races remembered him as a hero from the Spanish flu epidemic, but his determined efforts had taken a mental toll on the man. Now he was withered in body and soul. Whatever mind he had left was in a near constant fog. He was the sad ruin of a man and a life.

Some doctors from Harper Bay had opened a clinic in Stonebridge; they served white folk in the front of it and colored folk in the back. They did not live in the county, but rotated their visits among themselves between the Stonebridge clinic and their office in Harper Bay.

Doc Mack served as the jailhouse doctor and coroner. Tobit heard his ravaged voice directing the deputy, "Sit 'im ovah there, Del."

As Tobit followed the guiding hand to a sitting position, he could smell the doctor's breath as the man leaned in. "All right then. Let's see what we got here."

The doctor murmured something to himself and then spoke again, "You see this?"

"I see something, a lighter gray", replied Tobit. "Most of what I see is either darkness or a very dark gray."

"Well, it looks like that bird feces burnt your eyes", said Doc Mack. "Damndest thing, eh? Of course, bird feces is very acidic, but I've never seen such as this. No suh, not ever. Feeling any pain, Toby?"

"Just some burning from time to time. It was much worse last night."

"Hmmm. Well, I'll give you an ointment. Can't say that it will help, but it'll help prevent infection. I can see that your eyes look hazed over, maybe burned by the acid in the bird feces."

The doctor pulled down the lower lid of each eye and gently placed some ointment there. "Now blink. It'll feel gummy for a bit. I know a doctor in Chapel Hill who might look at you. He'll take on colored cases if they're interesting. I'd reckon a shat upon eye gone blind might be interesting enough.

"But, I warn you, he's expensive and he is not given to charity work. Can't pay him with eggs or a bag of potatoes."

"I don't have much money at this time", explained Tobit in a quiet voice.

"No, reckon not", sighed Doc Macklin with rum-infused breath. "Truth be tol', I doubt I could afford him either."

There was silence for a moment before Macklin continued, "I reckon I'm not much help. Not much use at all."

The voice was so laden with anguish that Tobit reached out until his hand found that of the doctor. He squeezed.

"You've done as much as you can, Dr. Macklin. I appreciate it. Many of us appreciate all you have done for us all these years. We remember the flu years. We remember you worked yourself to exhaustion. We will *never* forget."

He released the hand then, and gave an emphatic nod of his head and repeated, "Never."

Silence again, then a cough with a boozy exhalation, and finally the doctor spoke in a low, cracking voice, "Thank you for that, Tobit."

The smell of the man faded as his footsteps retreated. Tobit heard him call out softly, "Deputy, I've done about all I can do here. Make sure someone helps him get that ointment in his eyes."

The sound of the doctor retreated completely from the room. Tobit felt the deputy's arm.

"Come with me, Mister Toby."

He was led back down into the colored jail. Sam and Will took over at the cell and guided him to the wooden ledge. As he sat down he heard Gaines telling his cell mates, "If he is here tonight, you boys make sure he gets some of this here ointment in his eyes before lights out. Doc says just put a bit on his lower eyelids. Make sure your hands is clean, though, hear?"

"We'll takes care", Sam assured the deputy. He walked over to Tobit and put the tube of ointment into the pocket of the older man's overalls. "Keep that right there, Mister Toby. Will and me gonna look after you."

Four

Just before noon, Francis "Crafty" Forgeron came striding his bow-legged way into the offices of the sheriff's department. He was dressed as though he was intent on womanizing on a Saturday night in a large city. He was wearing a suit and his best cowboy boots with silver-tipped toes.

He saw a junior deputy on a stool behind the counter. The young man was turned to face an electric tabletop fan. The fan was on high, and between the rattling of its wire cage, and the wobbly swooshes of the ceiling fans in the room, the young man had not heard Forgeron entering—neither did Del Gaines at his desk off to one side behind the counter.

Forgeron was clutching a handful of documents that he slapped down on the scarred wooden counter. "Where's the sheriff? I've got all the paperwork for the release of Tobit Messager."

The deputy behind the counter spun around on his stool, startled and taken aback at the small man's abrupt and aggressive manner. From his desk behind the counter Gaines gave a chuckle. "Reckon maybe you better go get the sheriff, Ernie."

The wide-eyed deputy nodded and headed back into the warren of offices. After a few minutes, Sheriff Oliver preceded him into the room. The sheriff's pale, round face became flushed and his eyes narrowed. "Forgeron; figures. What you stickin' your nose into this business for?"

"You just worry about this paperwork here", replied Forgeron, slapping his hand again on the papers he had placed on the counter.

Oliver picked up the papers and began glancing through them. "Looks mostly in order. Of course, there's the issue of the stable his mule destroyed."

Forgeron reached in his pocket and tossed a nickel onto the counter. "That should cover that ol' heap of timber. Keep the change, but I'll be wanting a receipt."

"I don't much like your attitude", scowled Oliver as the last rattle of the nickel faded.

"I don't much like *you*", replied Forgeron. "Now, I expect you should get the man out of jail before I get really mad."

"Are you threatening me?"

"Sheriff, you know I have too much respect for a badge to threaten anyone wearing it. Two of my brothers wear badges, remember? However, should you want to take off that badge and step outside, I'd be very interested in seeing if you can pull my boot out from your behind as quickly as I can put it there."

"I don't think you're gonna like it much if you get me riled up, Forgeron", growled the sheriff.

"I've faced two hundred pounds of charging German carrying a Mauser 98 with fixed bayonet in his hands", replied Forgeron with a laugh. "So what makes you think I'd worry about a soft, strutting, pudgy little popinjay like you?"

Oliver glared at the man. He sifted through his mind for some angle to use against him, but he knew of Forgeron's brothers and their positions further up the legal chain. It just was not worth it. Finally he snorted, "You gotta be the most nigger lovin' man I ever heard tell."

"*Sheriff*"; it was Del Gaines with a warning tone.

Oliver turned around to his chief deputy. "Process the prisoner, Gaines."

With that the sheriff strode angrily back to his office. Forgeron called after him, "Don't forget my receipt."

A smile hinted on Del's face as he rose from his desk. "I'll go get Mister Toby. Ernie, write the man a receipt."

The junior deputy pulled out a receipt book and pen, but just stared at it for a moment in confusion. "How should I make this out?"

"Paid by Frank Forgeron, five cents for damages allegedly inflicted by Joe-boy Messager to an unused pile of timber known as old stables", said Gaines as he headed toward the door that opened onto the stairs of the colored jail. "Better put full payment to be determined. Wouldn't want you to get fired."

Tobit was sitting on the ledge when he heard the door open and the heavy footfall of Del Gaines. He was alone because his two cell mates had been taken out for a work detail. He judged the chief deputy to be halfway down the steps when he heard lighter footsteps scurrying down and past the heavier.

"I'll gets him ready, Deputy", called out the winded voice of Ben Cobb, followed by the rattle of shackles.

"Dangit, Ben; you near 'bout ran me off the steps", muttered Gaines. "We don't need shackles; Mister Toby is being released."

The door to the cell opened, and Tobit heard the trustee entering and then speaking just above a whisper, "Looks like someone done come to get they pet Geechee. This way with me, Toby."

The hand barely touched Tobit's arm, guiding him toward the door. Suddenly Tobit turned, grasping by instinct the trustee's shoulders. He bowed his head so that he guessed his eyes would be looking into Cobb's face. "I understand, Ben. I understand. I have known such anger. If I have been arrogant, I ask you to forgive me."

Tobit released the smaller man and heard him shuffle away. He could not see Ben Cobb shaking in fear, anger, frustration, and shame. Chief Deputy Gaines had also been startled by Tobit's sudden action and had hurried into the cell, but the trustee was already released before he got there.

Gaines reached out to take Tobit's arm and began guiding him toward the stairwell. He turned back to look at the still-shaking trustee. "Imagine that, *him* asking *you* for forgiveness."

Ben Cobb made his way shakily to his own unlocked cell and sat heavily upon the creaking cot. A series of emotions swept across him like a panicked and retreating army. Finally the trustee buried his face in his hands and began to sob.

"Crafty Forgeron posted your bail, Mister Toby", the chief deputy explained as he guided the blind man up the steps. "Doc Mack ruled that the boy's death was a suicide."

"Suicide?" said Tobit, halting in his tracks with one hand against the wall of the stairwell. "Suicide? Deputy, that was no suicide. Look at the rope, Deputy; you can see it has been dragged over a tree limb with weight on it. Go to the tree and you can see the limb it was dragged over. Nobody commits suicide by pulling themselves over a tree limb."

A hand was placed on Tobit's back, urging him forward. "I wouldn't make too much noise about this, Mister Toby. Suicide is still a crime, so the sheriff might still press on with this. If you lay low, the charges of disturbing the scene of a crime will probably be dropped."

"Somebody killed that boy", protested Tobit as he continued up the steps. "Doesn't anyone care about that? I know he was a colored boy, but he was just a child."

"Mister Toby—"

"Deputy, what if it ain't just a colored boy next time? What if it is some little white young'un? What if the same people who did this to James kill again? I couldn't live with that on my conscience, Deputy. Not even as the price for my freedom. Can you?"

Gaines said nothing, but the hand on Tobit's back became more firm and insistent. They entered into the muggy currents of fan-blown air, and the hand grasped Tobit's shoulder to bring him to a halt.

"Here he is", said the deputy to Forgeron. "You better get him out of here before he gets into more trouble. Wait, his personal effects are in this here envelope."

Tobit heard the passing of the envelope and then Frank Forgeron's voice. "Come on with me, Tobit. I'm taking you on home."

"Mister Tobit," called out Del Gaines, "please, be careful what you say. Be careful."

Tobit did not reply to either of them. He just let himself be led out of the building and into the cab of Forgeron's truck. When Crafty had started the truck and was pulling onto the road, Tobit ventured to speak. "How much was the bail, Frank?"

"Don't worry about that", replied Forgeron. "You ain't plannin' on jumping bail are you? So I'll get it back. Reverend Walker has been on the phone with a lawyer from up 'round Raleigh, a colored fellow. He thinks he can get him to take the case. Oliver won't be expecting some NAACP lawyer to be getting involved, but this fellow figures that with a lynching, maybe the Klan and a corrupt sheriff involved, and them out to get a respectable man like yourself, this is one they can make a statement with."

"The sheriff is saying it was suicide, Frank. It just wasn't. I saw the fraying of the rope having been pulled over the branch. The boy surely didn't beat himself up like that. I cannot believe Doc Mack would go along with such a determination."

"He did it for you, Tobit", said Forgeron. "That's what I would guess, anyway. Maybe he's just scared of the Klan. Poor ol' Doc is a washed-out man. I sometimes think he cared too much for too long and it has sucked him dry of hope."

"He broke himself during the Spanish flu years", said Tobit.

"Well, if it is proved that he falsified the information for a death certificate, it will be the end of his doctoring", said Forgeron. "I'll make some calls up to Raleigh. I don't know if it will do any good, but Washington isn't so friendly with the Klan these days. I reckon them Nazis got 'em worried; the two groups being cut from the same cloth, as it were. I do know, however, that the state has been lookin' into the moonshining in this county."

"I spoke of the rope and the tree to the chief deputy", said Tobit.

"Gaines is a good sort of man", replied Forgeron. "But, I'm not sure he's one to rock the boat. He just wants to get to retirement with as little fuss as possible."

"I can understand that", Tobit sighed. "He saw his father near about ruined by the Crash. I wouldn't reckon he'd want to risk ruin coming down on his own wife and children."

"I reckon you heard that ol' mule of yours got back home?" asked Forgeron.

Tobit laughed, "Ol' Joe-boy got a mind of his own. Was he hurt by that stable collapsing?"

"Only some scratches", reported Forgeron. "Mason's done put some ointment on 'im. Joe-boy is still ornery and stubborn with no loss of appetite. Now, that dog of yours, he's 'bout beside himself with you being gone."

"Okra ain't quite right in the head, Frank, but he's more right in the head now than when I first took him in. I think there's something in that dog. Don't know why, 'xactly, but I can see it waking over time."

"I'll take your word for it", laughed Forgeron. "I can tell you he makes a passable watchdog."

"I appreciate you and Mason taking care of Anna and Tobias like that, Frank."

"Don't worry about it. I reckon if anyone got by us, by the time Anna was through with 'em they'd be running back into our arms!"

The next two months dragged on with Tobit trying to acclimate to his situation. He had learned to milk the cow despite the perpetual mist before his eyes. He thought he could collect eggs, but Anna would have none of that for fear he might put his hand in a nest with a snake in it. Okra served as snake alarm elsewhere, but nobody deemed it wise to let the dog into the chicken coop.

A bill for the ruined stable came in the mail. It was a ridiculous charge, probably driven by Sheriff Oliver's anger at the NAACP lawyer having finagled that all charges against Tobit be dismissed, coupled with his becoming an object of ridicule for having supposedly arrested a mule. Forgeron got wind of the charges and stormed into the sheriff's office and nearly got himself arrested despite his connections, but in the end he got the bill reduced and paid it himself.

Tobit protested that generosity, but Forgeron only told him, "You can pay me back as you're able."

"I don't know when that'll be", replied Tobit. "I am near about useless. I can't scavenge for junk, can't do woodworking. If it weren't for Anna's houseworking, and Tobias working with you, we'd be starving for sure, and that fate always seems lurking 'round each new day.

"It weighs on me. It weighs on me too that Tobias can't go to college. I didn't get to finish college because of the trouble that came upon my father in Harper Bay. Now this has kept my son out altogether."

"The boy is a natural mechanic", offered Forgeron.

"I know. I know. It's just that such things are the only things a Negro seems allowed to do in the South", Tobit replied. "I at least wanted him to study engineering or some such."

"Well, now that he's out of school for good, the money from the shop should help keep your heads above water", suggested Forgeron. "And don't be thinkin' there is any charity involved. That boy's worth every penny I pay him. I reckon in another year or two he'll be a better mechanic than I am. He learns faster and keeps up with the changes better than I do."

What Forgeron did not tell Tobit was that the legal assistance he had given to a Negro came with a price. A great many white folk had stopped buying gas from his station, or bringing their vehicles to him for repair. He did not fret on it too much because this had happened before. He knew that eventually they would grow tired of the higher prices and lower competence of his competitors and gradually return to his shop. His place was newer and cleaner as well. It was a financial strain, but one for which he was prepared and would weather.

It surprised him one day when Hank Johns pulled his Cadillac in for a fill-up and oil check. Johns was a Klan member and near the top of the heap. He was a tall, lean man with a slight stoop. He owned farmland, timberland, and a fishery. He was a perplexing man because he was usually polite, moderately kind, and even at times generous to Negroes, but if he were asked about that he would just shrug and say, "I am kind also to children, dogs, and even pigs as it is warranted."

Forgeron sometimes suspected that Johns saw the Klan mostly as a way to control other men, and therefore useful to him for business purposes, more than believing any of the Klan rhetoric. He was suspicious of the appearance of the man at his shop, but dutifully fueled the car, checked the oil, and cleaned the windshield while Johns ventured in to get a Pepsi out of the cold chest.

Tobias was behind the counter, standing on a short ladder so he could pull a fan belt off the wall. Descending he saw Johns and nodded politely, wishing to bring no further troubles upon his boss. The leading Klansman smiled, but did not incline his own head. "Good morning, Toby Two. How is your pappy faring? Any improvement?"

"No, sir", replied Tobias, casting his gaze on the ground so as to hide his ire. "He is about the same."

"That's a shame, that's a shame", said Johns as he opened his Pepsi. "Some folk think that he is uppity. Reckon maybe he is. At the same time, though, he is a hardworking colored man. Always was. Your people could do with more folk such as him, except maybe without the uppity. You remember that, boy. You work hard, mind your manners, and the white man will help you along."

"I best get back to work then", said Tobias, passing through the door into the workshop area.

Johns finished his Pepsi and placed the empty bottle on the counter as he waited for his car to be serviced. When Forgeron came into the shop, Johns gestured to the empty bottle. "I got this here Pepsi too."

Forgeron nodded and went behind the counter to the cash register. "You should get those wipers checked out before too long."

"Thank you, Crafty. I'll tend to it next week", replied Johns. Then he lowered his voice, as if to keep it from carrying into the adjacent work bays. "Look here, I want to talk to you 'bout something. About that colored boy that was hanged a few months back."

"You mean the one who hanged himself by wrapping a rope around his neck and dragging himself into the air?" snorted Forgeron.

"I don't know about all that", replied Johns. "What I do know is that the Klan had nothing to do with it. I wanted to pass that on to you, so's you could pass it on to others."

56

Forgeron looked up from the cash register with a hard expression on his face. "Then just who do you think did it?"

"That I don't know", admitted Johns. "I can't even say as it might not have been someone who belongs to the Klan, or one of those worthless types who pretend to. Could even have been some stupid rednecks, like them Dunlin brothers, who are always into mischief."

"Lynchin' ain't just mischief."

Johns nodded. He had to chew on his own arrogance to speak of this with Crafty. He let go a sigh to regain composure before continuing, "You might not believe me, but I can tell you there was no official Klan involvement in this. You might not believe me, but I *can* tell you why there would be no such involvement.

"A number of us higher ups don't want no trouble that can be avoided in this area. With everything going on in Europe and with them Orientals, the government is thinking there's gonna be another war. They are looking to build some new military bases. They are looking in this area. They already own a lot of the land, but they'll be wanting some they don't own.

"Well, Crafty, a number of us in the Klan own some land they'll find useful. We also own land that will become more valuable when them bases is built. So, I think you can see where we don't want nothing aggravating the chiefs in Washington. Especially with that Missus Roosevelt sticking her nose into things she shouldn't.

"So there it is. That is why we had nothing to do with whatever happened to that boy. You can pass that on to your big-shot brothers who can pass onto even bigger shots. Do that, and white folk might see to look past your interference on certain matters."

"Sounds a little more like a veiled threat than I am inclined to appreciate", said Forgeron. "But, it is useful information, and it will be passed on. Now, you owe me two dollars and five cents for the gas and the Pepsi."

Shaking his head, Hank Johns pulled three dollar bills out of his wallet and laid them on counter. "Eighteen cents a gallon. Just imagine what will happen if war does come. Anyways, you keep the change; maybe help out ol' Toby. I always did like that nigger in spite of his attitude."

With that Johns turned and walked calmly back to his car and drove off. Forgeron could only wonder about the complexity of people, but he reckoned he could not figure himself out, never mind everybody else. Tobit had once chuckled at the observation and offered, "Frank, I reckon you're like Saint Augustine. He said he was a mystery to himself."

"I reckon I am", muttered Forgeron to himself.

By the end of that week his white business was nearly back to normal.

Tobit was sitting at the kitchen table. Summer was fading and a comfortable breeze was blowing through the open windows. The sunlight was strong and brightened the haze, into which he stared. When he closed his eyes, he thought he could actually see the hint of a red glow, but reckoned it was most likely his imagination.

He heard a car in the drive, then a car door open and shut, then the car leaving, and then he heard Anna coming into the house. She seemed lighter of step than usual and was actually humming softly to herself. She entered into the kitchen and placed something on the table across from Tobit.

"Some kind of day", she said cheerily. "Cleaned the Ferguson's house, but you know that."

"I know it's a long walk for you", said Tobit.

"It would be", replied Anna. "But you know who I saw? Nan Wolfe! She was driving her grandmother to see some friends over by Sunset Crossing."

"Driving? The girl can't be old enough. Well, no, I reckon she is", decided Tobit. "She's near ten years older than Tobias. I should be more surprised that Nanella Walker is still alive."

"Missus Walker didn't recognize me at first", said Anna. "She's looking her age, sitting all shriveled up in the backseat. Still, she perked up when she remembered who I was. Nan has graduated from college and is working in Winston-Salem. Says she can't get her grandmother to move up there with her. Says Owen is doing well.

"But, anyway, they gave me a ride home. Good thing, too, or I'd have had every dog between here and the Ferguson house chasing me. You just lean over that table and use that nose of yours."

Tobit followed the directive, taking in a deep breath. His eyes opened wider despite his blindness. "Something smells like ham."

"Do tell", said Anna. "I reckon nothing smells like ham so much as ham smells like ham."

"Ham? Where did you get ham?" asked Tobit.

"I have my ways", teased Anna.

Tobit frowned. "Anna, where did you get the ham?"

Silence. Tobit could feel the coldness. Then he heard Anna speaking softly, "And where would I have gotten the ham, Tobit Freeman Messager? Do you think I would have stolen it? Missus Ferguson gave it to me in addition to my wages. In appreciation."

"I wouldn't have thought the Fergusons so generous", replied Tobit.

"You listen to me", Anna erupted. "You are a good man. You are a charitable man. But the good Lord knows you don't know how to accept charity and the good intentions of others. Far too proud, you have been, Tobit. I ain't one to think that God sends misfortune to teach a lesson, but I think he can want you to learn a lesson from it.

"Instead of even thinking for one moment that I might have stolen this ham, you might have considered maybe, just maybe, there is some charity in folk. Even in white folk like the Fergusons."

"I am sorry, Anna", pleaded Tobit. "I didn't think you stole it. You are the last person I would think that of. But you are right; I wasn't as charitable in my consideration of the Fergusons as they seem to have been of us. I am sorry."

He got up then and began to feel his way toward the front door. He heard Anna whisper his name and then felt her hand lightly on his arm. He gently brushed it away, shaking his head apologetically. "No, I'll be all right. I just need to sit and think a spell. That's all."

Even in his gray haze he knew the way to the front porch, but his emotions made him fumble along. Once on the porch he felt Okra's cold nose sniff at his fingers. Finally he sat clumsily into one of the rocking chairs. He heard Okra settling nearby with a grunt.

Tobit closed his eyes and leaned his head forward. *Lord, you are righteous and everything you do is just. All your deeds have meaning and mercy. Forgive me my sins. Forgive me the pride that makes me despair.*

I am tired, Lord. I feel as though I am a stranger in my own life. Your will be done, but I ask you, Lord, to release me. I fear I have no more strength. I ask that you command that my spirit be taken up into the eternity beyond this. It is better that I should die now, than to let this misery eat at my soul until it has no chance of ever beholding your face in glory. As your will would have it, Lord.

Then Tobit buried his hands in his face and began to weep.

Five

Sarah wept with her face in her hands. She was wracked with shame, anguish, dread, and sorrow. She had been walking through her father's store when she overheard two old women talking about her.

"There she is", whispered the first, Mama Ann, who cooked at the grill. "Just eighteen years old and already she's put three men in their graves."

The other woman nodded knowingly. "She's cursed; that's what it is. Beautiful girl, but what man would marry her now? She used to carry herself like the queen of Sheba; now I reckons she ain't so proud."

Sarah had held herself together until she was out of the store, but as she hurried home the weeping had begun and built with each tormented step she took. She hurried through the house and collapsed into the overstuffed chair beside her bedroom window.

There was shame because she had been nearly relieved when the latest fiancé had died. Tom Bryant had been twenty years her senior. After two of her previous fiancés had died, her father had been desperate to see her married.

It did not register upon him what she might want, even though she had suggested she should probably join the Oblate Sisters of Providence. Her father, Jubal Tomkins, was more than resistant, and in the end the order suggested she give the notion more discernment, because they felt she was reacting to grief and fear rather than a true calling.

Tom Bryant was selected by her father because he was a financially stable farmer, and willing. He was a widower with five children, two of whom were actually older than Sarah. He was also a boorish man, greedy, and intemperate in his appetites.

Sarah was surprised that her parents should favor a marriage to such a rough and undignified man. Her mother, Rose, was particularly fussy about colored folk bettering themselves by speaking as the elite and educated white class spoke, and by minding that their manners were always polite and proper. To his credit, however, Bryant was a hardworking man. Many saw it as a grim irony that he should die while working. The front wheel of his tractor had broken away as he was turning sharply to begin a new row. The tractor had overturned and crushed Bryant beneath it.

Sarah had hated the way he looked at her, but she was the only surviving child of her parents, and they were both desperate for grandchildren. When fiancé number two had died, Jubal became sure that it had happened because God did not want his child married to a non-Catholic.

Tom Bryant had been a Catholic, albeit not a particularly devout one, and so he had become fiancé number three. Jubal Tomkins was a good man, but a muted form of madness seemed to have descended upon him and to deepen with each passing of a future son-in-law. It seemed, in fact, to Sarah that a superstitious madness had descended upon her whole family.

Sarah managed to lift her head and look out the window into the early autumn sky. It seemed almost a macabre joke now that her father had resisted her first betrothal. She had still been shy of her sixteenth birthday when William Gem, having just turned eighteen, had asked her to marry him. Her father had thought her too young.

She realized now that she had been. She was infatuated with William. He was a tall, athletic young man much admired for his skill as a baseball player. She had been smitten with the idea of William Gem rather than the actuality of him. He was smitten with her beauty, but knew nothing of her heart, soul, or mind.

Her father had finally relented, perhaps also tempted by the idea of his daughter wed to such an admired young fellow. William had promised to convert to Catholicism, though he had said to Sarah, "Providing y'all ain't gonna cut my pecker or nothing like that!"

Sarah explained to him that circumcision was a Jewish rite, not Catholic. She was very glad William had said it to her rather than her father. That would have been the end of the proposed marriage.

After Jubal had finally relented and let Sarah accept the proposal, William had celebrated overmuch. It was said he still smelled of alcohol when he stepped on the mound to pitch. A line drive had hit him in the chest. It was the sort of hit he had fielded many times before, but this time his reaction was slow, and it struck him full force in the chest. His heart was stopped, and he was dead before they could even lift him from the field to take him to the hospital.

Next had been Walter Vesper. He was a bookish young man also eighteen years of age. Sarah had rebounded into his arms, carried by her grief. He had been sensitive and gentle. From among her fiancés he had perhaps been the only real stirring of love in her heart.

Walter had drowned a week before the wedding. It was then that the superstition first began to grow. Walter had never been a strong swimmer, and folk could not help but wonder why he would be out swimming at night, even an overly warm night as it had been.

It was then that Jubal Tomkins began acting as if he were some Old Testament patriarch arranging for the marriage of his daughter. Rose Tomkins tried to dissuade her husband, but he was a strong-willed man. Sarah was so dispirited that she offered no resistance. Rose had seen Sarah's expression before—after a great fire had raged through Harper Bay and she had watched the stunned, confused refugees marching listlessly from their ruined and smoldering neighborhoods.

When Bryant had died, even Rose began giving way to the belief in some curse haunting her daughter. Jubal seemed resigned to his family line ending with him. Sarah lived in a constant state of depression and despair. Her mother's insistence that she not associate with what she called "farm folk" or "street people" left Sarah with no friends. She was an exile in her own home and imprisoned by the weight of loneliness.

Looking out the window, Sarah saw Amos Asher loading a customer's car with provisions. Tall, dark, and with a stern face cast as if from iron, Asher saw her gazing from the window. He gave her a slight, formal nod of the head before returning to the store.

With Jubal trapped in a resigned listlessness, Amos Asher had taken on much of the operation of the store. Folk said he had a grim face made for poker. No emotion seemed to ever flicker upon it, but it was too hard, too stern to be truly described as stoic. Still, he was efficient at his job and kept the business running.

It had come to this, thought Sarah, turning from the window and burying her face once again in her hands. All of her family was paralyzed by superstitious dread. They were resigned to this reality and could see no way out of it.

There was one way, though, for Sarah. She had thought of it. A razor in the bath, or a rope thrown over the exposed beam in her closet, and then it would be over. But when she thought of her father and mother, she would pray to God that he would take her from this life—that he would at least spare them the shame of such a suicide.

She lifted her face toward the sky outside and her hands toward the window. "Please, my Lord, set me free from all of this. I can't stand the sneering, the insults. I don't know how much longer I can bear this loneliness. I ask that you think of my father and my mother and the misery this has brought upon them. I can see no cure except by your hands."

Then she wrenched herself away from the prayer, embarrassed by what she thought to be a selfish plea. She threw herself onto her bed and was convulsed by tearless sobbing.

Frank Forgeron was in the sales room when he saw the man walking up the road toward his gas station. He noticed first the guitar case and a small duffle thrown over one of the man's shoulders. In the dappled shade he could not quite make out the features. He assumed it was probably a Negro vagrant. Who else would be walking along the road carrying a guitar and a duffle?

Then he was not so sure. He felt embarrassed at himself for having made the assumption. He was discomforted by his own prejudice. It was difficult to tell what race the man might be. He was tall and well proportioned, with skin darker than the average white man, but no darker than some white field workers he had seen. As the man drew nearer he saw that there was a slight coppery tone to the skin. The hair was black, but cut so short as to deny the context of texture.

As the stranger was approaching the door to the sales room, Frank saw that the man was not shabbily dressed. His loose suit was clean and in good repair. His hat was only slightly worn at the brim, and his shoes were well cobbled, if more functional than dressy. And the eyes, Berber eyes, thought Frank.

The door opened and the man stepped in. Frank was not sure of the age, maybe midthirties? The man removed his hat politely and bowed his head slightly. Frank thought then he had to be a Negro because almost no white men were so deferential. Maybe he was from South America?

"Good afternoon, sir", said the man. His voice was pleasant with an elusive, almost striking quality to it. "I am called Astier Freeman Losrouge, but when I'm playing this guitar, mostly I am known as Ace Redbone."

"Good afternoon, Mister Redbone", replied Forgeron. If the man was surprised at the respectful return greeting, it did not show on his face. Maybe he was white after all; most Negroes would be rather startled at being addressed by a white stranger as mister. But, no, Redbone was a Negro name, a mulatto name.

"Is there anything I can do for you?"

"Well, sir," Ace Redbone began to explain, "I am looking for a distant relative—"

"Tobit Messenger", Forgeron interrupted. "Tobit *Freeman* Messenger."

"Why, yes", smiled Ace Redbone. "Freeman is a family name."

"I am Frank Forgeron. Well, Mister Redbone—"

"Ace."

"Well, Ace, your luck has been extraordinary. Tobit Messenger lives not five miles from here. Better yet, his son, Tobias, is right next door in the service bay. He works for me."

"Providential!" replied Ace Redbone with a laugh.

"Tobias!" shouted Forgeron as he turned around toward the work bays. "Somebody's here to see you!"

After just a few moments Tobias appeared, still wiping his hands with a rag. "Yes, sir?"

"This here fella says he's a relative of yours", explained Forgeron. "He sure 'nough got them Messenger eyes."

Forgeron turned around to face Ace Redbone. "This here is Tobias Freeman Messenger. I'll let you introduce yourself because I already forgot that mouthful of names."

A soft, congenial laugh rolled up from Ace Redbone as he extended his hand toward Tobias. "Good to meet you, young man. I am called Astier Freeman Losrouge, the name given by a common great grandfather, Augustine Freeman Messenger."

Tobias hastily finished wiping his right hand before grasping the hand offered. "Pleased to meet you, Mister Losrouge."

"Since we're cousins, just call me Ace; most folk do. Mister Forgeron here is right that my full name is a mouthful." He gestured with his head toward the guitar case protruding over his shoulder. "When I am performing, I go by Ace Redbone. I played a club near Wilmington, and then Harper Bay. I knew that there was family in Harper Bay once, but I learned that y'all had moved down past Stonebridge, so I thought I'd see if I could track you down. I like to look up family when I travel, then when I get back to Louisiana I can fill the home folk in on the happenings and happenstance of their relatives."

"Well, I'm thinking my father would surely want to meet you, Ace", replied Tobias. "He's told me the family story many times over the years."

Ace laughed. "Too many times to suit a young man's interest, I'm guessing."

Tobias smiled and nodded sheepishly. "Maybe a time or two too many."

"Look," said Forgeron, "why don't you take off now, Tobias? In fact, I can give y'all a lift over to your house."

"I don't mind walking, Mister Forgeron", said Ace. "In fact, I like walking."

"Sir, you don't have to close the station on account of me", protested Tobias. "I've walked home more often than not. And if Ace don't mind the walk, there's no need to close up."

"All right then", said Forgeron, shrugging. He extended his hand to Ace Redbone. "But you call me Frank."

"Frank it is!" Ace answered cheerily as he shook Forgeron's hand.

Okra was stretched out in the dappled shade a few feet from the front porch. Here he could keep half an eye on Tobit and Anna as they sat on the swing, but also could survey the majority of the yard as well. It was a lazy afternoon; he could only muster enough energy to squirm back and forth on his back with his feet pawing the air. When the itch was addressed he remained supine with his feet drawn only a little closer to his chest.

He drifted in and out of sleep to the creaking of the swing. He dreamed the dreams of dogs: chasing rabbits, following interesting scents, stalking cats, leaping into the mule cart for a ride, and the praise of his master. The dreams would echo even into his drowsy wakefulness.

Then there was something else. He rolled onto his side and his black nose twitched at the air. He could *feel* something. It was almost as it would be if some change was working in the weather. He could often sense the approach of a storm long before even the scent or sound of it, but there was no telltale movement of air or creaking of trees today. All he could sense was that *something* new to his experience was in the world.

65

Pondering this as best a dog might do, Okra rose to his feet and stretched. With his ears pricked alert he trotted down the drive. Near the road he heard voices and immediately recognized one of them. Having learned not to go past the drive, he pranced and quivered in anticipation at this unexpected treat. He could usually sense the time of the day and would go to the end of the drive to await Tobias' return from work, but this day the event was early and had caught him off guard.

Then he saw Tobias and a stranger approaching, and he barked excitedly and leapt in circles. An early return was worthy of greater celebration. Finally, the two humans were near enough that Okra could stand shifty-pawed at their feet. Tobias reached down and rubbed the dog's ears.

"This here is Okra", he said to the other man.

Ace Redbone let his guitar case and duffle slip from his shoulder and then eased them to the ground so that he could go to one knee to greet the dog. Okra surprised Tobias by not even sniffing the man before insinuating himself between Ace's knees so he could be petted.

"Well, he's taken to you right off!" laughed Tobias.

"I get along well with dogs", replied Ace with a chuckle of his own as he rubbed the dog's neck and then along the spine. Okra turned to present the sweet spot just above the base of his tail, which the man dutifully scratched.

"Okra, eh? Fried or gumbo?" Ace asked of the dog, who only lolled his tongue in appreciation of the back scratching.

"You would think", said Tobias. "But you have to know my father. He says Okra is some ol' African word that means 'soul'. First time he saw this dog when it was a pup he lifted him up and looked into that face and said, 'This little fellow, now, he's got some soul to him.' So he named him Okra."

"Ghana", said Ace, after a moment of consideration. "It's from a language spoken around the Gold Coast, part of the old Ghana Empire."

Tobias raised an eyebrow before shaking his head with mock consternation. "It must run in the family."

Ace laughed and shrugged. "I reckon so. The things that stick in our heads."

He hefted his guitar case and duffle back onto his shoulder, and the three of them turned into the drive and headed toward the house.

Anna saw them from the porch. "It's Tobias. He has someone with him."

"Who?" asked Tobit.

Anna shook her head, forgetting that her husband could not see her. "I can't tell. A tall man. Taller even than Tobias by a bit. Light-skinned, but I don't think he's a white man. He's carrying a guitar case and some sort of bag."

After a few minutes Anna rose from the swing, and as Tobit followed she guided him with her hand to face the visitor. Ace removed his hat and nodded.

"This is Astier Freeman Losrouge", announced Tobias. "These are my parents, your cousins, I reckon, Anna and Tobit."

"I am mighty pleased to meet you. Folks mostly call me Ace Redbone."

Tobit laughed; he imagined Anna looking at him with a startled and disapproving expression, so he explained his mirth. "*L'os rouge*; it's French for the bone red, or redbone."

He turned then toward the voice of the newcomer. "My French is hit or miss, and I'm afraid I have passed even less of it on to my son than was passed on to me.

"By your middle name, I take it we are related."

"Yessir", replied Ace. "My mother's mother was Marie, the third daughter of Augustine Freeman Messager. My grandmother married a Louis D'Aubrage, a mullato, and my father, Vincent Losrouge, was also of mixed race.

"I was coming to North Carolina to play a club in Wilmington and then Harper Bay. I have a few weeks before another date in Charlotte, so I thought I'd look you up.

"Last word we had back in Louisiana was after the Harper Bay situation had brought you back to the bayou, and when you left there nobody knew where you'd gone, other than you had headed back to Carolina. Fortunately, some people in Harper Bay pointed me this way."

"We have lost touch", replied Tobit.

"He for sure has those Messager eyes!" Anna softly exclaimed.

"You are most welcomed", continued Tobit. He gestured vaguely behind him. "If you have walked all the way from Crafty's, I'm sure you could do with a sit-down."

"You must be thirsty, but I'm afraid all we have to offer is some cool water", Anna apologized as Ace and Tobias walked up onto the porch.

"That suits me just fine, ma'am", replied Ace as he let his case and duffle down onto the floor and took a seat in the rocking chair that Tobias indicated. Okra happily walked up and rested his muzzle on Ace's knee.

"Okra seems taken with cousin Ace", Tobias informed his father as his mother went to fetch some water.

"That speaks well of you, Ace", said Tobit. "Okra is a keen judge of character."

"Dogs often are", allowed Ace as he scratched the cleft between Okra's ears.

"How is it with the family in Louisiana?" asked Tobit as Anna brought out a pitcher of water and some glasses. The conversation turned into an hour of discussion on the complexity of marriages and relationships that dizzied poor Tobias, but he saw his father's interest rise at the mention of one name, Jubal Tomkins.

"Jubal", said Tobit, repeating the name Ace had mentioned.

"Yes, sir", replied Ace. "His first wife was our cousin Jeanette. She passed away sadly young. I heard he is near Newton Grove now. I was going to go visit him after I leave here, if I can track him down."

"I knew Jubal", said Tobit in slow recollection. "My father and I lent him some money when he was trying to start up a store, but he was in Danville, Virginia, at that time. I hadn't heard about poor Jeanette."

"From what I understand," said Ace, after a long swallow of water, "when Jeanette died he sold the store in Danville and opened one in Sampson County somewhere. He remarried some years later."

"Ah, he never did repay me", said Tobit. "Though, I can hardly blame him. We lost touch with one another after my father got run out of Harper Bay."

"The colored folk in Harper Bay still talk about what an injustice that was, Mister Tobit. I reckon it was just after that, too, that the Lord called Jeanette.

"You know, you should get word to him. What I heard of Jubal Tomkins I 'spect he frets to this day about owing you that money. If he checked at Harper Bay just after your family left, he might not have known where to find you. From what I heard nobody in Harper Bay was sure where your father had set back down until some years later."

"I think Jubal would have tried to find me", agreed Tobit. "I wouldn't expect payment now; although, two hundred dollars would be a treasure for us in our present circumstances."

"It might put his mind to ease, sir", pressed Ace. "I heard he's done very well indeed, so the repayment shouldn't tax him overmuch."

"I don't know", Tobit sighed. "I still don't know where to find him."

"Well, I'm going up to find him anyway", replied Ace. "Why don't you write a letter so he'll know that I've talked to you. In fact, Tobias here could come with me. Jubal might feel more comfortable repaying the loan to a young man that is the spittin' image of you!"

"We can't even afford bus fare", noted Tobit.

"Well, we can walk", suggested Ace. "Maybe hitch a ride or two."

"Walk all the way to Sampson County? Hitching isn't the safest way for a Negro to travel", said Tobit.

"No, but I often find that other colored folk will let you ride on the back of their trucks or wagons", replied Ace. "We are going to have to do a fair amount of hitching up around the Newton Grove area anyway to track Jubal down."

"I don't think I want my boy walking all the way to Newton Grove", Anna softly interjected into the conversation.

"I am eighteen years old."

"And he'll have cousin Ace with him. Ace has done a lot of travelling without having come to harm", said Tobit before reminding her, "Two hundred dollars."

"Ma'am, I'll see that he gets there, and more than that I'll see that he gets back", Ace reassured her. "I keep three dollar bills in my wallet for emergencies, and so I won't be arrested as a vagrant. Least wise, I have never been arrested before."

"It makes me nervous", Anna continued to protest.

"Two hundred dollars", repeated Tobias.

Anna looked at him with the gentle reproach of a mother, but finally she gave a near imperceptible shrug. She shifted her gaze to Ace then, arching her eyebrows to accentuate her words, "You best bring this here boy back safe and sound."

Ace Redbone laughed lightly before he grew serious and nodded. "Yes, ma'am."

Anna took a deep breath then and exhaled it as she put her hands onto her knees. "Well then, I need to get started with supper. Cousin Ace, we don't have anything fancy, but the least we can do is feed you and give you a bed for the night. Also, you let me have any clothes in that bag of yours and I'll clean 'em. No argument about that."

"No, ma'am."

After supper, while Anna was washing Ace Redbone's clothes, Tobias pulled out his grandfather's old atlas and turned to the map of North Carolina. With Tobit's insight and knowledge of the state, Tobias and Ace plotted out their trip.

It was decided that they would go farther up county to avoid Harper Bay. Tobit offered his opinions of which were the safest counties and towns for a couple of colored men to be walking and hitching. They managed to cobble together a gerrymandered route in the direction of Newton Grove.

"It might gnaw at your souls," Tobit instructed them, "but you have to be as deferential as you can to the white folk you meet."

"I understand how to play the game", Ace Redbone assured him. "That's why I never take more than three dollars on me. Too much money and they will think you a thief; or, worse in their minds, an uppity Negro.

"I will also put off these clothes I am wearing. I put them on special for meeting you, my cousins."

He turned then to Tobias. "Wear something clean, but not too fancy."

"That's right", said Tobit in agreement. "Unfortunately you must play the part of the sort of colored man who meets a white man's expectations of what he considers to be a good Negro."

"That should be easy enough", replied Tobias with a shrug. "Other than the suit of Daddy's that I wear when we go to church, I ain't got nothing fancy."

Tobias paused then said, "Daddy, what about Mister Forgeron? I hate to leave him shorthanded, and I truly hate to leave him without so much as a word."

"I will tell him", Tobit assured his son. "After y'all leave, I'll hitch up Joe-boy and your mother can take me over to Frank's place. I tell you, Ace, hitching up Joe-boy is one of those things I could do in the dark.

"Now, if we tell Frank before you're gone, he'll insist on taking you all the way to Newton Grove. We can't let him do that. He's done more than is good for him already, and if two colored men driven by a white man start asking around Sampson County for the whereabouts of another colored man, every Negro in the county will clam up, or drive Frank into bankruptcy bribing them."

Ace, despite his protest, was given Tobias' bed, and Tobias slept on a camp cot in the same room. Okra had followed them up the stairs, and it was only with what seemed great reluctance that he finally came down to take his place on the large burlap bag filled with rags that Anna had placed in the foyer. This was his usual sleeping place, just outside of Anna and Tobit's bedroom.

They could leave the entry door open, with a simple hook lock on the screen door, and Okra and his dog senses would act as sentry. This allowed the whole house to cool overnight so that it would resist the building heat of the day. Soon it would be too cool at night and not warm enough for this during the day, but it was still in Okra's mind that this was where he should be at night.

In the dark Anna lay sleepless for a long time. Finally, she quietly said, "Tobit?"

"Love?" was his drowsy reply.

"Why are we letting our boy go with this man we don't really know? I understand that he is your cousin, judging by what he says and those Berber eyes of his, but still, we don't really *know* him."

Tobit shifted onto his back and shrugged. "I'm not sure. I just trust him. It seems proper somehow that I should. It's difficult to explain, but somehow it's as if my soul itself trusts him. Besides, Okra trusts him."

"That dog", huffed Anna as she rolled her eyes in the dark. "He does seem taken with our cousin Ace."

"Indeed he does", Tobit said, yawning. "And Okra has a sense about people. Many dogs do, but in this one it seems exceptionally honed."

"I supposed so", Anna sighed.

Tobit reached in the dark and patted her arm. "It's as if God has sent cousin Ace to present this opportunity in our hour of greatest need."

"I hope so", replied Anna with yet another sigh. "I guess I'm just a mother and mothers worry."

"And may God bless them for it", chuckled Tobit, as he turned over to tuck himself into a sleeping position with his back pressing against his wife.

71

Anna was up earlier than normal in the morning. She taxed her larder to prepare Ace and Tobias nearly more breakfast than they could eat. She packed them biscuits and hard-boiled eggs to take with them, as well as some dried beef and a few of the early, barely ripe apples from their trees.

"Now, y'all save that jerky and those apples for later, since they won't spoil. Eat the biscuits and eggs first. I've got some crackers in here too, for later."

"I reckon we'd have figured out the proper order to eating our supplies, Mama", Tobias teased her. "But don't load us down too much."

"What have you got packed?" asked Tobit.

"Sleeping rolls, some clothes, cooking kit, some hooks and fishing line, a canteen", replied Tobias. "Oh, and some matches because I never was much use with tinder."

"Don't worry, I could start a fire in a hurricane", said Ace. He was dressed now in a dark gray suit not too unlike the one they had met him in, except that it was more worn, with patches on the elbows and fraying on the cuffs of both coat and pants.

"Well, I guess you are ready then", said Tobit.

"Lord", sighed Anna.

"I'll bring him back to you", promised Ace, with his face beaming from beneath the broad-brimmed hat. He winked at her and it made her laugh at her own worries.

"Wouldn't it lighten your load to leave your guitar here?" asked Tobias as they began hefting their burdens.

"White folk trust a colored man travelling the countryside toting a guitar more than they do one without", explained Ace, standing with the guitar case slung over one shoulder and his duffle over the other. Tobias nodded his head, facing his travelling companion with a worn canvas backpack hefted between his own shoulders.

"Time to go", announced Ace, and he and Tobias stepped from the porch and headed down the drive.

"Lord, Lord, Lord", fretted Anna.

Tobit searched for her hand and gave it a squeeze. Then he heard Anna clucking her tongue lightly.

"You better call that dog of yours; he's following them. He's even left the drive after them."

Tobit prepared to do just that, but then paused, and finally said, "No, let him go. He'll look after your boy for you."

"But he'll be a nuisance", Anna protested.

"If that were so, Ace or Tobias would have sent him back, don't you reckon?"

"I suppose so."

"And, besides, it comforts you that he should be with Tobias on the journey, doesn't it?"

Anna nodded as she admitted, "Yes, I suppose it does. I can't tell you why, but it does."

"Well, there you go", replied Tobit, squeezing her hand again. "Let him go; both of them, Anna, the boy and the dog. No, let me rephrase that, our young man and the dog."

"He'll always be something of a boy to me", whispered Anna.

"I know, woman; I know."

Six

Okra ranged around Tobias and Ace. Sometimes he trotted a little ahead of them, pausing on occasion so as to keep them in sight. Or he might be distracted by some interesting scent and they would pass him. He would then run or trot to quickly catch up. Other times he walked easily beside them.

Tobias was tempted to shoo him back home when Okra had dared to step onto the roadway to follow them, but Ace had pointed out that Anna or Tobit would have called the dog back if they had not wanted him to go with them.

"Besides, we'll be camping under the stars more than a few nights. It will be good to have such alert senses with us", added Ace. "He shouldn't hinder our hitching much, because most farmers will be willing to let him jump into the back of the truck or cart they're driving."

Tobias reluctantly agreed, "I guess I would just feel better if he were home looking after my mother and father."

"They have Joe-boy", replied Ace with a wink. "From what I hear tell, ain't nobody wants to cross with that ornery mule. Tore down an entire building!"

Tobias laughed, "Yes, he did. Weren't much of a building, barely able to stand on its own, but he sure enough brought it down!"

"Like Samson in the temple of the Philistines!" Ace declared.

Tobias laughed again and his worries eased. Okra adjusted his gait so that he could sniff his young master's hand in curiosity. Tobias rubbed at the tall ears.

"You know, Ace, this will be the first time I have ever slept anywhere besides my own bed. Least since I was a baby. Well, except a few times of the year when we would go to little Washington on a Saturday night and spend the night in Miss Bolen's boarding house, so we could go to Mass on Sunday."

"Truly?" marveled Ace Redbone. "Your daddy never took you camping or some such?"

"No. He was often busy, and then when the Crash came, he had to work double hard", said Tobias, shrugging. "He did take me fishing from time to time. Usually just to the banks of the creek at the back of our property. A few times we went down to Landmere and put out onto the sound in a boat he would borrow."

"Pretty blue water out on the sound", noted Ace.

"Yes, it was", mused Tobias. "Though there was one day when a storm rolled up all of a suddenlike. Actually saw a waterspout some ways off. Lord, my daddy was rowin', and prayin', up his own storm trying to get us back to the shore."

Tobias laughed at the memory. "Mind you, I was praying just as hard as my daddy!"

"Nothing wrong with praying", replied Ace. "You'll be okay with ol' Ace Redbone looking after you. Why, I've slept under the stars for many a night, and just about the only bad thing to happen, aside from getting rained on a few times, is being bitten by snake. Shoot, that ain't happened but a half dozen times."

"What?"

"No, no", laughed Ace. "I have never really been bitten by a snake. Though, you hear tell of it happening, especially when an evening starts off warm and then goes cool. The snakes are active early on, but then when the cool of night descends they are attracted to the warmth of a human body."

"That's it", said Tobias, shaking his head. "I'm sleeping in a tree."

"Just don't make it a pine", Ace warned him. "Redbugs seem to love pine trees. Of course, a possum might find a sleeping roll a comfy, warm place in the chill of the night. I'd hate you to wake up with your toes nibbled off."

"I'm staying up all night."

Ace laughed and slapped Tobias on the back. "Now, you see why it's a good thing to have Okra with us? I don't think you have to worry about snakes, possums, raccoons, foxes, bobcats, cougars, or bears sneaking up on us with ol' Okra around."

Tobias shrugged sheepishly, before looking down at the dog as it trotted beside him. "Okra, you stay real close to me tonight, you hear?"

They were closing in on the northwestern boundary of the county by early afternoon. The land around them was swampy and desolate. The

75

last farm had been passed nearly an hour before. Tobias reckoned they had less than two miles to the county line.

They had both been quiet the past several hours, with only the softly whistled tunes from Ace. Okra had been trotting happily with his dog grin and lolling tongue. Then a slight wave of tension passed over him. He stopped and turned to look back the way they had come. His head tilted and a slight bristle shown between his shoulders.

"Look here", said Ace, his own gaze following that fixed by the dog into the distance. "Let's say we just step into those trees over yonder. Might be time for a break in the shade."

With Ace in the lead, the three of them stepped off the road and through a fanlike veil of wax myrtle and into a grove of scrubby oaks. As the two men released their burdens to sit on the loamy soil, Okra let out a low, rolling growl about the same time they heard the sound of tires on the road.

Ace quieted the dog with a touch of his fingers to the muzzle. He and Tobias looked through the patchwork veil of wax myrtle. A white car appeared down the roadway travelling at a moderate speed.

Tobias looked over to Ace Redbone and said. "That's Sheriff Oliver's car."

Ace nodded, putting his finger to his own lips as a sign for silence. The car slowed slightly, as if it were a sentient thing that sensed something elusive, but then eased back into its previous pace. Soon it disappeared around a bend in the road.

"Well then," said Ace, "let's just take a bit of a break here."

"Reckon what he's doing so near the county line?" asked Tobias. "I can't explain it, but his appearing like that just gave me a creep across my back."

"Well, who can know", said Ace, shrugging, as he offered Tobias half a biscuit.

"I suppose he'll probably be turning up Tellman Road and patrolling back toward Stonebridge", decided Tobias.

"That would make sense", said Ace as he gave a bite of biscuit to Okra. "All the same, we'll rest a while to make sure he doesn't turn back up this road. Just as well he doesn't see us given the trouble your father has had with him. See how useful ol' Okra here is?"

Tobias was about to take a bite of cheese, but he broke off a small piece and offered it to his father's dog. As the dog ate, Tobias gazed off into the haphazard pattern of trees, with a perplexed frown upon his face.

"How is it that a man like the sheriff prospers, while a man like my father suffers so?"

A slight smile came back to him from Ace Redbone. "It rains on the just and the unjust."

"That has always seemed a shabby answer", complained Tobias. "I've heard it before. God works in mysterious ways. My ways are not your ways. Where were you, Job, when I laid the foundations of the world?"

"Not understanding a thing doesn't make it wrong", Ace said, shrugging. "Many things don't make sense unless you can stand back from them, and we can't stand so far back as does God."

The musician gestured toward the growth of trees Tobias had been absently gazing upon. "If you had never seen a forest from a distance before, standing in the midst of it you would be hard-pressed to imagine the greater reality of it. Or, as they say, sometimes you can't see the forest for the trees."

Tobias arched an eyebrow in skepticism, but then just shrugged. Ace laughed as he stood and gathered up his duffle and guitar case. "Reckon we can get going again. Okra, you run out ahead of us a ways and keep those overgrown ears of yours alert for the sound of the sheriff's car."

As if he understood every word, Okra forged ahead and set out along the road toward the county line. They had crossed the line and gone perhaps a mile past it when Okra suddenly stopped on the side of the road. They saw the slight rise of his hackles as he stared intently around a shallow curve in the road.

Ace and Tobias looked at one another and then with mutual shrugs walked slowly to where the dog stood. Now they could see a truck pulled to one side of the road and the figures of three young men standing around it.

"The Dunlin boys", said Tobias in a low, cautious voice. "That looks like Lenny Morris with them. I didn't know he was hanging around with them. They're the bunch that came by our house the night my father was arrested."

"Looks like they are having motor trouble", decided Ace. He gestured with his head for Tobias to follow him.

"I don't know if this is a good idea", responded Tobias as he followed the older man. "These here boys are always up to some sort of trouble."

The hood of the truck was lifted and the two brothers were both peering under it. The Morris boy was just standing off to one side looking uncertain and useless. He was a thin boy, on his way to being tall. His jeans and his plaid shirt were cleaner and newer than what the Dunlin boys were wearing. He was pale and had reddish brown hair, and green-brown eyes that grew wide as he saw Ace and Tobias approaching.

Morris said something and the two Dunlin boys emerged from out of the engine bay of their truck. Both were big-boned, the older a little heavier set than the younger. Both had thick, unkempt black hair and dark brown eyes set in dark wells. The older boy stepped forward, glaring. "What you niggers lookin' at?"

"Just saw that it looked like your truck has broken down", replied Ace amiably, as his fingertips brushed Okra to stop the low growl beginning in the dog's throat. "It happens this young man is a very good mechanic. Maybe he could lend you a hand?"

Both Dunlin boys sneered; Lenny Morris seemed mostly interested in the ground. The older boy crossed his arms. "What makes you think we need help from a nigger?"

Ace shrugged. "Mostly a broke-down truck, but even if you don't need the help, doesn't seem any harm in offering it."

"He's the boy that works for that nigger-lover Crafty, ain't he?" said the younger boy to his brother. There was a nodded reply.

"I don't care if he were Crafty himself", said the older boy. "We don't need no niggers or no nigger lovers helping us."

"As you wish", replied Ace. He touched the brim of his hat with a smile before turning to his travelling companions. "Come along, Tobias, Okra. Looks like these gentlemen have things under control."

"Smart-ass nigger", growled the older boy as he turned to plant his head back beneath the hood.

Ace did not reply, though he gave Lenny Morris a good-natured wink when the young man's gaze skipped across his own. Lenny just became all the more interested in the cracked pavement.

When they were past the truck, Tobias whispered, "Were you trying to give me a conniption fit? Some folk think those boys might be the ones who hung Jamie Farmer."

"Best we don't show fear then, right?" said Ace as he continued the same steady, nonchalant pace. Okra picked up on his confidence and trotted out again to a modest lead.

About an hour later Tobias indicated a side road. "That's the Harper Bay road. We go down that about ten miles and then we'll come to the Greenville road. We'll take that for about five miles, and we can cross over to the road that will take us through Goldsboro, and we'll have avoided Larson County."

"Like it showed on the map?" asked Ace pointedly, but with a smile.

Tobias laughed at himself. "Yes, sir, like on the map. It's a narrow road, and not in very good shape. A lot of people use it as a shortcut though."

After another two and a half hours they came to a wide black-water creek. A rickety wood bridge spanned the dark waters. To the south of the bridge, swampy woodland crept to the edge of the creek, and to the north tawny and green marsh grasses and cattails began to spread as the creek formed at the outflow of a large, shallow pond. They stood for a moment appreciating the light of the lowering sun casting a golden glow across the marsh grass.

"Catfish Creek", Tobias informed Ace. "There's a reason they call it that."

"All the trout?" deadpanned Ace, with a sly look at his younger companion.

Tobias laughed, "Has anyone ever said you have a bit of attitude, Ace? The catfish in that creek are big. Huge. Legendary!"

"That big?" mused Ace. "Well, I'd like to see such a thing. You've got fishing line, so let's test it out."

"I don't know that my line can hold the weight of one of those cats", replied Tobias.

"Double it up", suggested Ace. He motioned for Tobias to follow him down to the muddy bank. "I'll show you."

After Tobias had pulled the fishing line from his pack, Ace twisted two strands through the hook and then tied the two strands together with a knot about every six inches. He looked up and winked at Tobias. "Now, I'm not saying that it doubles the strength, but it should hold all but the most legendary of catfish."

Tobias nodded and turned to investigate the nearby shrubby growth. He finally selected a long, lean, and springy sapling that he broke off near the ground before bending to cut the tenacious, fibrous portion of wood with his pocket knife.

"A lot of folk plant bamboo near good fishing spots, but I don't see any around here, so this will have to do", he explained to Ace.

Tobias then pulled off his boots and socks before rolling up his pant legs. Then, using the sapling as a stave, he eased himself into the water. When the water was near his knees, he began using the sapling to feel ahead and around him. Nodding to himself, he retreated carefully back onto the bank.

He said, "I'm just testing how deep the water is likely to be." He tied the line to the sapling and then broke off a handful of dried reed. "This will have to do as a float. I want about three feet of line dropped into the water, so I'll tie it around these reeds about three feet from the hook. Cats don't feed just on the bottom, but they love to slink along down there looking for easy pickings, or to ambush live prey."

"Sounds like someone taught you a lot about fishing", suggested Ace.

Tobias nodded. "Most folk know a lot about fishing in the county. Since the Crash, fish is all the meat some folk get."

Finished with his rigging of the line, he pursed his lips and a look of concentration passed across his face. "Bait. If I had a fine net I'd get some minnows. Some folk even use ivory soap! Oily fish are really good. Well, I'll just have to improvise."

He went to his pack and pulled out the jerky, biting off a small piece. He chewed it slowly and lightly, but rather than swallowing let it fall into his hand. Then he broke off a bit of cheese. He pierced the jerky with the hook, and then rubbed the cheese on the hook and about a foot of the twin line.

"Got to get some sort of scent into the water", he said. "That's why I like oily fish when I can get it."

With that he walked about two feet into the water and cast the line out ahead and to his right so that it could drift along the slow current. "Nothing to do now, but wait."

Ace nodded and moved back away from the creek bank and settled in the dappled shade of a river birch. He pulled his guitar out and began softly strumming. Tobias chuckled quietly when he recognized the tune *We Shall Gather by the River*.

For half an hour in the slanting light of late afternoon Tobias patiently cast his line, let it drift, and then carefully removed it from the dark water to cast again. Suddenly the reed float bobbed and disappeared. Tobias gave a slight whip to his sapling fishing pole, and the entire line became taut.

Tobias' eyes went wide when he saw the broad, black back of a cat roll out of the water before it lurched swiftly back toward the bottom of the creek. What he saw of it indicated the creature was longer than his arm. He began backpeddling with as much finesse as he could as he tried to drag the creature into shallower water without breaking the line or sapling. Behind him Okra was barking and growling at the dark form in the water.

When he reached the dry bank, he stumbled and went to his knees, all the while still pulling along the sapling. He could see the cat flopping and twisting in the water. His hands were at the end of the sapling and he was considering grabbing the line itself when he saw Ace forging into the creek, with pants rolled up above his knees.

Ace reached for the cat, and his fingers had barely brushed its skin when it went suddenly still. Careful of the barbs, the musician pulled it onto the dry bank while Tobias dropped the sapling pole, shushed Okra, and hurried to help with the fish.

"I don't think that's the biggest to ever come out of this creek, but it's a big one", marveled Tobias. "It's too big to be a blackback, but it's darker than a flathead. What do you reckon, twenty-five pounds?"

"More than that, maybe even thirty-five", chuckled Ace, as he sat down next to the beached fish on the dry bank.

"All the fight went out of it when you got to it", said Tobias.

Ace nodded. "Good thing. I wouldn't have wanted to wrestle with that monster in its own element. I reckon it's old and its heart just burst from the struggle. You fought a great battle with that thing, Tobias. I was afraid it was going to drag you back in, especially after you lost your balance and fell."

"Phew", replied Tobias, blowing air through his lips as he finally relaxed. He appraised his adversary as Okra sniffed at it suspiciously. "It's a shame, really. That's more cat than you, me, and Okra can eat in a single sitting, but we've got no way of preserving it."

"I guess we'll count our blessings and eat our fill", said Ace. "It looks like that cat's fight took some energy out'n you. Maybe we should look for a place to camp for the night, and we can get some eating done."

"I don't fancy camping on this creek bank", replied Tobias. "There could be gators, and for sure mocs, and for all I know this here cat might have avenging relatives.

"There used to be an old logging shed about two miles farther down the road. It doesn't have any walls, just a tin roof mounted to some poles, but it should keep us dry in case of rain."

Ace looked up to the sky and nodded. "It does look as if a shower could pop up before too awful long. All right then, let's get on with it."

They dried their feet and legs, replaced their footwear, and gathered their packs and gear. They lashed the catfish to the sapling, and with each of them holding it by one hand carried the fish between them.

They came to the logging shed, where the paved road made a sweeping curve while the dirt road proceeded straight on. Tobias gestured toward the curved paved road. "I'll bet that can be confusing at night, if you miss the sign back there warning you."

The shed was set to one side about thirty yards down the rutted dirt road. Originally it had been fifteen feet wide by about thirty feet long, but the back half of it looked to have been collapsed by a windstorm. Ace checked the creosote posts holding up the remaining peeled and rusted tin roof.

"They are solid", he reported. "What's left of the roof looks like it should give us some shelter. Better get us some dry wood before the rain comes."

The two of them began scrounging in the scrubby woodland for dead wood. Okra trotted around investigating the area with his nose. He would spend time with one of them and then run to join the other for a while.

Ace returned with his fourth armload of broken tree limbs and dropped them into the pile they had gathered. As he was brushing the dust and dirt from his clothes and hands, Tobias returned with a small armload just before the first spatters of rain began tapping on the tin roof. The young man's expression was a mask of worry. Ace tilted his head and offered an inquisitive look.

"The Dunlin boys, and Lenny", explained Tobias. "I saw them going down the road. Going to Harper Bay, I guess."

"Must have fixed their truck", said Ace.

"Well, they saw me, no doubt. They slowed down and shouted something, but I couldn't make it out. I just pretended not to hear them and picked up some more wood before heading back here. Those boys ain't right in the head, Ace. I'm telling you, they're dangerous."

"Maybe so, but they continued on, didn't they?"

"Yeah", replied Tobias with a sigh. "But it still makes me nervous."

"That's why we have Okra", Ace reminded him. "We can sleep sound enough tonight, and it's unlikely any critters, even the Dunlin boys, are going to be sneaking up on us."

"I reckon", conceded Tobias, chuckling at his own worry now.

"It does us good sometimes to consider why people like the Dunlin brothers might be so mean", continued Ace. "We have to protect ourselves against their actions, but try to imagine what their life has been.

"I suppose both of us have seen a colored man just turn mean, or simply lose his temper in a very violent manner, because of the humiliation piled upon him. Too often it is not those who cause him harm who feel his wrath.

"So we should be wary but understanding, even with the Dunlin brothers."

While Ace commenced assembling some of the wood for a fire, Tobias began cleaning the catfish. The rain had begun to come down hard and the gloom of evening was hurried upon them. Beneath the drumming of water on the tin roof, Tobias soon had the catfish clean and filleted.

The dark had increased, but Ace had a decent fire going to drive back the cool, damp night. Tobias was about to begin cooking when they heard a sharp retort that caused him to jump nearly out of his skin, thinking that someone was shooting at them. Ace pointed back along the dirt road toward the paved road.

Tobias saw weak, yellow headlights bouncing slowly toward them. He heard a sputtering motor that finally coughed and quit. The headlights rolled to a bouncing stop. The rain had faded to an erratic drizzle, and he could make out that the vehicle was some sort of bus, much to his relief, having feared it was the Dunlin brothers.

"Reckon we should see if they need some help", suggested Ace. He turned and wagged his finger at Okra. "You come with us, brother dog. Don't want to tempt you with unattended catfish."

They walked down to where the bus had rolled to a stop. There was a small, old white man hunched behind the wheel. Ace lifted his hat in greeting, calling out, "Evening, sir. Can we be of any assistance?"

After a moment the man let go his white-knuckle clench of the steering wheel and cautiously exited the bus. His gaze was careful and calculating. Tobias thought he was probably trying to ascertain to which race Ace might belong. Ace asked again, "Can we be of any help?"

The little man pulled himself up to what Tobias guessed was all of five foot, three inches in height before replying in what Tobias recognized as a substantial Lebanese accent.

"Depends. Either of you know anything about motor vehicles?"

"As it turns out," replied Ace with a chuckle, "this here young man, Tobias Freeman Messager, is a mechanic of competent and blooming skill. Works for Crafty Forgeron, back near Stonebridge."

"Crafty?" repeated the old man, with a perplexed look upon his face that turned discerning. "Wait ... Messager? Are you related to Toby Messager from Harper Bay?"

Tobias was about to offer a qualified reply, but Ace spoke first. "None other than Tobit's son!"

"Well, I'll be", said the man as he cast an appraising eye on the son of Tobit. "What a small world it can be. I knew your father, years ago. My father used to do some business with Tobiel Messager. Me and Toby would sometimes play checkers while our fathers tended to business. Or we might have a contest to see who could throw a green pinecone the furthest. Though Toby, being a strapping fellow, always won those. But now, when we contested who could throw a cone closest to a particular mark, well those were my games! Toby Messager's boy, eh? Well, I'll be."

"Indeed", interrupted Ace.

"Sir," said Tobias, "do you reckon that old bus can make it to that shed yonder? It's awful dark, but I can take a look at it for you. If you could get at least the front portion under the shed, I could do it without getting rained on."

"I can try", replied the old man. Just before he turned to go back into the bus he looked at Tobias again. "I don't reckon your father ever mentioned Jake Choory?"

"Well, sir, he didn't like to talk much about his days in Harper Bay."

"No, I don't suppose he would", agreed the old man, nodding his head. He looked at Tobias and pointed his finger for emphasis. "Let me tell you, what happened there was a shame, but ain't none of it should fall on Tobiel or Tobit."

He was about to board the bus again, but halted for the second time to ask of Tobias, "How is your father? He's still with us?"

"Oh yes, sir. He's had some trouble recently, but he's still with us, thank the Lord."

"Thank the Lord, indeed", said Jake Choory before finally going back into the bus.

The vehicle chugged back into erratic life and lurched toward the shed. Jake had to restart it three times, each time with more difficulty, before it finally rolled to a halt with the engine bay and a few feet of cabin beneath the tin roof.

Having walked alongside the slow progress, Tobias looked up and waved his hand to indicate that was far enough. He was startled to see behind Jake, in the dark interior of the bus, four white faces peering from even whiter vertical halos. Nuns.

The bus door opened and Jake Choory hopped to the ground, turning back to address the four nuns. "Sisters, you can come out and stretch your legs a bit. You'll be fine here, I warrant, if young Tobias here is a fraction of the fine fellow his father was."

In a softly spoken aside, Choory offered to Ace and Tobias, "The elder sister, Sister Charlotte, can seem a bit daft at times. She's from overseas and she's old. Mostly she's sharp as a tack, but sometimes she says some odd things."

Ace smiled and doffed his hat to the sisters. "Mister Choory speaks the truth, sisters. Tobias is a fine young man. A fine Catholic young man!"

The four faces rose and proceeded toward the bus exit. It was then that Tobias saw there was a fifth haloed face; this one was a round, cherublike ebony face. A Negro nun, imagine that, he thought.

The sisters stepped out of the bus with Choory assisting each. One of them helped him with a particularly elderly nun. When they were all out of the bus, Jake pulled himself erect and stood with one arm and hand behind his back. It seemed to be how he expected official introductions might be made in a formal setting, despite the fact that an old logging shed alongside an unpaved road was hardly that.

"Gentlemen," he began, "I would note, as they so often have, that these religious sisters are not nuns, for they are not cloistered and work among us."

He then nodded his head toward the elderly sister. "First, Sister Charlotte. She is, you might say, the ranking sister of this group."

He pronounced her name with exaggerated emphasis as *sharr-lotta*. "Sister Charlotte is originally from Germany, though she spent many years in Spain."

Sister Charlotte nodded her head formally as Ace and Tobias doffed their hats to her. This ritual was repeated as the other sisters were introduced. Sister Marie Regina was the next oldest, who seemed the implementer of Sister Charlotte's will. Her accent suggested she was from the South. Sister Elizabeth Maria was a chubby, smiling young woman with a barely discernable Middle Atlantic states accent. Next was Sister Mary Teresa, who was probably the third oldest of the group, but with a quiet and subservient demeanor. She sounded as if she might be from New York. Finally was Sister Mary Lenora, the Negro sister and youngest of them all. She had no particularly discernable accent.

"Sister Mary Lenora is on loan to us from the Oblate Sisters of Providence", said Sister Charlotte in a peculiar German-Spanish accent. "We think she can help our mission at Saint Aurelius Parish in Harper Bay. Then she will be on to mission work in Cuba."

"Sisters," replied Ace, "I am called Astiel Freeman Losrouge, more commonly called Ace, a travelling musician haling from Louisiana. This young man is Tobias Freeman Messager, a cousin and accomplished mechanic haling from near Harper Bay."

With introductions complete, Jake Choory fetched folding campaign chairs from the back of the bus and arrayed them near the fire for the sisters because a chill was coming on with the night. Tobias moved to inspect the bus. He saw that only the front quarter had seats. The rest, accessed by a door in the rear, had been cleared of seats and partitioned for use as storage and hauling.

"A '26 Z-29 Yellow Coach", he surmised, with Ace at his elbow. "Well used and abused by the looks of it."

"It doesn't look yellow", noted Ace.

"No, but it once was", replied Tobias as he turned to see Okra investigating the sisters, who seemed to be fussing over him. "Sisters, if Okra becomes a nuisance, feel free to set him straight."

They assured him they were fine, as the dog paraded from one to another for attention. Tobias turned his own attention back to the bus, going to raise the hood. He peered into the engine bay, pointing to a spot on the dirty bulkhead. "See, yellow. Well, the engine is getting fuel, I can smell it. It's so dark, though, I can hardly see a thing. Do you have a lantern or a flashlight, Mister Choory?"

"No, I am sorry to say", said the little Lebanese man.

"What about I get a lit branch from the fire?" suggested Ace.

"Well, I don't relish having my head in that engine bay with an open flame for light, given the strong smell of fuel. I would venture it is some sort of electrical ignition problem. What was the progression of the problem, Mister Choory?"

"Well, it started to running rough some ten miles ago. It cut off a couple of times, kind of chugging like. Each time it got harder to restart."

"Electrical", sighed Tobias. "And it looks a mess under the hood. I don't know what I can do in this light."

"Ah, it will have to wait until morning", decided Ace, turning toward the women. "Sisters, I am afraid you will have to be guests of Ace and Tobias' Logging Shed Hotel. I am pleased, however, to announce that in addition to being a first-rate mechanic, young Tobias is reputed to be an excellent cook in regards to catfish, of which we happen to have a surplus."

"Can we not just walk to the convent?" asked Sister Charlotte.

Sister Marie Regina leaned over to speak softly to her superior. "Sister, I told you, we are some miles away from Harper Bay yet."

"Yes, of course", said Sister Charlotte.

In short order it was decided that the sisters would sleep in the seating section of the bus. The men would bed down in the partitioned storage section. Sister Charlotte instructed that the stores be inspected for items they could add to the meal.

So it was that in addition to the catfish some potatoes, carrots, lard, flour, and seasoning became available to Chef Tobias. Seeing, and amused by, the young man's discomfort, sisters Elizabeth Maria and Mary Lenora took on the preparation of potatoes and carrots, allowing Tobias to concentrate on panfrying the catfish.

Ace and Jake rigged up a table and benches with old planks and cinder blocks. When it was time to eat, the men sat across from the sisters. Sister Charlotte prayed for grace over the food and then all began to eat.

There was much praise for Tobias' catfish, and he had to admit that it was a particularly tasty catch. Near the end of the meal, Ace built up the fire at the rear of the shed because a cold drizzle had begun again. The benches and camp chairs were rearranged around the fire after the two youngest sisters had cleaned up after the meal and packed away their supplies, while Tobias packed away his kit.

Ace Redbone spoke to the sisters of the journey he and Tobias had taken up. He told them of the tribulations of Tobit. He laid before them the tale of young Jamie Farmer.

"The poor child, and your poor father", said Sister Charlotte as she looked into Tobias' eyes.

"It seems so unjust, Sister", replied Tobias. "I think worst of all for him is that he feels exiled from even his own faith. We speak of it sometimes, of the comfort of the Mass, the consolation even from the scent of incense and the Latin chants."

While Tobias spoke, Ace had taken his guitar from the case and casually checked the tuning before beginning to play a few soft tunes. Then he began to sing. He had an excellent, wide-ranging tenor voice. He sung a few Negro spirituals. The sisters especially liked *There Is a Balm in Gilead*. After that he delighted Sister Charlotte with hymns in Latin, German, and Spanish.

"Oh, what delight!" she exclaimed, clasping her hands together. Then her wistful expression turned sad. "I was born in Bavaria, Mister Losrouge, but my family moved to Prussia in my youth. There we faced the irrationality of Bismarck's Kulturkampf. Those were terrible days, when they tried to root Catholicism from all aspects of life in Germany.

"We moved for a short while into Austria, and I entered the order there. I then went to Spain because I was adept at languages, first to study, and then to teach."

Her expression had turned so dour that Sister Marie Regina took her hand and softly squeezed it. Sister Charlotte managed a smile. "I was teaching introductory German, French, and English at a large school for girls in San Cyprian, a small town near the Pyrenees Mountains when the civil war erupted.

"Such horror, San Cyprian was in a no-man's-land between the Nationalists and the Republicans. The order directed us that we should leave for France, but we begged that we be allowed to stay with our girls."

"Sister, you need not—" began Marie Regina, but her words were cut off by a shake of Sister Charlotte's head.

"No, I must", replied the older woman quietly. "The Communists came and burnt the school. The people of the town smuggled us into the countryside, but several of them were shot for it.

"It became a nightmare of hiding and clandestine movements, almost always at night. We arrived finally in Colinaverde, a larger town. We were to wait there for transport across the mountains and into France.

"The next morning a force of Communists and Republicans arrived. They began rounding up the priests and sisters from the local parishes, but suddenly a force of Nationalists also arrived, and there was a day and a half of skirmishes before both sides withdrew into the hills.

"This complicated things for us, very much. We knew the Republican side would arrest us, but were not sure that the Nationalists wouldn't turn us away from the border. We hid in that poor, ravaged city for three days. We did what we could for the wounded and the homeless, but finally our guides decided we must make an attempt to slip between the two forces.

"It did not go well. Two of our sisters were captured, along with a priest that was travelling with us. The rest of us had to watch from our hiding place as they were shot at the side of the road by the Communists."

Sister Marie Regina interrupted her. "You must understand that Sister Charlotte and others wanted to intervene. They wanted to go down to plead for the release of the others, but the guides would not allow it. They said there was nothing that could be done and to reveal themselves would put everyone at risk."

Sister Charlotte was staring now at the fire, and Tobias tried to imagine what she might see in those crackling flames, but decided he rather not know. Finally she began again. "The executions were so swift and haphazard. One moment there was talking, arguing, and the next a Communist leader just fires his pistol and kills the priest and our sisters. We hid for another day, not even daring to bury our fallen sisters and the priest, because the guides were certain they were left there to draw us out."

Sister Charlotte hung her head with a sigh, gathering internal strength. "Finally shepherds came out of the hills and buried the bodies under a pile of stones, a 'cairn' I think you call it in English. Then we knew we could move on.

"We passed through another village. It was deserted. The church was burnt, and the old pastor and his young assistant were hanging from a nearby tree. We took them down and buried them.

"It was not far from the border when we came upon the bodies of the Communists. There must have been fifteen of them who died in a battle with the Nationalists. It looked as if the Nationalists hung another six of them.

"May God forgive me, but I felt such elation at this, seeing it as an avenging, though I could not even be sure these were the same men who had been murdering our brothers and sisters. I was burning with such sadness, anger, and shame.

"It was after this that we were discovered by a Republican force of twelve men. By the mercy of God they were not, however, Communists, but Basque separatists. While allied with the Republicans, they were devout Catholics and had become irate with the Communist faction. The dispute had erupted into a skirmish where two of their men had been killed.

"It was heartbreaking, though, to hear these good Catholic men speaking gleefully of having killed seven of the Communists. It stung me with my own elation at the dead Communists we had stumbled across."

Sister Charlotte sank into a grim silence, seeming to ponder the sins of her past. Marie Regina softly picked up the tale. "The Basque militiamen were not from the immediate area, but they used their knowledge and skill in the Pyrenees to guide the refugees safely over the mountains and into France.

"Still, it was a long and twisting journey that took them another week of dreadful hunger, sleeplessness, and fear."

"The last stretch was most anxious", said Sister Charlotte with a sigh. "The Basque were not welcomed by the French, so they had to leave us before the last few kilometers. At the top of each rise in the path we could see the border station, but then we would descend again, not knowing what might await us, hidden behind the twists and turns along the way.

"Many of the refugees feared the French would turn them back, and they melted away to try and find entry where there was no official presence. The captain of the station, it turned out, however, was a good man. He arranged transport for us to a refugee station. From there, those of us from the order were processed to another refugee camp near Lourdes where we were to rest and recover."

Sister Charlotte shook her head in sad, confused wonder. "It was there that I was offered a chance to come to America and work with the Negro missions. America seemed such a safe place, for all its imperfections.

"I was onboard the ship when word came to us of the bombing of Guernica. What hope could there be for the decent people of that tortured land? Madness gripped both sides, and God's essence was betrayed and violated in one way or another no matter where you turned.

"I stayed in the cabin the entire voyage. In the wake of Guernica my accent would not have created much welcome for the other sisters travelling with me. But now I am in America. I have been working for the schools and medical clinics the Church has founded for the Negro. Your people have known a long history of the sort of sorrow I saw being inflicted upon the people of Spain. I am honored to serve."

From time to time, as she spoke, Ace had been feathering a melody from the strings of his guitar. *I have seen my Jesus crucified*, he began to softly sing. The sisters joined him in the whispered song. Tobias and Jake Choory did not know the words, but they sat still and listened.

Okra sensed the sorrow shrouding Tobias' heart, so the good dog rose and trotted to rest his chin upon the young man's thigh. His strange, dark dog eyes gazed longingly at his young master's face. They seemed to offer and entreat: *Love. Love. Love.*

Seven

Ace stoked up the fire again so that the sisters could have enough light to read and pray. The three men and the dog retreated nearer the bus. Jake Choory went into the storage section and found blankets, which he took to the front for the sisters to use that night.

"All manner of things in the back there", said Choory. "Every parish where we stop, the people donate to the sister's work. Catholics in the South are a peculiar sort. Most of them want to assist the Negroes, except that they should worship in the same church building with them.

"It is not maybe so bad in Harper Bay as elsewhere, bad as it might be. I suppose that when my folk came over they brought a dose of what was not lily-white with them."

He chuckled then as he rearranged some of the items in the back of the bus so that the men would have places to sleep. "I was a very young man when we came from Lebanon. My family was among the first. None of us spoke much English, and for sure nobody at Harper Bay spoke Arabic. We made do for a while with a mix of English and French.

"We were Maronites, you know. Still, the bishop welcomed us into the diocese. We had no Maronite priest, but since we were in communion with Rome we started attending the local Roman churches.

"They were shocked to see us, I tell you. I don't suppose they ever considered there were Christians in Lebanon, or had ever heard of Lebanon."

When he was done prepping for the night, Choory stood back and appraised the bus. "This old beast had seen better days before it was donated to the sisters. I don't know what we will do if Tobias cannot get it running as it should."

"We will get you to a telephone", said Ace. "Then you can call someone to come up from Harper Bay and collect the sisters."

"They may already be looking for them", suggested Tobias.

"Probably not; we were running early."

"A new day brings new possibilities", declared Ace with a firm conviction. "I have heard nothing but bragging on Tobias' turn of a wrench."

The sisters had finished their prayers and readings. Choory assisted them each into the bus. He had made pillows for them out of pillow cases stuffed with towels that had been donated. He beamed at their praise and gratitude.

Before Sister Charlotte boarded the bus, she paused to look up into the night sky. She seemed confused. Tobias thought perhaps she was just tired, or maybe she was given to coming and going in presence of mind the way some elderly people were.

"Look, the sky is clearing", she said absently. The three men and Marie Regina glanced up to see patches of hard, cold stars. She smiled at the stars, and then she looked at Ace. Her expression became earnest and intent, as if trying to bring forth some memory packed far away in her mind. "You are familiar to me. I think I have seen you before. In Colinaverde, I think. I saw you walking among the wounded. You were offering them comfort and aid. You didn't care if they were Republican or Nationalist."

She smiled as she looked at Ace and whispered, "Of course, you were a woman then."

With that she turned so Choory could help her into the bus. Jake shrugged at Tobias and Ace. Sister Marie Regina looked at Ace with an apologetic expression. She was about to say something, but Ace shook his head that it was not necessary.

When the sisters were aboard and secure, Jake gestured to the other two men. "I am worn out and I haven't been walking all day like you two. Let's get some sleep."

He paused then near Ace, gesturing with his hand, "Ladies first."

Tobias could not help but laugh despite Ace Redbone's admonishing gaze. Then the musician allowed a reluctant chuckle himself. Near the back door of the bus he paused. He glanced around at the clearing sky.

"I think I would rather it had rained", he said. "It will be cooler now."

"Something else", prodded Tobias, trying to read his companion.

"Well, just not so likely that there would be any prowling critters in a good rain", said Ace. Then he gestured with his head toward the bus. "I'm going to sit by the fire a bit. Me and Okra here. We'll be joining you before too awful long."

Tobias studied the inky night of the scrubby forest around them. Then he said, "Yes, ma'am."

When everyone aboard the bus had slipped into sound slumber, Ace Redbone put a rolled-up blanket under one arm and nodded toward the dark-forested aisles. "Come along, Okra. Let's get ourselves into the night."

The dog followed at his heels as they moved between the tree trunks. They came finally to a small area near the road where for some reason the old growth had never been cut down. The tall hardwoods had lost most of their leaves as autumn slipped over the forest. The trees formed a vault of strong limbs, and a lacy canopy of finer branches through which shone the starlight.

Ace seated himself beside an ancient oak. Okra lay dutifully beside him. After only a few moments the dog's ears perked higher than normal as the sound of tires on the road came coasting to a motorless halt, and there followed the creaking of suspension as the vehicle pulled to the side of the road. The musician let his fingers brush lightly across Okra's neck and back so that the raised hackles were lowered.

There came the sound of whispered voices, and Okra tilted his head to look at Ace Redbone. The dog was uncertain as to why he should not raise an alarm, but Ace just slowly shook his head to maintain the silence. The whispering ceased but was replaced with the muffled sound of feet on the leaf-mold forest floor.

Three figures emerged from the density of the pine growth into the clearer space beneath the star-domed old growth. The lead figure was fifteen feet away when Ace Redbone rose smoothly to his feet. The newcomers went still.

Ace fixed his gaze on the leader. "Lester Murphy Dunlin, what are you doing out this time of the night, sneaking around in the woods?"

The oldest Dunlin brother overcame his surprise and took a single, deliberate step forward. He was carrying a clublike length of wood, which he slapped against the palm of his hand. "Look here, boys, it's that smart-ass nigger that was with Toby Two. We been lookin' for you, yeller man."

"Looks as if you have found me", said Ace with a slow smile. He looked then to the younger Dunlin brother, who was holding an old butcher's knife that had been sharpened over the years until it was a slender thing worthless for its original intent. "Michael David Dunlin, what are you thinking of doing with that?"

"How do you—" began Michael Dunlin, but he was cut off by his older brother.

"Toby Two told him our names", snapped Lester Dunlin. He motioned with his hand and his two companions fanned out. His brother moved to the left of him. Lenny Morris, carrying a five-foot length of sapling, moved to his right.

"It'll be easier this way", sneered Lester. "First this one, then Toby Two. Time to teach 'em a lesson."

Lester charged forward, with his companions hesitating only a moment in his wake. Ace slipped effortless to one side. The speed and smoothness of his evasion caused Lester to trip over the roots of the ancient oak. He skidded face-first over the chaotic roots, losing the grip of his club, which became tangled in his brother's feet.

Michael Dunlin's momentum sent him into his own sprawl. His instinct to catch himself caused the skinny knife to be stabbed into one of the oak's large surface roots. The knife snapped off at the hilt, leaving the blade driven uselessly into the root.

Both of the young men began scrambling in a panic as Ace Redbone approached them with a grim countenance. Regaining their feet, they fled back toward the road. Lenny Morris had been frozen by the sudden burst of confrontation, and he was shoved aside by the retreat of the Dunlin brothers, causing him to lose his footing and fall square on his backside. When Ace turned toward him the young man leapt to his feet, abandoning his stave as he tried to run after his companions.

"Okra."

With the whisper from Ace the dog burst after Lenny. He grabbed the tail of the boy's shirt. Lenny screamed in fright when he felt the tug. The fabric gave way and a palm-sized patch tore from the shirt. The sudden release caused Lenny to fall onto his face in the leaf mold.

The boy turned over onto his back, holding out his hands in front of him defensively and pleading, "Mister, Mister, I didn't want to come here."

Ace had stopped so that he was standing over the boy, looking down upon him. "You should *not* have come, it would seem."

"Please, please."

From the road there came the noise of the truck motor turning over, and then the crunch of the tires as it pulled onto the pavement and trundled away. Ace had looked up from the boy to listen to the retreating vehicle.

Turning his gaze back to the frightened face, he spoke, "Leonard Levi Morris, it seems that those boys you hoped were your friends have abandoned you. Now you are alone here in the woods with the person the lot of you were seeking to beat, maybe even stab."

Lenny began to cry, and his hands dropped to cover the shame on his face. Ace Redbone squatted beside him then, silent for a very long moment. When at last the boy was able to open his eyes and peer beyond his own fingers, Ace spoke again to him, "Leonard, I know why you are with those boys. I know that you are afraid. You are afraid that they would know the truth about you. You are afraid that people in these parts would realize that your middle name is from your mother's maiden name."

A stunned amazement stilled the tears, and Ace continued, "A Jewish girl who married a man of Jewish-Welsh decent. What would they think? What would they do? Not only those two warped boys who just now abandoned you, but what of so many of the other folk who look down upon Negroes, Jews, and Papists?

"Do you know why they are like that, Leonard? Because they have let themselves be made small and uncertain, so they try to make others smaller still."

Lenny closed his eyes, and a tormented groan emerged from his throat. "Mister—"

"Hush just now", said Ace softly. "I'm still talking. There's more that causes your fear. The death of your mother. Your father's retreat from the world around him. His bringing you to Stonebridge, a place alien and confusing to you.

"Yet, there is still more. There was the man in the car. I know what he tried to convince you to do. I know that you ran off into the woods and hid. I know that you saw young Jamie get into that car only a few minutes later.

"From your hiding place you wanted to scream at him to run, but fear paralyzed you. The same sort of fear that overwhelmed poor Jamie and molded him that day into a sad, compliant child."

Tears were falling again from the corners of Lenny's eyes as he stared in disbelief at Ace Redbone. An expression of compassion was returned to him as Ace continued, "Now I will tell you how your fear can be undone. There is a man I want you to talk to. He has in his power the ability to protect you, and to bring justice. I will tell you where to find him, and what you must say. Do you want to be healed, Leonard? Do you want to walk without this fear?"

Slowly, Leonard Levi Morris nodded his head. Ace Redbone smiled softly and spoke gently to the boy for a few more moments. Then the man stood up and offered the boy his hand.

When Lenny was on his feet, Ace draped the blanket he had carried into the forest around the boy's shoulders. "You have a long walk and the night has grown chilled."

Ace then retrieved the stave and gave it over to Lenny. "Take this. It will give you some courage on your way."

Then the man called to Okra. The dog trotted softly to him. Ace smiled and retrieved the patch of green plaid shirt from the dog's mouth. He turned and pushed it gently into the boy's shirt pocket. "You have been given a gift this night, Leonard Levi Morris. It is decreed that to whom much has been given, much is expected. Keep that piece of cloth to remind you of that."

The boy nodded blankly. Ace smiled, "Well, go now. Go now, you son of the race of Israel, circumcised on the eighth day. Go now, you son of the tribes of Judah and Levi. Go now, you Hebrew of Hebrew parentage, and remember that your Lord will *never* forget a covenant he has made."

Lenny straightened then and a firm hope woke in his eyes. He turned with as much resolution as ever he had known and walked purposefully from the forest.

Ace watched him. He smiled. He looked down at Okra. "What a marvelous beast you are becoming. Now, let us return to our friends and your young master."

The morning was crisp and cooler than normal for this time of the year. Tobias wanted to just stay curled up in the blanket in his little nook in the storage area, but remembered that he needed to investigate the problem with the bus.

Okra was happy to have him awake, prancing back and forth between his young master and where the sisters were huddled around the fire. Sister Mary Lenora handed Tobias a cup of coffee and a rewarmed biscuit with melted cheese between the halves.

"I trust you slept well", said Sister Charlotte.

"I did, Sister", replied Tobias. "A little longer than I had intended. I hope you slept well too."

"Oh indeed", said the sister, smiling and staring into the fading gray and growing azure sky. "I slept as if rocked in the arms of angels."

"Well, they cricked my neck", complained Jake Choory. "I'm too old to sleep all scrunched up with boxes and such."

Ace laughed. "Maybe Tobias can help you get home to your own bed tonight."

When he had finished his breakfast, Tobias made his way back to the motor bay of the truck, with Choory, Redbone, and Okra following him. The coffee had more fully wakened and warmed him. He was ready to get to work, except he said, "I don't suppose you have any tools?"

"Hmm", mumbled Jake, but he raised his hand as if requesting a moment. He went into the front of the bus, disappearing as if looking under the driver's seat. Then he reappeared and exited the bus carrying a small, shallow, greasy cardboard box.

Presented with a haphazard collection of grubby tools, Tobias shook his head. "Not much to work with here, but let me see what I can do."

Jake and Ace stood with arms crossed watching him. Okra sat between them tilting his head to one side and then the other as he tried to decipher his young master's activity. Without looking up from the bay, Tobias spoke to them as he worked, "It's a mess under here. We could just about take our pick of what's wrong.

"Jake, turn it over for me."

Choory nodded and went into the bus and tried to start it. After a few cranks Tobias called out to him, "That's enough. The coil is working, anyway. Now, let's see if I can get a plug out."

Jake came back around to the front of the bus, resuming his arms-crossed observation. In a few minutes Tobias straightened himself out, holding up a spark plug. "Well, this isn't helping. Pretty fouled up. I need to clean them. Do you reckon one of the sisters might have a fingernail file?"

"I don't know; they're not given to cosmetic vanities", replied Choory, but then a look of sudden comprehension spread over his face. "What I do know is there is some sandpaper in the back of the bus."

"Grit?"

"Fairly fine, I guess."

"Worth a try."

While Jake hurried off to scrounge up the sandpaper, Tobias began working to pull the remaining plugs. He carefully sanded off the carbon and oil smudge on each plug, blowing or flicking off with his fingernails any grit that might stick to the plug. Then he replaced each plug.

"Well, let's try it again."

Choory returned to the driver's seat and turned the motor. There was a chug, chug, a backfire, and then the motor rumbled into life. Tobias leaned into the engine bay to raise the revs a few times and then indicated for Jake to turn the motor off.

"That should get you to Harper Bay", he said when Choory had rejoined him. "Do you know when was the last time the plugs were changed?"

"I suppose maybe eight months ago when we had it serviced. They certainly billed us for plugs."

"Hmmm. Well, if they in fact replaced the plugs, then you probably have some bad valves, maybe rings too. Sounds like it could be both."

"But it will get us to town?" asked Sister Marie Regina as the women joined the men.

"Yes, I was just tellin' Mister Choory," replied Tobias before turning back to Jake, "I'm not sure how long our business is going to take, but in a few weeks call Crafty's and ask for me. If you can bring it to me, I can give it a go-over. I'll only charge for the parts, and I'll let you know what I think that will be before I go on with any repairs. Mister Forgeron won't mind me donating my own time."

"That is very generous of you", said Choory.

"Indeed, it is", echoed Sister Charlotte.

"Well, you sisters have been very kind and generous to us", said Tobias.

"Oh no, young man," protested Sister Marie Regina as the younger sisters began repacking and rearranging the bus for the continuation of their trip, "we offered you a few vegetables and lent you some blankets. You provided us with fish for our dinner, a fire to warm us, and repaired our bus."

She turned then to look at Ace. "And you had to have been up most of the night. Every time I woke I would see you standing guard over the camp."

Sister Charlotte was nodding her head emphatically even as her gaze seemed far away.

Tobias shrugged again. "Sister, you gave us a gift. You treated us like men. Like we were equal in station to any other men. You cannot understand, I think, what that might mean to us. Sister Mary Lenora could explain it."

Sister Charlotte's gaze refocused on the here and now. She held up a hand. "Just a moment, young man. Sister Marie, would you fetch for me my satchel?"

In a few moments Marie Regina returned with a battered, stiff-sided, brown leather satchel. Sister Charlotte placed it on the step of the bus. She carefully removed a folded towel from out of the satchel and then pulled from within a small box. She opened this and pulled out an even smaller box, which she handed to Tobias.

"Last night, you spoke of the scent of incense when you walked into the church, and how you missed that", she explained. "This is a bit of incense I have carried with me all the way from France. It was given to me by an old man who was on pilgrimage to Lourdes. He was a retired groundskeeper at the Basilian abbey at Grottaferrata in Italy. He said the incense had been made by a holy man on the Island of Patmos; so you see, it is a precious thing, from the island of Revelation itself."

She turned then to the satchel and brought out another box. When she opened this, one strand of straw spilled over the sides. She brought forth one of four glass vials, no longer than her smallest finger. She set this in a small cardboard box with some of the straw and presented this also to Tobias.

"This is water from Lourdes", she said. "Wash your father's eyes. If the Lord wills it, maybe it will help."

"Sister, I don't know what to say", muttered Tobias. He was awed by the personal generosity of the sister's gesture.

Sister Charlotte waved off his gratitude, and the distance returned to her gaze as she turned toward Ace Redbone. "Mister Losrouge, I do not believe there is anything I could give you."

Ace smiled, "Like the young man said, Sister, you have given much."

She was about to speak again, but then seemed to think better of it. Instead, she smiled and turned to enter the bus with the assistance of Sister Marie Regina. When the door had closed behind them, Ace and Tobias called to Okra and stood back as the bus chugged to life and began its whining reverse out from under the shed.

Returning the waves from the bus windows, they watched as it trundled down the dirt road, and then, after a squeal of its brakes as Jake Choory checked the road, it disappeared onto the pavement and behind the screen of scruffy pines.

"That was something", mused Tobias aloud as he investigated the peculiar gifts the sister had given him.

"It was", agreed Ace. "Providential."

"Well, she sure was a pleasant lady", decided Tobias. "Although she seemed a bit addled from time to time. I suppose that happens to a lot of older folk."

Ace arched an eyebrow. "It does. But sometimes there is an aura of the other world around the wisest and the holiest."

"Well, she certainly seemed taken with you", chuckled Tobias.

Ace winked at him. "And that is why I believe she is a saint."

It was midafternoon and Frank Forgeron was focused intently on his work. He was a little backed up with the absence of Tobias. He was not put out by that. He had been more put out by the fact that the Messagers had not come to him for help. Yet, he understood when Tobit explained to him that sometimes colored folk needed to do things for themselves.

"You are a generous man", said Tobit, his hazy, unseeing eyes fixed on where Forgeron had been standing. "But you can understand, I think, how it is that a man doesn't feel he is a man until he can take care of himself in such ways as God might will it.

"Frank, our people need to have some part in their salvation in the world of men."

Caught up in his work and pondering the words of Tobit Messager, Frank hadn't noticed the peculiar sight of the boy approaching his repair shop. It startled him when the blanket-draped young man suddenly appeared at the open bay door holding a length of sapling like a prophet's staff.

For a moment they just stared at each other, but the young man seemed to dredge up from within himself some motivation to speak.

"Mister Forgeron? Frank Forgeron?"

Frank's brow furrowed. He recognized the boy, though he didn't know him well. He nodded. The young man then seemed to draw himself more erect.

"Sir, I am Leonard Levi Morris. I have something to tell. Mister Ace Redbone said I should tell it to you."

Eight

Though tired from her work in the house of others, Anna had house-cleaning that had to be done in her own home. She sent Tobit out to socialize with Joe-boy. Her husband needed some exercise, and he needed to keep his mind occupied. Ever since Tobias had left, Tobit had been sleeping restlessly. He dreamed often of Tobias, seeming to imagine trials and tribulations the boy might be experiencing on his journey.

Anna had been at her housework only a few minutes when she heard the creaking suspension of Reverend Walker's car as he drove it slowly up the driveway. As she came out of the house onto the porch, she saw Tobit feeling his way along from the barn with a bamboo stick. She walked over to take him by one arm.

"Has to be Gaston", he guessed. "I don't know anyone else who drives so slow as that. Joe-boy is like swift Mercury in comparison."

"Shush", she giggled. "Don't exaggerate."

With Anna guiding her husband, they made their way back to the walk that led to their porch. They stood there in front of the steps as they waited for Gaston Walker to go through his deliberate preparations for exiting the car. When he heard the reverend's car door shut, Tobit called out to him, "Good afternoon, Gaston. What brings you this way? Not that you need a reason to visit an old friend."

"Indeed, indeed", returned Reverend Walker. "But, I bring news."

"Come on up on the porch then and have a sit-down", said Anna. The two men seated themselves on the rocking chairs, and Anna took her place on the swing.

"I don't suppose you have heard about Doctor Macklin?" asked Gaston. When both Messagers shook their heads, he continued, "His house burned down last night. It started in his clinic, but the house was a complete loss. He was fortunate to survive. Well, he might not make it yet, but he was alive when they took him to the hospital in Harper Bay."

"How did it happen?" asked Anna. Walker shrugged, but remembering that Tobit could not see he replied, "Not rightly sure. There are rumors."

"There are always rumors", Tobit sighed.

"Always", agreed Gaston Walker with a soft, grim chuckle. "There is some talk that he left a Bunsen burner on because he was drunk. No explanation for why he might have had it burning to begin with.

"Others say he had stopped drinking but he had a breakdown because of it and set the place on fire himself. I know he had stopped drinking, and it was a struggle for him, but I doubt that story.

"Others say it was an electrical short. Given that it is an ordinary story, and that Doc's place was in poor repair, it might be the most likely."

"We'll keep him in our prayers", said Tobit, to which Anna emphatically nodded her head.

"Any word from your boy?" asked Gaston.

"He called Frank Forgeron, who relayed to us that they were near to Goldsboro", replied Anna. "It has taken them longer than they thought it would because of the heavy rain, but they are safe so far."

Gaston shook his head. "You should have let me take Tobias to look for your cousin."

Tobit laughed, "God bless you, Gaston, but we should like to have Tobias home before Christmas."

Gaston chuckled at his own expense. "Well, I could have let the young man drive. But, we have been over this, I think I understand, and I certainly respect your decision."

"You have a flock to tend to, and we weren't sure how long it would take to find Jubal", said Tobit. "But your offer is appreciated."

"And pray we don't regret our decision", Anna softly added.

In the bright midmorning sun filling the office, Del Gaines considered the paperwork on his desk and the amount of time left until lunch. He did not see how he could finish it before he had to be in court that afternoon, but there was nothing to do but try. He picked up the first stack of papers and prepared himself for tedium.

It was just then that the door to the office opened and a man approached the counter. He was a lean man of medium height, dressed in a crisp, conservative suit and carrying a briefcase. His eyes were sparkling sharp as he appraised the room and the deputy. He nodded his head in a curt, officious manner and set the briefcase on the floor.

"Deputy, I am Fredric Forgeron, State Bureau of Investigation", he said as he laid his identification on the counter. "I am here to investigate the death of a James Farmer. I will need to see the sheriff."

Del looked over the ID, and his eyes grew slightly wider at the investigator's announced intent. "I'm Chief Deputy Gaines. The sheriff is in court this morning."

"Then while we wait, I have some questions for you."

"Yes, sir", replied Gaines. "I'm the only one in the office until lunch. Everyone else is tied up over at court. We're a small office, you see, a small county. Can we talk here? At my desk, maybe?"

"That will be sufficient", said Forgeron as he picked up the briefcase and went around behind the counter and sat behind Del's desk. He gestured for the deputy to sit across from him before beginning to pull a file from his briefcase.

With the file open before him, and a pen and notebook at the ready, Fredric Forgeron turned his intense stare upon the deputy. Gaines squirmed slightly in discomfort, but then steeled himself and asked, "Are you Crafty Forgeron's brother?"

"I am Francis Forgeron's brother", said the investigator. "Which I should imagine would be almost impossible to *not* determine, since there are few Forgerons in this state, and fewer still that work for the SBI. In fact, there is only one. I am that one."

Well, he certainly has the Forgeron sarcasm, thought Del Gaines before speaking again. "Is this an official inquiry?"

Forgeron pulled a sheet of paper from the file and turned it around so Del could read it. "This is an official notice of inquiry."

Del glanced over it, nodding. "Yes, sir."

"Good", said Forgeron, pulling the piece of paper back around and returning it to the file. "Now, you saw the body?"

"Yes", replied Gaines.

"Deputy, this will go faster if you give me complete answers so that I don't have to fish for them."

"Understood. Mister Toby—Tobit Messager—brought the body into town. He had found it hanging in a tree about twelve miles outside of

Stonebridge. He claimed it had been hanging there for about three days and that the department ignored notice of it."

"Had the department done so?"

"I don't know, sir. There was no record of such a notification."

"Deputy, do you believe it to be a suicide? Based on your observations?"

Del Gaines spent a long moment in silence. He dreaded confrontations of this sort. He dreaded making difficult decisions. Finally he sighed and replied, "No. No, sir. I do not."

"Despite the medical report?"

"I suppose I could be wrong. But Mister Toby pointed out some issues that my own observations confirmed. The body was hung with an ineffective slip knot. It had been badly beaten before death occurred. I went to the scene of the hanging, and there were signs on the tree limb that someone had pulled the body up by the rope.

"Sir, I believe the boy was killed and *then* hung."

Forgeron had been taking notes; he nodded when the deputy finished. When he looked up, his hard stare was softer, though still searching. "Deputy, why were you silent on these observations?"

Del looked at the desktop. "It was not officially my investigation. And I suppose because the sheriff said it was a suicide. Doc Mack filled out a report saying it was a suicide."

Almost he shrugged his shoulders, but instead he sat more erect and looked directly at Forgeron. "Mostly, sir, it is because I am a coward."

The investigator did not flinch; he drove his gaze even deeper into Del's eyes. "Deputy, are you tired of being a coward?"

"Yes, sir, I am."

The next day Del Gaines drove Forgeron to the scene of the hanging. He had no idea how the interview with the sheriff had gone. It was nearly two hours in length, and neither man emerged from it with any hint in their expressions of what had transpired. Forgeron did say that the county had been subject to a review and clandestine investigation into illegal whisky distillation.

After the investigator had examined the hanging tree, he had Del drive him over to Tobit's house. Sitting on the porch, they went over Tobit's account. Then it was a drive over to talk to Gaston Walker and Mason Newberry.

Finally they drove to Harper Bay. At St. Luke's Hospital they tried to interview Dr. Macklin, but he was not conscious. It was late in the afternoon by then, and neither had eaten since breakfast, so they stopped at a diner for a late lunch, or early supper.

As they waited for their food, Forgeron passed over a piece of paper to Del. "The report Doctor Macklin gave on James Farmer's death. Does that, by any chance, look like Macklin's signature?"

Del frowned and shrugged. "Hard to say, sir. Doc Mack has a drinking problem. His handwriting was bad, even for a doctor. I have to say it looks about as much like Doc's handwriting as it doesn't."

Forgeron nodded. He turned his head to look out the window, into the long shadows of the descending sun. The waitress brought them their food. As the plates clattered onto the tabletop, Fredric Forgeron turned his gaze to the chief deputy.

"Del, I have something I want you to see."

"Yes, sir?"

"Just call me Fred", said Forgeron. "I've decided that you are clean in this. I have decided that you may be guilty of uncertain omission, but you are not guilty in any way of commission.

"What I have here is a statement of a young man named Leonard Morris."

"I know Lenny", Del frowned as he took the papers Forgeron handed him. "Poor kid has had it rough. I hate to think he was involved with Jamie's death."

"What you read there will be upsetting", said Forgeron. "In ways you might not have imagined. Lenny is in Raleigh. He is safe."

Del read the papers. His face deepened into a frown. Then the frown melted into disbelief. Then his face went white. He looked up at Forgeron, but no words would come.

"You know what we have to do next, don't you, Del?"

The chief deputy could only nod.

Because of the rain, Tobias and Ace Redbone made very little progress. They spent one night in a barn a farmer generously allowed them to use, and another they spent huddled beneath the leaking roof of a mostly collapsed house. In two and a half days they had managed less than twenty miles.

Then the weather changed and their luck with it. From Tobias' point of view it came from the unlikeliest of sources, a white man who travelled the area repairing cotton gins. He was busy this time of year, as the cotton was being harvested and baled.

"It's a shame the way you people are treated", was all he said when a Negro foreman introduced them. The repairman gestured to the back of his panel truck.

"A '35, Dodge", Tobias explained to Ace while they rode. "Hydraulic brakes, six-cylinder motor with floating mounts. That two-level roof lets you move around back here without bumping your head so much. Some folk call 'em humpbacks because of the roof."

"That's good to know", replied Ace.

The driver let them off near Goldsboro, and after thanking him they made their way southward, with Okra ranging around them as always along the narrow road. Tobias had been lost in thought for the entire ride, and he still remained pensive as they walked.

"What is troubling you, Tobias?"

"I was just wondering about things", sighed the younger man. "It's not that I don't believe, mind you, of a fashion, but things like what happened to my father, or to Sister Charlotte. I don't know."

"Then there is this holy water, or whatever, that she brought from Lourdes. Do you think it can make a miracle?"

"I think only God can make a miracle", said Ace, shrugging.

"Then this water is just water?"

"I didn't say that. It may well be a tool that God uses."

"Why don't he just cure folk?"

"Because the miracle isn't always a cure, I reckon."

"I don't understand."

"Nobody understands all but God", replied Ace. "Look, human beings are tangible creatures, right? They have touch; they can be touched. Maybe something like this water, the faith it instills, is a way God touches a human in a physical sense. Perhaps that tangible sensation stirs their faith."

"I dunno", sighed Tobias. "Sounds to me like you're saying it is all in their minds."

"The mind is how we *know* anything, is it not? Is the mind not most how we are like God?" suggested Ace. "The soul reflected in the mind.

Does it matter if some shock to the mind, to the psychology as these mind doctors say, is what instigates the cure or the understanding or the comforting? Is it really any less miraculous? Is it not *still* a miracle?"

"I suppose", replied Tobias. He lifted his gaze to the road ahead, wanting to shake his mood. "What do you know of this man, Jubal, that my father calls a cousin?"

"Only what I have heard tell", said Ace. "He has done well for himself, but he has only one child, a daughter. From all accounts she is a beautiful young lady. Dark, tall, well formed, and graceful. Folk say she is rather like a young queen or princess from the stories of ol' Africa.

"But they say too that she is afflicted. Three times she has been betrothed, and each time death has come for her fiancé before the marriage ceremony could be performed. Some folk talk of a curse. Others say there is a demon who prowls at the edge of her life, a lustful demon who would keep her for itself."

"People talk crazy sometimes", noted Tobias.

"Yes, yes, they do", replied Ace with a chuckle. "But, might it not be similar to the miracles? Afflictions, curses, can be a physical manifestation of something from beyond, something spiritual."

Tobias felt a strange surge in himself. He frowned, considering Ace's words. "Seems a shame, though. Has she done anything to deserve such affliction?"

"It rains on the just and the unjust", Ace reminded him. "Remember when the Christ spoke, in Luke's Gospel, of those killed when the tower at Siloam fell upon them. How he challenged the notion that they were somehow more guilty than others who were spared. By no means, he declared!

"For whatever reason, be it the work of evil or pure chance, misfortune comes, but even with such misfortune God will knit something from which we might learn and be blessed. Of that you can be sure."

Uncertainty created a slight frown on Tobias' face. "When we get back home, you should spend a few weeks talking to my father. You sound just like him."

"Ah, he is a wise man, then", replied the smiling Ace Redbone.

Okra recognized the lightening of the mood and pranced alongside them for a moment, sniffing at their fingers with his pointy nose before going forth to range ahead of them again.

"What is the daughter's name?"

"Sarah", replied Ace. "A sweet girl. A dutiful daughter. A young woman with as much beauty in her soul as is upon her body."

Tobias sighed.

They spent a day asking for Jubal, but nobody knew him. They spent the night in the open and then spent another day walking and inquiring with little results to show.

They spent the second night sleeping on the pews of the Good Samaritan Missionary Baptist Church. It was a very old-frame church with no steeple, sagging in the middle, with two windows boarded over, and badly in need of paint. There was an ancient colored man working at repairing the wooden steps.

As they had walked by the place, Ace had called out a greeting. That simple act turned into a conversation. It turned out the old man was the pastor of the church. He heard the story of their journey and had insisted that they sleep in the church that night. He even graciously allowed that Okra could also sleep in the church.

Tobias marveled at how so many people just seemed to instinctually trust Ace Redbone. Not, of course, that there was anything in the church worth stealing. The pastor told them that the church dated back even to the days of slavery. One of the plantation owners, with his days nearing an end, became very concerned for the souls of his slaves. The congregation was dwindling now, attracted by newer churches and younger preachers.

When the old man had finally given up on his work and walked to his equally ramshackle parsonage, Ace had suggested that he and Tobias show their gratitude by finishing the repair of the steps and the stoop. The pastor had left his tools just inside the church.

So they spent a couple of hours replacing boards. Being two and younger, they accomplished this task much more quickly than the preacher could have done. They then spent an hour more cleaning up the inside of the church: clearing out dust, cobwebs, and washing the remaining windows.

"I wish we could get a hold of some paint", mused Tobias.

Ace stood in the middle of the church. He smiled a little, closing his eyes, and his head swaying slightly. "Do you hear?"

"Just the boards creaking beneath your feet, and the sound of frogs and crickets from outside."

"Ah, I hear the echo of songs from days gone by. Generations of hope. Songs rising to the Lord like incense."

Tobias frowned. "You are beginning to sound as addled as Sister Charlotte."

"The world would be a better place if all folk were as addled as the saintly sister", Ace admonished him. "Or as righteous as Pastor Williams. I am afraid that this old church shall never rebound, but it has served the Lord long and well."

Okra woofed his approval, causing Tobias to laugh. "I tell you, sometimes having that dog along is just like having my daddy along with us."

Then the young man's expression grew perplexed as he saw the dog's ears prick and his head tilt as if considering unseen things within the church. "I hate it when a dog does that. Like they're seeing ghosts or some such."

"Ghost? No. The memories of the Lord, maybe. The memories of the Lord from when this place was filled with song and prayer. The Lord remembering the lives and the spirits that stretched eagerly, hopefully, and desperately to him from within this place. The Lord ne'er forgets."

"Yeah, that's a lot less crazy than ghosts", said Tobias.

"We should sleep", Ace decided aloud.

They each picked a pew. Before he laid himself down, Tobias pulled his rosary from out of his pocket and began to pray. He imagined the prayer drifting like incense to Heaven.

When he finally laid himself down for sleep, he dreamed. All the night he dreamed. He dreamed of this church filled with people. These were no ghostly folk. They were vibrant and alive. The air was filled with their song.

He saw Ace sitting among them, joining in their song. Then the musician rose and walked to the front of the church and he went to his knees. Then he bent forward until his forehead was on the floor. The song of the congregation rose into a seamless crescendo. Ace rose erect upon his knees and threw his arms wide in supplication before the plain wooden cross hanging on the wall.

Tobias' eyes grew wide, for there was now on this cross a corpus where there had not been one. The features seemed to shift as if to reflect back the images of everyone who gazed upon it. The congregation surged forward and fell upon their knees on either side of Ace Redbone, and like him they threw wide their arms.

Then Ace seemed to grow and his features became illuminated as if from within. Around him flowed light, rising as in a great arch, and color flowed like water within it. The congregation fell upon their faces before the cross, and then rose and began to march past Ace with a song of exaltation upon their lips.

Ace rose in a swirl of winged flowing light and walked straight toward the cross, and every man, woman, and child in the church strode past him. Tobias watched as they seemed to pass *through* the cross. They cast wide their arms in joyous supplication.

It was surreal because it was more real than anything he knew in the waking world. Then the shouts began: "Hallelujah!" "Amen!"—like the rhythm of great battle drums, and they flowed to rattle the very gates of Hell and to make tremble its walls.

Then Ace knelt and kissed the feet of the crucified Christ. Those feet were astonishingly real, bloodstained and with the last lingering warmth of life as the sacrifice became complete. Ace turned a gaze of burning beauty upon Tobias before following the memory of the congregations into a brilliance Tobias could not bear.

Tobias trembled at the terrible beauty of it. Then he felt his gaze pulled to the back of the church, where he saw Okra standing near the doors, watching the great celebration with his head inquisitively tilted.

Tobias turned then to look once more at the generations of worship; when he turned back to look again upon Okra, he was startled to see standing there, instead, his father. Tobit was observing the memories of the Lord with seeing eyes. There was a pleased smile upon Tobit's face. His eyes drifted over the sight of it all until they settled upon the face of his son, and his smile became brighter still.

Then Tobias saw his father turn around and open the doors of this little clapboard church, but instead of opening onto the outside, Tobit stepped into another church. This one was very large. Candlelight lit the interior. Tobias saw at once that it was a majestic vaulted church.

He watched as his father walked down the aisle filled with a seemingly endless flow of people. Tobit went to the altar rail and knelt. Tobias saw a robed figure placing what he assumed to be a Host upon his father's tongue, except that there seemed to be a faint light upon the bread.

Again and again he saw the scene repeated, his father walking the aisle and taking the glowing Host. Each time it seemed that a light grew within Tobit until at last he was himself a source of incredible brightness.

All the other communicants shone with him until Tobias had to narrow his eyes against the glory. This great light flowed out over the world.

Then Tobias had a vision of a great number of people wrapped in heavy gray robes kneeling upon stony ground; they were in a wide arc with their backs to the ominous gates and craggy walls of Hell. Each lifted face was ash streaked, but they were gazing with expectant hope into the distance. Suddenly, on the horizon of this dismal plain, there burst forth the light that rose from Tobit and his companions.

The light swept over the robed figures, and the gray fabric became as dust, and each of them was revealed in a glory of light and color. The light washed against the incoherent gate and walls that looked as if they had been built by a maddened hoard of workers, each obsessed with their own work and vision, considering nothing of those who had toiled beside them. And it burst through every crack and crevice until the wretched construct crumbled and the light as of countless suns shone fierce into everything that was, had ever been, or would ever be.

Just as Tobias thought he could bear no more, Okra stepped out of the light and walked calmly toward him and into the tired clapboard church. Tobias started awake. He did not feel frightened, only a peculiar comforting awe. He pulled himself into a sitting position on the rickety pew and looked back at the doors.

Okra was sitting there, looking at him with the eyes of Tobit. I must still be dreaming, sighed Tobias to himself as he lay back on the pew.

Ace, Tobias, and Okra slipped away from the Good Samaritan Missionary Baptist Church in the gray predawn. Ace had suggested that they leave before the pastor should see all the work they had done and feel obliged to offer some payment.

"A hot breakfast would have been nice, though", said Tobias as he chewed a piece of jerky. "But it is probably better that we leave rather than tax his pantry. I just hope we don't make the old man feel guilty."

Ace smiled. "No, he will make payment into *caritas*, as your father would say. Pastor Williams probably has paid more than his measure over the course of his life."

"I don't half the time understand what you're saying", laughed Tobias. "But I usually like the half I do."

"You seem out of sorts this morning", said Ace. "Was that pew too hard for your delicate back?"

"It was none too comfortable, but no, it's not that", replied Tobias with a rueful chuckle. "I just had strange dreams all night long. I can't hardly remember them, but the feeling lingers. I dreamed of singing, chanting, Communion, Purgatory, and I don't know what all else."

"I told you the memories of the Lord were in that place", Ace reminded him with a wink. "And the Lord remembers things that have yet to even happen."

They walked until near dusk, and then began searching for a campsite. With his usual acumen for such things, Ace found them a place off the road where the sandy soil had drained away the rain and the sun had made it relatively dry. They would be screened from the road, thus spared any hassles from passing law enforcement. Tobias was so tired that he slept as soundly as he had since having left home.

When morning came, Okra woofed impatiently at them. He was eager for the journey to be resumed. After a brief breakfast from their dwindling supply, they were on their way again. A few miles down the road they came upon a man waiting where a driveway met the pavement. Just off the road were a few battered shanties.

The man was in his middle years, shabbily dressed like most field laborers would be. He was a tall, big-boned, lanky fellow, who gazed, without quite staring, in interest at the approaching men and dog, something mildly new and different to his work-a-day world.

Ace Redbone doffed his hat. "Good morning to you. Do you by any chance know of Jubal Tomkins? We asked Pastor Williams at the Good Samaritan Missionary Baptist Church, but while he knew the name he knew little else."

"Preacher Bill don't remember so good nowadays. I know of Jubal. He owns a store 'bout twenty-five miles from here, over near Newton Grove. Jubal's Generals is what folk calls it. It's on Cut Creek Road, just where Masterson Farm Road joins up with it."

"Thank you", replied Ace before turning to Tobias. "Well, that's quite a walk still left to us."

"Mister," began the man, "I work as a field hand for the Mastersons. They gots land all and 'round 'bout here. I be waitin' for George Battle to pick me up. He should be 'round most any time. I'm sure he'll let you ride in back of the truck.

"We're working down near the train depot today. That's five miles or so from here. They gots trucks and mule carts coming and going from that place. Good chance, I reckon, that you could catch a ride on one of those trucks that would take you near Jubal's, if not right to it."

"That sounds promising, sir!" replied Ace. "I think we will do just that thing; thank you.

"I am called Ace Redbone. This young man is Tobias Messager. This here dog is Okra."

The man nodded to both of them. "I am Davis Johnson, but most folk here about jus' calls me Beetle, on account of the way I crawled when I was a baby."

"Like a beetle", said Ace with a smile.

"That be it", replied Davis Johnson known as Beetle.

"And you don't mind?" asked Tobias.

"Not at all. I reckon I did when I was a younger man. Didn't seem such a good name for attracting the ladies, but I ended up married to a fine girl who thought it was cute."

"So Beetle it is", said Ace.

"Pleased to meet your 'quaintance, Ace", said Beetle. He stiffly lowered himself into a squat because Okra had approached him and sat down at his feet, pawing lightly at his pant leg.

"Pleased to meet you too, Okra", laughed Beetle as he shook the dog's paw. "But be careful now, folks around here love them some fried okra!"

The introductions finished just as there came the racket and rumble of a truck heading toward them down the road. Beetle nodded toward it. "That's George."

The noisy truck geared down and moaned to a halt in front of them. There were two men in the cab, the driver and a man dozing with his head lolling against the door frame. Beetle called out to the driver, "George, you mind if these here two fellas hops in the back with me to ride to the depot?"

"Makes no nevermind to me", the short, burly driver said and shrugged. "I wasn't sure you'd be out here this mornin', Beetle. You looked like you might not be able to work today when we dropped you off last night."

"Feedin' a family is mighty motivatin', George", replied Beetle as he gestured for Ace, Tobias, and Okra to follow him to the back of the vehicle.

They climbed into the back of the truck, with Ace and Tobias offering their hands to help Beetle. It was obvious that he was struggling. Okra mounted with a single bound.

"Show off", said Beetle to the dog before nodding his thanks to Ace and Tobias. "I cricked my back somethin' wicked yesterday. Yessir, something wicked. Dangdest thing; weren't even liftin' nothing heavy. Just turn't funny and felt a pain."

The truck had started moving again. Beetle slid to sit with his back pressed against the side. Tobias looked around him; the floor was dusted with cotton puffs and dried bits of cotton husk. He looked to Ace and patted the floor of the truck. "A Mack BV. Probably '27 or '28 model."

"The boy is a walking encyclopedia on motorized conveyance", Ace explained to Beetle. "Now, where about does your back hurt?"

"About midway down, I reckon", said Beetle, shrugging.

"Right in the middle, the spine?"

"Well, yes, sir, though it's gotten to ache all over."

"Sharp pain in the spine?"

"Like a giant sting, and then it shoots off lines of pain. Don't hurt all the time, except that the rest of my back is aching now."

"The ache is dull?"

"It is", said Beetle.

"The ache is because you're holding yourself different than normal, so as to avoid the sharp pain. Sounds like you have tweaked a nerve", said Ace as he got up and moved over beside Beetle. "Slide forward so I can get behind you."

Not without uncertainty, Beetle did as directed. Ace slipped quickly behind him and slipped one arm under one of Beetle's and then placed a hand in the middle of the man's back. Suddenly Ace pulled up sharply and twisted a bit.

"Damnation!" shouted Beetle in alarm and pain, but then his expression melted into confusion.

"Go ahead", Ace chuckled. "Test it."

Beetle leaned forward a bit, then more. Then he leaned to one side and the other. Then he twisted a bit with his eyes growing wide in wonder. "Why, I'll be. I'll be. Don't feel no pain at all! Well, it be achy still, but no sharp pain at all. I'll be."

"Just a little something I picked up over the years", Ace explained to Beetle and the equally amazed Tobias. Okra just sat happily thumping his tail against the floor of the truck.

"Well, I sure owe you many thanks, Mister Ace", marveled Beetle. "I weren't lookin' forward to this day of work. Not at all. Sometimes they lets me take inventory and do some organizing. I'm right good at that sort of thing. Mister Masterson says I'm the best ciphering colored man he's ever known. But today is a loadin' day, so I wasn't looking forward to all the toting and pushin' that's gonna be going on."

"Take it as a thank you for getting us a ride on this truck", replied Ace.

"You is sure welcome."

The depot was no more than a side track and a cluster of storage sheds. Set about a quarter mile back along an unpaved road sprawled the wood and tin-sided cotton gin. Already there was a line of mule carts waiting to unload at the gin, and a few carts with ginned cotton heading toward the box cars poised beside a long brick-and-mortar loading dock.

Ace Redbone and Tobias were considering their options when George Battle came waddling toward them. There was another man with him, an older, tall, thin man with blotchy skin the color of creamed coffee with cinnamon stains. Beneath the man's floppy hat they saw tightly curled, reddish hair.

"Beetle says you fellas is looking for a ride to Jubal's", said George. "This here is Red Greene. He drives for the Mastersons too. He's goin' over to Newton Grove and he'll be goin' through Cut Creek, where Jubal has his store. You're welcome to ride, he says."

Ace doffed his hat. "Thank you kindly, Mister Red."

Red Greene shrugged and motioned for them to follow. He led them to a truck, indicating that they should jump into the back. Ace gave Tobias a playful, but stern, gaze, indicating that he did not care to know what kind of truck this was.

They had climbed into the back with Okra, and the mechanical beast of burden had growled to life, when Tobias leaned over and half whispered to Ace, "Did you notice that Mister Red Greene is actually yellow?"

"Hush that", replied the chuckling Ace. "Your mamma would rap your knuckles for impertinence toward someone doing us a favor."

Okra gave a low growling whine, and Ace nodded at him. "See, Okra knows it too."

"This is another Mack, by the way", said Tobias as he looked around the back of the truck. "Much newer. I reckon the Masterson bunch likes them some Macks. This is faster than having to ride a mule cart."

"I think I'd prefer the fresh air of a mule cart", noted Ace.

"Suppose it would be fresher air. The exhaust is being sucked back in on us. Hold on a minute."

Tobias got up and made his way toward the front of the bed. There was a flap of the otherwise taut canvas that formed the roof of the truck bed. He rolled it up and tucked it tightly into the metal frame.

When he had done so, the air current changed. Bits of cotton fluff and dried husks were swept up off the floor and swirled at the back of the truck before being pulled away into the open air. Soon the truck was mostly swept clean and the air much fresher as well.

The truck was faster than a mule cart, but it still moved at a deliberate pace, and it took them over thirty minutes to cover twenty miles. Finally the truck began gearing down and slowed to a stop. Ace, Tobias, and Okra hopped from the back. They stood to one side and waved their thanks to Red Greene as the truck growled back into movement and pulled away from them.

They found themselves in a small community. There were a half dozen clapboard houses on either side of the main road. A larger house stood across one corner of a T-section road and a well-maintained commercial building stood on the other. There were a few smaller houses strewn along Cut Creek Road, and some agricultural utility buildings farther down Masterson Farm Road.

Ace gestured toward the large commercial building. "That would be Jubal's store, I suppose. Now, Okra, you be close by us. There are more automobiles buzzing here about than you are used to."

The dog dutifully fell into a heeling position near his young master as the two men headed toward the building. When their angle to it changed they saw a sign reading Jubal's General Store. There was a small parking area between the store and another, less refined building that bore a sign reading Jubal's Feed and Grain.

The Feed and Grain was busier at this time of the morning than was the General Store. As they approached the store they saw a very tall, big-boned man striding from the Feed and Grain. He was a very dark fellow. His face seemed hard edged, as if hurriedly chiseled from black adamant. Above his high cheekbones were eyes nearly as black as his skin. He wore a crisp forest-green shirt tucked neatly into sharply creased khaki pants.

"Excuse me, sir", called out Ace.

The big man stopped, paused for a discernable moment, and then turned to face them. His expression was both haughty and suspicious. He did not reply, but only raised an eyebrow in question.

"We are looking for Jubal Tomkins", explained Ace. Then he winked and nodded at the sign hanging above and behind the big man. "Jubal's General Store seems a good place to look. Is he around?"

No mirth appeared on the man's face, and the sense of suspicion grew. "What do you want with Mister Jubal?"

"Well, first to see him. Then we have a matter to discuss with him. We are his cousins by marriage, you see? Well, by his first marriage."

The information was absorbed into the big man. He nodded slowly, but his suspicion seemed hardly eased at all. Finally he blinked. "In these trying times, he seems to have a lot of distant family members interested in talking to him. Seems to me that cousins by a first marriage are hardly family at all. I try to look out for him, so he's not takin' advantage of because of his success."

Tobias found this stern man's resistance to Ace's charm to be almost refreshing, were it not for the haughtiness in his voice. Ace only smiled and reached into his back pocket to pull out his wallet. From it he withdrew a single dollar bill. He held it out in front of himself like a token. "See this? I want to purchase something. Are you going turn a customer away from Mister Jubal? Do you think he would approve of that?"

The hard man did not return the smile; he half turned so that he was looking at the front of the store. "You know how to use a door?"

"We will go into the store", replied Ace. "If he is not there, we would be obliged to you for finding him. Tell him that Astier Freeman Losrouge and Tobias Freeman Messager would like to speak to him.

"I take it you *do* work for Mister Jubal."

"I am his foreman", said the man.

"Then I thank you in advance, Amos Asher, for your assistance."

The man seemed slightly startled at the sound of his own name upon the lips of a stranger. When the two men and the dog walked away from him he called out, "That dog cain't go in the store. Dogs ain't allowed in the store."

"He's with us", replied Ace, holding the door open so that Tobias and Okra could proceed in. Then he pulled it closed behind him, shutting out the sight of Amos Asher.

Nine

The chief deputy's car pulled into Chuck Oliver's driveway and rolled to a stop behind the sheriff's white sedan. Del and Fredric Forgeron exited at the same time. Forgeron walked around the sheriff's vehicle, inspecting the interior through the closed windows. Then he gestured to the steps.

The two men walked up to the front door. Del rapped with the shiny brass knocker three times. There was no reply. He did so again. Silence still. He turned to look at the white car, as if it might have disappeared. With a shrug he knocked solidly upon the door with his fist.

When there was still no reply, Forgeron tested the doorknob. The door creaked open a bit, so he pushed it fully open, and both men stepped into the foyer of the house. Like the exterior, the interior was clean and neatly ordered. It was well appointed and the windows draped with rich, heavy fabric that shut out most of the waning light of the day.

To one side of the foyer was a double-width opening with pocket doors pulled three-quarters open. From within the room to which it opened they could see the faint glow of a dying coal fire in a fireplace. A single lamp offered a soft light that served to silhouette rather than illuminate a figure sitting at a desk in the room.

"Chuck?"

"Del? What you doing here?" was the softly spoken reply. "And why are you just walkin' in like that?"

"We knocked, Sheriff", noted Forgeron as he and the chief deputy moved into the room.

"You seem an intelligent man", replied Oliver. "Smart enough to figure that if I didn't answer a knock, I didn't want to be disturbed."

"Mister Forgeron and I have some things we have to discuss with you, Chuck", Del cautiously offered.

"Sheriff Oliver. I am Sheriff Charles Oliver", intoned the voice in reply.

Forgeron casually reached over to turn on another lamp. Its light was as soft as the first lamp, but it brought Oliver from out of the shadows. The sheriff's eyes were red and moist. He was gazing blankly at his visitors. A glass and a bottle sat on the desktop.

"Are you drinking, Chuck?" asked the perplexed chief deputy. "I ain't never known you to drink."

Oliver's gaze lowered to the glass of amber fluid. He smiled, lifted it to his lips, and took a swallow. He smiled again.

"Proper stuff. Not that gawd-awful moonshine."

"This is a dry county", noted Forgeron.

Oliver sneered, "Cain't sell it or buy it here, but ain't no law against owning it."

Then the sheriff began a chuckle that melted into a sigh. He reached with a fingertip to angle the bottle back, and then he shrugged. "I reckon it's good stuff. It was a ... *gift*."

He let the bottle drop back square on its bottom. It rocked back and forth for a moment, but Oliver did not seem to notice or care that it might fall over. "Truth is, I don't hardly ever drink. My daddy, now he was a drinkin' man. He could drink most men under the table. Bastard."

Oliver sat back then, the chair creaking with the shift of his weight as he crossed his arms. He cocked his head and fixed the gaze of his red, bleary eyes on the two visitors. "So what does my chief deputy and mister high and mighty state investigator want to see me about that's so damned urgent they jus' come barging into my home when I'm tryin' to relax?

"Tell me, state man, you love niggers as much as your brother?"

"I don't reckon I'm as fond of them as Felton is. Probably comes from working up there in Washington with the Roosevelts."

"What? I'm talkin' about Crafty."

"Ah, Francis? Well no, he probably likes colored folk more than most white men. But I do believe they have been shabbily treated and that their rights should be respected."

"Rights", snorted Oliver. Then he leaned forward. Despite the room having cooled as the coal fire died, his face glistened with sweat. He had a smirk on his lips and motioned conspiratorially with his hand, as if the two visitors should lean in closer.

"Your brother, that Francis, he likes to treat the nigger whores proper. I heard maybe he really likes ol' Toby's woman. Now as colored women go, she's better than most I reckon. Thing is, Francis can go over there and get all *crafty* with her now and Toby cain't see a damned thing they do!"

He started laughing at his own puerile wit until Del Gaines' admonishing, "Chuck."

In an instant Oliver's expression turned angry and he slapped his hands down hard upon the desktop, causing the whiskey bottle to fall over and some papers to skid away and waft to the floor. "Don't you talk that way to me, *Deputy*. You forget yourself. I am the sheriff. You are just a pansy who didn't have the guts to take the job. You, always thinking you can call me in because you think I'm gettin' out of line—"

"Sheriff Charles Oliver", interrupted Forgeron as he pulled some folded papers from out of his suit coat. "We have here a sworn statement from a Leonard Morris."

"The Jew boy", hissed Oliver. He reached for the glass on the desk, saw it was empty, and then noticed the bottle had fallen over. He seemed lost in perturbation at this before picking the bottle up and determining that some of the whiskey had survived the spill.

He began pouring the fluid into the glass, but his hands were shaking and as much spilled down the outside of the glass as the inside. He considered the spilled liquid, but then just put the glass to his lips and drained it with a single gulp.

"That boy's daddy didn't think I knew they were Jews", he continued after he tossed the glass at the nearly dead embers in the fireplace. "But I make it my business to know things. I know'd more things than anyone could guess."

He seemed well pleased with himself as he placed his hands flat on the desk in front of him. Forgeron had merely kept slowly unfolding the papers he had produced. He looked down officiously on the drunken sheriff.

"Leonard Levi Morris states that near Merchants Corner you pulled over to offer him a ride. He says that you seemed agitated and not quite right. Something about it frightened him, so he said he told you he would prefer to walk.

"The young man continues, saying that you became angry and asked him if he thought Jews were too good to ride with a white man. He said then you got suddenly less angry and told him there was no reason that you couldn't be his friend, and that a Jew boy might need a friend in a county where the Klan was so powerful.

"He said you reached over and opened the door and said to him that you knew some secrets he might like. It was then that he ran off into the woods. He said you were screaming for the 'Jew boy' to come back.

"He watched from hiding as you cruised back and forth for a while. Then he said he saw Jamie Farmer walking down the road and saw you pull over. He said you spoke to the boy. Said the boy seemed scared stiff. Young Morris says he wanted to scream out to the colored boy to run, but was too afraid of you.

"Then he said you leaned over and opened the door. He saw the boy get in, very slowly. Said he thought he might be crying. Then he saw you drive off and turn down the logging road where James Farmer was later found hanging."

"Jews are liars!" shouted Oliver, his piggy eyes gone wide, wild, and wreathed in bloodshot red. "That boy was a queer! Both of them was. They were probably sodomizing one another! Probably that Jew boy kill't that nigger boy to keep him from telling."

Forgeron ignored the outburst and continued, "Then, Sheriff, there is the matter of the medical report presented by Doctor Cicero Macklin considering the death of James Farmer."

"The drunk", said Oliver with a snort that was cut off by the realization of his own condition.

"The report was inconsistent with the observations of a Tobit Messager and your own chief deputy. I went with the deputy to the scene of the alleged suicide. The evidence remaining there did not indicate it was a suicide."

"So the drunk doctor fouled it up", said the sheriff, reaching for the glass before remembering he had thrown it into the fireplace.

"Did you not also see the body? Surely your powers of observation are not so lacking as to think that boy had hung himself? Then there is the fire at the doctor's house. It seems to have burnt especially fierce where his records are kept. The deputy and I went to Harper Bay to interview him in the hospital."

Forgeron let the words hang on that statement and did not indicate that they had not actually been able to interview Macklin. Oliver's features went blank, and his eyes distant.

"He was an abomination, that boy", he intoned in a flat voice. Then a sneer ticked to life as his lips drew tight. He reached for the whiskey bottle, studying it for a moment before draining the contents. Then the bottle joined the glass in the fireplace with a crash.

"*Abomination*. It's one of the secrets I know", he snickered. His face had become so twisted that Del and Fredric both tensed. The deputy looked as if he might be sick. Oliver looked at one, then at the other, and a vicious smile spread across his face. "My father liked nigger whores 'bout as much as your brother. Liked 'em young."

He laughed, and then snarled, "He was mean when he was drunk. He was mean."

He frowned, glowering, "Do you know that once he got so pissed at me that he started beating me with a mule whip? I ain't never seen anyone so mad in all my life. I cain't even remember what I had done. Then, suddenly, Toby comes round the corner of the barn, and he just grabs my father's wrist. Some grip that nigger had, considering the rage that had aholt of my daddy. He just looks at my father and says *no*. Just like that my father drops the whip and walks off. We didn't see him for weeks after. Off drunk.

"Now, what right had that nigger to put his hands on my father? We can't let them be goin' about puttin' their hands on white people. My daddy ought to have turned that whip on him. The judge spoilt that nigger. They have to be kept in place.

"Like that girl; daddy said she would like it before he was done with her. She mostly just moaned and cried, blubbering all over herself. Then he says, 'Do her, boy, do her.'

"I ain't wantin' no nigger girl. He yells at me, 'You a queer, boy? Do her. That's right, do her. She ain't nothing but what we make of her. None of them niggers is nothing', he laughs.

"That girl, bad enough she's scared, but then she looks at me as if I'm disgusting, as if the thought of me makes her sick. I don't know who I hated more then, my daddy or that bitch. I showed 'em. Both of 'em."

His gaze was frozen into some faraway place, hard, angry, and devoid of all else. "'That's it, boy. That's it.' Then he says to me, 'Maybe you got some manhood after all.' Then he tells her, 'Whore, you tell anyone 'bout this and we kill you and your whole damned family.'"

His eyes came partly back into the room. "He tol' me we could kill her, but it was better to let her live with knowing what she was. Said maybe she'd have a baby and we'd whiten up their race. He thought that was real funny. Then he looked at me and told me I was probably too queer to kill the bitch anyway."

His gaze leveled coldly on each of his visitors. "That's what he said to me. Didn't have it in me to kill nobody. Guess he found out different, that night in Atlanta when he was whorin' and gamblin'."

Moved by their police instincts, Del and Fredric had each eased away from one another to the left and right of Oliver. Their hands slowly went closer to their holstered weapons, Del's to his hip, and Fredric's to the inside of his suit coat in the pretense of putting away the folded papers.

Oliver did not bother to look at them. He was smiling and rolled his chair back a bit from the desk, and his gaze fell to his lap. Both men saw a shotgun laid across his thighs.

"Relax, gentlemen; I mean you no harm. My ol' daddy had this made special for me when I was a young'un. Had it made in Belgium and gave it to me for my seventh birthday. A four-ten gauge, twenty-inch barrel. It don't recoil much at all. Beautifully made child's shotgun, this is. I reckon it to be the only good and beautiful thing he ever passed on to me. The last time that ever he showed me any affection at all.

"He ruined everything. Thought I was a coward. A pansy boy. Didn't have it in me, he said. Stupid son of a bitch. He found out I had it in me when I used this here very gun to blow him away."

He looked into empty air with eyes that were plaintive, wishful, and childlike. "I wish Mister Toby was here. Maybe he could help me understand it all."

Then he suddenly was aware once again of Gaines and Forgeron. In a single, smooth motion he raised the shotgun beneath his own chin, angled it toward the back of his head, and pulled the trigger.

Del Gaines watched in disbelief, not even blinking at the sound of the discharge. He saw a volcanic spray of skin, bone, hair, brains, and blood erupt from the back of Oliver's skull. The sheriff's face bulged for a moment and then caved in upon itself as his body was hurled backward and slithered as if boneless from the chair into the floor.

"Chuck", was all the deputy could croak. He moved to go behind the desk, but Forgeron grabbed his arm. He looked over to see the investigator shaking his head.

"There's nothing can be done for him", whispered Forgeron as he led the chief deputy outside onto the porch.

They left behind the smell of coal soot, whiskey, gunpowder, and blood. The fresh air washed over them. Del Gaines stumbled to the steps. He leaned forward with hands clasping his stomach and was sick.

"He seemed entirely immune to your great charm", teased Tobias as he watched through the window as the tall, stern figure of Amos Asher strode purposefully toward the Feed and Grain. Ace only gave him one of those ever so slight, condescending smiles that somehow made the young man feel like a mere boy.

Tobias shrugged and turned to inspect the store. It was as clean and orderly as any he had ever seen. It was well stocked, too, given the economic distress of the area. It was moderately busy as well.

"Now, this is the way to run a business", said Tobias, noticing the evident similarity in philosophy between Jubal and Crafty. "Well ordered and clean."

"That would be thanks to Amos", said a short, plump woman from behind a counter to their right.

"And your biscuits, Mama Ann", called out a customer. Her dark, round face beamed in pleasure.

"I reckon it plays a part, it does", she admitted. "It was Amos what got me this here job, though. See, I makes biscuits in the mornin'. I puts cheese in 'em and the workers love 'em for breakfast!"

"Shucks, sometimes white folks even comes in, or sends in they help to buy some of 'em", added the man who had first praised her.

"Amos makes sure they is priced right", continued Mama Ann. "He says that they could be sold for much more, but by sellin' 'em only a little above cost, we are helpin' the local folk. He convinced Mister Jubal that the increased traffic would pay off more in the end than raising the price would."

She leaned over the counter, with her ample bosom squeezed against the wooden edge. Her round face took on a conspiratorial tone.

"Truth is, Amos is the one what makes this place work", she said quietly. "Yessir, he is one smart man. Fine lookin' man too!"

She giggled at her own observation as she looked over the two newcomers. "You is some fine lookin' boys too, so don't be gettin' jealous now. I ain't much on high yellers, but this here guitar man sho' is fine. You two must be kin, 'cause you gots the same eyes."

She looked from one to the other before continuing, "Though you is much darker, young'un. I suspect if this here guitar man is yo' daddy, he mus' have spent a lot of time away from the house."

"We are distant cousins", Ace chided her in his teasing, charming manner.

"I didn't mean no harm, guitar man", replied Mama Ann with a giggling apology.

"I am called Astier Freeman Losrouge, and this fine young man is Tobias Freeman Messager. Most folk just call me Ace. They call him Tobias. I caution you not to call him Toby. His daddy's name is Tobit, and there have been folk who think it funny to call the son Toby Too, or Toby Two", said Ace Redbone, holding up two fingers on the last name. "Now, the way I hear tell it, he once sliced a man from crotch to throat for calling him Toby Too!"

"Lawdy", breathed in Mama Ann with manufactured shock.

"He's tougher than he looks", cautioned Ace.

"He would have to be, now, wouldn't he!" replied Mama Ann with a wheezing laugh that degenerated into a short coughing spell.

"We're here to see Jubal Tomkins. He is a distant cousin of ours", explained Ace. The coughing fit was truncated by genuine shock.

"I hope you hasn't taken no offense by what I said about Amos runnin' this here place", said Mama Ann.

Ace winked at her. "We'll keep it as a secret between the three of us."

"And half the people in this store", muttered Tobias under his breath.

It was then that they saw a man passing by the window, with Amos Asher walking a little behind him. He was not as tall as Amos Asher, but was not a short man despite a weighted stoop to his posture. He was of medium build, with paunchiness around the middle. He was wearing a patched suit coat over a pair of overalls, over a blue cotton shirt. He had on a well-worn, wide-brimmed hat, and a white towel was rolled up and draped over his neck. Later they would learn the towel was something he used to keep grain dust from getting down the back of his shirt when he was over at the Feed and Grain.

This man moved with the slow gait of a stunned survivor. He entered the store, looking around the small crowd for anyone he did not know, and froze his gaze on Ace and Tobias.

"Well, I'll be", he began before trailing off. "If you ain't the spittin' image of a man I used to know. Ol' Tobit Messager. Yessir, spittin' image."

"I am Tobias Freeman Messager. My father is Tobit Freeman Messager."

"Lawd! I'll be. Well look at you", said the man. "I feel like I am back twenty or thirty years in time! I am Jubal Tomkins, and your father was a friend of mine, a relative by marriage for a spell."

He looked over at Ace Redbone, and raised a thick finger to his own eyes as he spoke, "Now, them eyes. Them Messager eyes. You gots to be his kin. Is Toby your daddy too?"

"No, sir", answered Ace. "I am called Astier Freeman Losrouge, a cousin from Louisiana."

Jubal nodded. "I was wonderin' if Toby had been messin' with some white women there for a minute."

"He is innocent of that charge", replied Ace. "Though obviously there has been some mixin' back somewhere in the line that produced me."

"Well, don' matter, I welcome you both", announced Jubal. "You ain't had no breakfast yet, have you? No? Mama Ann, fix these young men up with your famous biscuits and some coffee."

Jubal turned to Amos Asher. "I want to do some catching up with these two men. If you would, go over to the Feed and Grain and make sure they take care of Nate's order for him."

With only a terse nod, Asher left the General Store in his ever deliberate stride. After Mama Ann had given a biscuit and a cup of coffee to each of the two visitors, Jubal nodded his head to indicate the rear of the store.

"Come along back to my office."

After passing through a storage area nearly as neat and orderly as the public area of the store, they emerged into what had once been a porch that had run the entire length of the back of the building. Half the porch had been enclosed with a series of tall windows.

"Right there is Amos' desk", explained Jubal, indicating a tidy desk set catacorner to the wall that divided the entry room from Jubal's office. "He is the neatest man that ever I saw."

They entered Jubal's office, which wasn't nearly so uncluttered, but appeared well ordered nonetheless. He gestured to a couple of upholstered chairs for his visitors to occupy. They were scruffy and well worn, probably reassigned to the office once they were no longer suitable for his home.

The windows lining the outer wall looked over a softly rolling landscape. Large oak trees were scattered about, and a line of evergreens had been planted on the west boundary many years ago, probably to screen off the sight of the Feed and Grain.

To the north could be seen a shallow creek of clear water. It made two cascades over the course of passing through the property, and then ran more quickly into a long, narrow, dark lake sheltered by willows. The northern bank of the creek and the pond were quite steep, with reddish clay streaking the earth.

"Cut Creek", said Jubal, noticing the gazes of his visitors. "Reckon it's called that because it's cut through those folded ridges, way back before even the Injuns came to these parts. It gathers up in this here pond and then flows out over yonder to the river."

He gestured to a building near the western line of evergreens. "That right there is a little chapel I built back when my Sarah was born. Lawd, I was so proud of her and mighty thankful to almighty God. I reckoned she would be the first of many, but it hasn't turned out that way.

"We goes to church over in Newton Grove, but sometimes I like to sit a while and ponder and pray over things."

He let go a long sigh. "Right much to worry over and pray for these days."

He shook his head, and sat down behind his desk. "Well, enough of that. Tell me how things are with your father, Tobias. He was a fine man when I knew him. In fact I owe him some money. He helped me get my start, him and his father. But then something happened back in Harper Bay and I couldn't find out where they'd gone an' gotten themselves off to."

Tobias told the tale of his grandfather and father being expelled from Harper Bay, of how they had gone first to Louisiana and then to Chatqua County. He told of how his father had worked for Judge Oliver, and of how he had been dismissed when the judge had passed way. Finally he told of his father's recent troubles and the reason he and Ace had trekked all this distance by foot.

"Walked almost all the way from Chatqua County", marveled Jubal. "Well, I'll be. Let me say, set your mind at ease. We have our troubles here, as you have heard, but we prosper nonetheless. I will pay your father and with a sensible interest."

"No, sir, no interest", Tobias interrupted him. "Daddy was insistent about that. He said he would never charge interest on a personal loan, and especially not to one made to a member of his family. He figures that you are still family. I reckon that's just the way my daddy is."

"It is indeed", replied Jubal. "Well, no interest. But I will see to it that you *ride* back home. You two should rest here a few days first. Is there anyone you can call that can run over and tell your folks that y'all made it here safe and sound?"

"Reverend Walker has a phone", said Tobias. "I know Mister Forgeron has one, and I know his schedule best. Yessir, I'll call Mister Forgeron."

Jubal had left them in the care of Mama Ann when he finally had to return to his business. She took them to a bunkhouse next to the Feed and Grain. It was only a single large room with cots strewn about, and a horse trough in one corner for use as a bathtub. She explained that Jubal rented it out to migrants, or to farmers who hired migrants during the harvest season, but it was unused at this time.

"Y'all put a little bit of spring into ol' Mister Jubal's step", she chuckled as she started water for boiling on the pot-bellied coal stove she had lit. "Thing's been tough for him lately. All these people actin' as if they is a curse on Miss Sarah.

"Mister Jubal should marry her off to Amos. He knows this here business. He ain't hardly scared of no curse and such. He is a strong, good lookin' man for sure. Don't let on I told you about it, but I think he fancies her. He just don't want to be intrudin' into the family's grief, or being a worry to them."

Clucking her tongue to herself, Mama Ann left and then returned with bedding and towels. "You know where the pump is, so gets all the water you need and takes y'all some nice long baths."

As she turned to leave again she gave Ace a wink. "Now, I reckon I'd wear that there boy plumb out, but should you need someone to scrub your back, you just calls me, hear?"

When the door shut behind her, Tobias gave Ace a teasing smirk. "Now, I reckon *there* is someone who ain't immune to your considerable charms."

Ace shot him a look before replying, "See if there is a way to lock that door."

Ten

The afternoon sun was slanting warm across the porch. Tobit sat with the sun on his face. Sometimes he might see a crease of red-gold, or a smudgy lightening of the endless gray void into which his eyes gazed. He had become self-conscious of that empty gaze, his nowhere stare.

When Gaston Walker became aware of this, he brought Tobit a pair of dark glasses. On an afternoon like this, sitting alone with only Anna on their own porch, Tobit would keep the glasses in his shirt pocket while seeking for some hope of color and light.

Tobit sat in his gray dark listening to the world around him, and musing on the strange dreams that continued to haunt his sleep. Dreams that were remembered upon waking more from the emotion they created than from events. What little he could remember was as if viewed from a distance or through an uncertain filter.

As he considered all this, there was a sound among sounds that particularly caught his attention: a rhythmic tick that countered the sound of the floorboards beneath Anna's feet as she pushed the swing.

"I am going to have to replace the eyebolts", Tobit decided aloud.
"Well, have Tobias replace them."
"Why in the world do you say that?"
"I can hear that there is a worn part to one of them, the one on the left, I reckon. That's the side you sit on most of the time, and I almost never swing anymore."
"Maybe Tobias can just inspect it to see how much it is worn", suggested Anna.
"That is sensible. I just don't want to take chances of the swing falling and dumping you out. Where would I find another woman to take care of an ol' blind man?"
"Hush."
"Okay, but I hear Frank's truck", replied Tobit, as he pulled his dark glasses from his pocket and placed them on his face.

"What? I don't—no, wait, yes, I hear it now", laughed Anna. "The way you hear these days I'd think you'd grown ears the size of Okra's."

Tobit brought his fingertips to examine the sides of his head, and then let go an exaggerated sigh. "Can't be too careful when you can't actually see yourself."

Frank Forgeron's truck turned into the drive and bounced its way along until he wheeled it to a stop. As he got out of the vehicle and made his bowlegged way toward the porch, he called out, "Don't get up on account of me. I got some news from Tobias."

"He's smiling", Anna noted for Tobit's sake.

Forgeron took a seat in the rocker next to Tobit. "He telephoned. He found that Jubal Tomkins you sent him to look for. He said he and Ace were right as rain, and that Mister Jubal was more than willing to repay the money he owes. He said they were going to spend a couple of days resting up, may even stay until Sunday so they can go to church with Jubal and his family.

"He said Jubal was insisting on having them driven back. Said he wanted to buy 'em a bus ticket, but Ace pointed out that you wouldn't likely let them back in the house if they didn't bring Okra back with 'em."

Tobit laughed. Forgeron shrugged to Anna before continuing, "He said Mister Jubal was prosperous, and in good health other than looking worn out some from worrying about some troubles his daughter has experienced.

"That was 'bout all he said, except that he didn't want to talk too long and run up Mister Jubal's phone bill."

"How did he sound?" asked Anna.

"Loud", chuckled Forgeron. "I had to remind him that the phone took care of the distance, no need for him to make his voice carry. I have to remind him of that near 'bout every time he answers the phone at work."

"He was that way when we had a phone", replied Tobit, adding his own chuckle to the consideration of his son's foible.

"I 'spect you heard about the sheriff?" asked Forgeron.

"No, we haven't had any visitors in three days", said Anna.

Forgeron shook his head. "Well, the man done kill't himself."

"Oh, Lord!" gasped Anna with a hand to her mouth.

"My brother and Del Gaines investigated this hanging of Jamie Farmer. You were right, Tobit; weren't no suicide. Fredric also had been investigating this moonshine business. He pretty much determined the sheriff was taking bribes. Exhorting bribes is what Fredric said."

Forgeron grew quiet a moment; he glanced up at Anna, his expression apologetic. "You'll forgive me, I hope, Anna. What I'm gonna tell now ain't pleasant.

"Turns out that Oliver is the one who killed that boy, and then hung his body up there like that. Worse, he done things to that boy. He may have done things to others. It seems he tried to do such a thing with that Lenny Morris boy."

Anna closed her eyes and she hugged her arms around her stomach. "Oh, Lord, no. Those poor children."

Forgeron's gaze had become distant and almost blank. "I don't even know how to say this. Seems Jamie might have been Oliver's son, or his brother. His father made him join in the raping of poor little Mabel."

A grim anger tensed in Tobit's sightless expression. "That worthless bastard ruined his son. Chuck was not a bad boy, Frank, but that father of his was darkness itself. I caught him once beating that boy like no man or beast deserves to be beaten. I stopped him, and I spoke to the judge about it. Judge Oliver sent him away to dry out, for all the good it did.

"I tried to help little Chuck, but the boy resented it. Some white folk, Frank, when they get beat down, all they got left is this sense that they are superior to colored folk. You take that away from them, even if you're trying to be kind, and it stirs a bitter, bitter resentment."

Frank nodded, without thinking that Tobit could not see him. "Well, turns out that the sheriff murdered his own father. Went down to Georgia and killed him. Blowed him away with a shotgun, and everyone thought it was some street fight over gambling or whoring.

"What you said, about trying to help him. I think you almost did. Fredric says one of the last things Charles Oliver said was that he wished you were there, that maybe you could help him make some sense of it all. Then he all a sudden pulls out a shotgun and blows a hole in his own head. A shotgun his daddy gave him years ago. Same shotgun he killed his daddy with, they say."

"How can the world be so wicked?" wondered Anna in a whisper.

"I wonder myself", sighed Frank Forgeron. "I for sure wondered about it many times during the war. Fredric ain't supposed to have tol' me some of this, so I'd ask you to keep it between us until the reports are official, or as official as they're going to get."

"What do you mean?" asked Tobit.

"I don't think they'll let the whole story out. It's jus' too much. They'll not want it reflecting badly on the area and the state. The whole experience tore up poor Fredric. He's usually a stern, kind of stoic fella, but this tore him up. He said more to me than he should have because he came by to see me, and we started drinking and the words started flowing from him.

"Anyway, it seems that they gonna make Del the interim sheriff until the next election. Fredric seems to think Del is clean enough that he can run for the job then if he wants it. Said he could see Del change as the investigation proceeded.

"I nearly forgot to tell you; they're pretty sure Oliver set fire to Doc's house. Tried to destroy his records and kill him so's he couldn't talk about that medical report. Oh, and Doc is conscious now, he's talkin' plenty, and what he's saying supports most of the conclusions Del and Fredric had come to."

"Poor Chuck", sighed Tobit. "I know that seems a strange thing to say, dark as he had become, but I don't reckon any of us know what it was like for him with a father like that."

"Lots of folk have fathers that bad, maybe worse, without going so evil", protested Anna.

"That's true enough", replied Tobit. "But ain't none of us know all the facts. What is done. When it is done. You say or do something to someone and you don't really know where they are at that moment. There's a whole pile of moments from their life just a teetering at any given time. It's hard to know if you might push them over some emotional cliff, or pull 'em up from an abyss.

"I reckon that's why we are warned by the Bible about judging the worth of another. God knows, though, and he'll take all into account."

"Well, I reckon we can judge the deeds", said Forgeron. "I reckon the county is better off without a sheriff like Oliver."

"No argument on that."

Ace and Tobias had been left to their own devices while Jubal attended to business. They roamed with Okra around the property, further admiring the store, investigating the operations of the Feed and Grain. They wandered down to Cut Creek.

The creek was not particularly deep, probably four feet at its greatest depth. The water was fairly clear as it ran along its path. It had cut smoothly through the sandy ridge that caused the rills, ditches, and gullies to form Cut Creek Pond. It had, over thousands of years, even cut through the coquina limestone. In some places it looked as if the coquina had been quarried by humans, but in others it bore the telltale, organic story of years upon years of water passing through the soft stone.

The line of evergreens screening the operations of the Feed and Grain from the house arced back toward the creek and thinned as it went. It terminated in a spur of sparsely spread hardwood, which in turn gave way to cypress trees along the edge of the creek.

Directly behind the house the ridge was so high that the banks of the creek were steep and nearly twenty feet in height. At the bottom of this clifflike bank were scattered cypress trees with their knobby knees rising from the creek itself. Scrubby, poorly situated brush and contorted trees sprang here and there along the sides of the bank.

"It's really kind of pretty", decided Tobias.

"It is", agreed Ace. "It's an interesting anomaly of geography and geology."

"Kind of pretty", repeated Tobias with a chuckle.

They investigated the little chapel. Okra was not pleased at being left outside. While he pouted at the doorway, Ace and Tobias explored inside.

It could maybe have held as many as fifteen people. The pews were little more than backless benches. The altar was simple but well made. A three-foot crucifix with a roughly hewn corpus was mounted on the wall. There was no tabernacle, but there was a space for one. The low altar rail terminated in wood pedestals at either end, and upon those stood two-foot high statues of Mary on one side and Joseph upon the other.

"They have Negro features", noted Tobias.

"Carved by some local craftsman, no doubt, but more finely done than the corpus", said Ace

"Reckon they ever have Mass in here?" wondered Tobias.

"I don't know. Probably just a place for praying and pondering."

"Well, between this place and that porch office, I sure would have liked to have been the man who sold Mister Jubal windows."

Ace laughed, "They appear to be salvaged from a number of different buildings. They are, in both places, arranged cleverly so as to make it pleasant to look upon."

"It is", said Tobias as he looked over the whitewashed tongue-and-groove timber that lined the interior walls of the chapel. There was even a small, pot-bellied coal stove in one corner at the rear of the building. The stove pipe poked through the wall and then ran out above the edge of the roof outside.

"Cousin Jubal must be a devout man", suggested Tobias.

"Or a fairly wealthy man trying hard to cling to his faith", said Ace.

While Ace made up to Okra for the indignation of his exclusion from the chapel by taking him for a walk through the sparse woodland around the pond, Tobias returned to the store, where he called Frank Forgeron. While he was talking to his boss, he saw two young women talking to Mama Ann, who had taken her place behind the counter.

They were attractive girls, though Tobias thought maybe they were trying too hard. Each had treated her hair so that it mimicked that of white women. They wore clothes that they thought were in fashion in big cities. They no doubt imagined that they would have fit right in at the nightclubs in Harlem.

He could not help but overhear and be distracted by their conversation with Mama Ann, who was leaning conspiratorially with arms resting on the counter. "The Bible says that the sins of the father will haunt the children. Let that be a lesson to y'all."

The young women nodded and leaned closer in as Mama Ann continued, "Now, I ain't sayin' that Mister Jubal has done any great wrong, mind. Could be that Sarah herself has sinned in some secret manner; who can say?

"Thing is, though, what's they gonna do to make things right with the Lord and ease his wrath? That's the question what wants answerin'. If I was Mister Jubal, I'd marry that girl off to Amos. He's strong enough to break this here curse."

"You reckon he is?" marveled one of the girls; both of them seemed to ponder this in a dreamy fashion.

"He some kinda fine", added the second.

Tobias had finished his phone call, and Mama Ann saw him from the corner of her eyes, as she did so she admonished the younger women. "Now, Amos is too old for the likes of you, and too settled. Whats you need is a fine lookin' young man like Tobias over yonder."

She gave Tobias a teasing wink. "What do you think of that, Tobias? Two fine lookin' girls like this. They is always lookin' for fun."

"That's for sure", giggled one of them. "Ain't nothing to do 'round here. You got a car? I'd love to find me a man with a car that could take me up to Raleigh or Durham."

Tobias shook his head. "Sorry, no car. I don't much care for big towns anyway."

"Reckon you girls could think of some fun that might be possible right around here", suggested Mama Ann with a self-delighted laugh.

Tobias smiled and shook his head ruefully before retreating out the door to join Ace and Okra in their explorations.

"You gentlemen jus' sit yourselves down", Jubal directed his guest, indicating two side chairs at his end of the long table. Rose Tomkins sat at the other end, while Amos Asher and Sarah were sitting across from the two guests. Mama Ann was sitting next to Ace Redbone. "Rose and Mama Ann done fixed up a fine dinner. Fried chicken, mashed taters, lima beans, collards, and hot biscuits, and some of the best banana puddin' I reckon you'll ever eat. I hope all that is fine enough for you."

"It'll be better than anything we've had since we left home", allowed Tobias. "We ain't eaten much 'cept old biscuits and jerky. Well, we did have some catfish, potatoes, and such with some nuns first night out."

"Sisters", Ace corrected him.

"Sisters? Sounds like a story", said Jubal as he heaped mashed potatoes on his plate. "Don't forget to try this gravy, done up fine as Thanksgiving Day."

"Not much of a story", replied Ace. "The bus carrying them to Harper Bay broke down and young Tobias here fixed it up for them."

He proceeded to sketch out the encounter. Jubal shook his head in light-hearted disbelief. "You mean to tell me there was a Negro nun?"

"Sister", said Ace. "Yessir. She's going up to Harper Bay to work at the colored church awhile before heading to Cuba for missionary work."

"Well, if that don't beat all", said Jubal. "You know, we're workin' on a colored church over there in Newton Grove. I reckon the white folk tired of us in their church. Didn't seem to bother them back in the day, but now the congregation is grown, both whites and colored, but the church is the same size. Maybe we're a might too close to suit 'em now."

"It seems a waste to send a fine black girl off with them nuns", said Mama Ann as she chewed a piece of chicken. "No offense, Mister Jubal, but that's one of them things I don't understand 'bout you Catholics, wasting women and men like that. She might have made a fine wife for some black man, and made lots of little colored chillins."

"I would reckon it is admirable", said Sarah without looking up from her plate.

"Sarah, dear, don't use the word 'reckon'", said Rose softly. "That's country talk."

An uncomfortable silence dogged the rest of the meal. When the last bite of dessert was eaten, Mama Ann and Sarah cleared the table. As she did so, Mama Ann called out from the kitchen, "Mister Ace, I sees you gots your guitar here. Why don't you give us some music?"

"Please, if you would", added Rose.

"I don't mind at all."

"Let's go into the parlor", said Jubal, leading them to the room. "Them dishes can wait."

Ace pulled his guitar out of its case and checked the tune. "Any requests?"

Jubal and Rose were mostly interested in old Negro spirituals. Amos just sat stiffly in a corner of the room, indifferent to it all. Sarah was sitting on the sofa, gazing out the window to the darkening world beyond. Tobias sat in a chair, angled to one side of the sofa. Mama Ann, sitting on the sofa next to Sarah, requested something new. "Maybe some of that Jazz or Blues music."

Ace played a number of spirituals, then a couple of Blues songs, an instrumental Jazz piece, and for good measure threw in a classical piece for Spanish guitar.

"You are a master", marveled Rose.

"He do play purty, but why don't you play something a little more throaty and all", said Mama Ann, rolling her shoulders in an attempt to be silky and suggestive.

Ace ignored her, turning instead to Jubal's daughter. "What about you Miss Sarah? There must be something you would enjoy."

She was silent for a long moment before softly replying, "Maybe something about the ocean?"

"Well, here is one I learned in England, *Nancy Lee*." As he sang, Ace called for them all to sing the chorus.

The sailor's wife the sailor's star shall be,
Yeo ho! We go across the sea;
The sailor's wife the sailor's star shall be,
The sailor's wife his star shall be!

They all joined in, excepting grim Amos Asher. When they had finished, Jubal bellowed with laughter, Rose clapped her hands in delight, Mama Ann chuckled, and even Sarah offered the first smile they had seen since meeting her.

"I reckon you mus' be parched", suggested Jubal. "Mama Ann, will you fetch some lemonade for our singer?"

As Mama Ann was waddling off, Tobias reached to turn a book resting on the sofa table toward him. It was a book of lighthouse illustrations. He looked at Sarah. "Is this yours?"

She nodded.

"She loves the ocean", said Jubal. "I got her that book for Christmas when she was just ten years old."

"She loves birds too", suggested Tobias, noting a similar book of illustration for the winged creatures.

"I do", said Sarah before her father could speak.

Tobias nodded. "Freedom on the wing, flying through the sky. I like the ocean too. It's like the planet breathing. It reminds me of things bigger than our piddlin' lives."

Sarah's eyes widened, and she nodded. "Yes, exactly. I wonder what it must be like, to see the world from high in the air. Like from a high mountain, only with your feet not bound to the earth."

"Nonsense", growled Amos from his chair in the corner. "We aren't meant for flying. The ocean sends killing storms."

"Dread beauty", Ace decided aloud, pinning Asher with a steely gaze that rose above his amiable smile.

Sarah had sunk back into herself, but Tobias would not let go so easily. "You have a beautiful voice."

"She does indeed", called Mama Ann as she came back into the room with lemonade and glasses. "But she ought not spend it pining for what cain't be changed."

"Mama Ann", said Rose in a tone both warning and pleading.

Sarah looked over to Ace and smiled. "I liked the sea song. It was happy and hopeful. Full of fun."

Tobias leaned toward her like a coconspirator and in an exaggerated, low voice said, "He is very charming."

Sarah actually laughed, "He is. Yes, he is."

"The lady likes songs of the sea and songs of fun!" announced Ace, and then he launched into a fast-paced rendition of *What Do You Do with a Drunken Sailor.*

That night, in the bunk house, as he lay in his cot staring at the pale, whitewashed plank ceiling, Tobias spoke into the dark, "Ace, when you first spoke of Sarah, something seemed to strike some familiar chord in me. It was as if I knew her story before you even told it. Then when I met her, when I heard her singing and saw something heavy lifted off from her if only for a moment or two ... I just wanted to grab that sadness and wrestle it from off of her, to beat it down into the ground."

The words lingered alone for a while, until as he pondered Tobias thought maybe Ace Redbone was asleep; but then came a soft, quiet reply. "I thought you might, Tobias Freeman Messager. I thought you might."

Ace Redbone and Tobias ate breakfast at the store: Mama Ann's biscuits with cheese again washed down with coffee. As they were leaving the store through the front door, there was a sharp, echoing retort from near the Feed and Grain, as if a large rifle had been discharged. Okra started and trotted to position himself behind Ace's protective legs.

An old man was loading his mule cart when the sound caused his mule to lurch forward in fright. The poor beast nearly bolted away completely, but Ace grabbed its halter and quickly calmed it. The old man hustled from the back of the cart.

"Thank you, mister; if'n he had charged out of here, he would done thrown me off the back. I'd have probably broke a leg, if not my neck or cracked my skull", said the shaken man. "It's that danged tractor of Jubal's; it's been acting up. Lawd, how I hates them things.

"Why, jus' yesterday down at the Mastersons' farm, the brakes on a truck fails and that big ol' hunk of metal jus' crashes into a warehouse and sets the place afire. Would likely have kill't some folk, but this ol' boy we calls Beetle, he holds up this gigantic beam so's the men could get out of there. One of 'em was the younger of the Masterson boys. Can you imagine that? Reckon they will give ol' Beetle a Christmas bonus this year? Cain't ever know 'bout white folk."

"We've met Beetle", cut in Tobias. "Was he hurt?"

"Nah, he was singed a bit, but nothin' bad like", replied the old man as he turned back to finish loading his cart. "I better gets this done afore that tractor fires off another blast."

"You hear that, Ace? Imagine if you hadn't fixed Mister Johnson's back. Ain't no telling how many men might have died if he hadn't been able to hold up that beam."

"No telling", replied Ace with a nod. "You know, you should check on cousin Jubal's tractor. Backfiring motors seem to be a clarion call for your skills. You know anything about tractors?"

"I know a bit", deadpanned Tobias.

As they turned into the Feed and Grain yard, they saw Jubal and a couple of other men standing around staring perplexedly at a blue-gray tractor.

"McCormick-Deering Farmall", noted Tobias.

"Not this time, young man. Even I can see that; it's written right on the side of the beast."

Tobias nodded. "It is. They're made by International Harvester. I'd reckon that one is a late twenties model year."

"Nineteen and twenty-seven", said Jubal as he overheard their approaching conversation.

"I give up", smiled Ace Redbone.

"If it backfires like that, it's most likely the carburetor or maybe the valves", Tobias informed his cousin Jubal. "Could be both. That's what's sneaky about mechanical things; it ain't always jus' one thing ailing them, but a number of things working toward trouble.

"Look here, Ace, this here little tank is for gasoline. That's what you use to start it. Then it runs off kerosene from the bigger tank. Gas is much more likely to backfire. Looks like cousin Jubal has added some new fuel filters and oil filter. That's smart."

"He knows about these things", explained Ace with droll amusement. "You might want him to take a look at it. I know he seems young, but he has been amazing me this whole trip with his knowledge of internal combustion machines."

"Best let him do it, boss," said one of the workmen, "before the thing gives one of us a heart attack."

"Or someone sues you for their animal dying from fright", added the other.

"Have at it then, Tobias", said Jubal with a shrug.

Within two hours Tobias had cleaned and adjusted the carburetor, as well as making a number of other mechanical adjustments to the machine. When it was started, the two workmen were in awe. One of them opined, "Well, boss, that's got to be as smooth as she has run since she was brand new!"

"Just remember how I adjusted it", Tobias told them. "And keep that fuel filter clean or it'll just get grit into the carburetor, and as bad as that might be, it's worse if it gets into the pistons."

"Well, I'll be", said Jubal. "Looks as if that Crafty fella taught you real good."

"We get some tractors into the shop", explained Tobias. "When I was fourteen Mister Forgeron had me start working on an ol' Model A he salvaged from a wreck."

"A Tudor Deluxe sedan", noted a poker-faced Ace Redbone.

"That's right", continued Tobias, completely missing Redbone's teasing humor. "I took that thing completely apart, and then put it back together again while replacing some of the worst parts with parts from another Model A."

"Just a regular Tudor sedan", added Ace with a wink for Jubal's benefit. This time Tobias cast him a look of suspicion.

"Well, that's fine, jus' fine", declared Jubal. "Now, son, you're gonna have to let me pay you somewhat of something for this."

"Oh no, sir", protested Tobias. "You've given us food and shelter."

Jubal laughed, pulled a few dollars out of his pocket, and stuffed them into the pocket of Tobias' shirt. "You are a fine young man, to be sure. But now, I swear you're jus' like your daddy. Both of you fine, generous men who jus' cain't seem to accept gratitude in return."

Since he had a time or two accused his father of that very same fault, all Tobias could do was chuckle sheepishly and accept the offer already residing in his pocket.

From the back porch of her family's house, Sarah watched Tobias throwing a stick for his dog to fetch. She had noticed immediately upon meeting the two men and the dog that there was a peculiar similarity to their eyes. The men, being cousins, seemed plausible enough, but the dog's eyes caused her to almost shiver.

In the conversation the night before, Tobias had said his father called them "Egyptian eyes". A bookish and well-educated girl, she recalled immediately the eye-lined images of Egyptians from art adorning the temples and tombs of the ancient land. Perhaps the dog's eyes would not have been so remarkable if they did not so eerily suggest those of his master.

She was perplexed too by the effect Tobias had upon her. He was attractive, tall, and finely enough built, but there was something else about him that intrigued her. She felt, in ways she could not completely understand, as if he actually *saw* her. She had become used to being considered beautiful, though she found it odd, and she had become used to being desired for that and her father's wealth, but Tobias seemed interested in *her*, who she was beyond all that.

It chilled her to think of it, because she could not help but also think of those three tombstones that haunted her life. She tried to put the young man out of her mind, but there he was. She wondered how, despite all that had happened in his own life, he could be so innocent and straightforward. There was toughness in him, but also a childlike playfulness as he exercised his strange dog.

She smiled, remembering him talking about automobiles, trucks, and such like. She had not really understood half of what he said, but felt that his open enthusiasm had helped her to comprehend more than she would have otherwise.

He is *alive*, she thought, and found herself drawn to that as a leaf unfurls to the sunlight.

Tobias heard the slap of the screen door. He turned to look over his shoulder as Okra darted after the thrown stick. He saw Sarah descending the steps from the back porch, her hand light upon the stair railing.

She was wearing a long, white dress that was somehow neither modern nor old-fashioned. He thought her beautiful. From when first he had seen her, he thought her beautiful. Tobias Freeman Messager was a contemplative young man. He thought that if you only ever saw a formal photograph of Sarah Tomkins you would not think her *that* beautiful, but to see her in the flow of life was another thing altogether.

Sorrow was like a veil draped over her, to be sure, but it could not obscure an intriguing grace. She was like a Nubian queen in the body of a servant. Somehow she could be regal, yet unassuming. There was a simple joy in her when she spoke of the soaring of gulls, or the crashing of waves.

"He has a lot of energy", she said of Okra as she approached. The dog was returning with the stick in his mouth. His pace quickened when he saw the young woman. He bounded to them, dropping the stick at Tobias' feet as if to fulfill some legal obligation, and then scooted up to fawn at Sarah's feet.

She laughed.

"He likes you", said Tobias to the obvious. "My daddy says Okra is a better judge of character than any man he's ever known."

"Then I feel suitably honored", said Sarah with a soft smile.

Tobias almost told her that she was beautiful when she smiled, but he swallowed the words and only smiled himself in return. It was a dark mark against the worthiness of the world, in his opinion, that she did not smile more.

"How did he come by the name Okra?" she asked.

"Ah, well. My father says it means 'soul' in some African language", explained Tobias. "You would have to know my father. He is a man who does right much thinking about things."

"Like father, like son?" suggested Sarah with an arch of an eyebrow.

"In some ways, I reckon. Not always about the same things. My mama says we're more alike than either of us can see. Daddy, he says I'm an enigma, because I seem to love machines *and* nature. I try sometimes to explain to him how machines are really jus' an extension of nature. He does allow how men can make nothing independent of nature."

He shut up then, thinking maybe his thoughts were too poorly expressed, but he saw that she was looking at him, perhaps a little bemused, but also intrigued.

"I reckon I'm talking too much", he offered sheepishly. "Reckon I shouldn't say 'reckon', either."

"Lord, do", chuckled Sarah. "My mother is always fussing at me. Telling me what I should say, what I should not say. She loves me and wants what's best for me, but I swear sometimes I just wanna shout out, 'Mam, I reckon I be talkin' however I wants t'be talkin' from now on!'

"You know, I called her Mam until I started school and she said I should call her Mother going forward. That's what she said, 'going forward'. Who talks to a six-year-old that way?"

"Your mother, I reckon", replied Tobias with a chuckle. "My mother and father are a little that way, though. I guess they're all just wanting us to learn proper manners so we can fit in better with cultured folk."

"Well, I reckon I should like to talk to you for hours on end", Sarah suddenly announced in an admission that surprised both of them. She flustered slightly, laughing to cover her embarrassment. "I don't have many friends. Everyone my age is put off by all the prim and proper manners my mother insists on."

Tobias shrugged. "It doesn't put me off at all. Of course, my mama always says that at least I am easy to get along with."

"Seems to me she is right", said Sarah.

Tobias offered her an amused and wry smile. "Oh, she often is, to hear her tell it."

"Where is your friend, your cousin Ace?"

"I think he's still at the bunkhouse."

"He is a peculiar man."

"You're telling me", snorted Tobias. "He just has a knack with people, and things always seem to work out when he puts his hand into it."

"My grandma would have said he is a man that can fill a room", mused Sarah. "Dominate a room just by being in it. But not in a grim or intimidating way. Not like Amos."

"Now, he *is* grim", allowed Tobias.

Sarah nodded her head. "He is a hardworking man, but he seems to always be burning with some cold anger. My daddy has come to depend on that man too much. He is a hard worker, but I just feel like he wants to own everything around him. To possess it and make it do what he wants."

"Dark ice", Tobias decided. "It's mighty strange when Amos and Ace are in the same room. They don't much seem to like one another. I confess it is nearly a relief to come across someone who is completely immune to my cousin's warmth and charm, but when the two of them are in the same room it's as if there were two different rooms, two different realities, layered over one another."

"I much prefer Ace's room", said Sarah.

"I seen you with Miss Sarah", said Mama Ann, wagging her finger at Tobias when he entered the store. "That girl is trouble, boy. You jus' remember ol' Mama Ann tells you so."

"The world is full of troubles", Tobias said in reply.

"Don't make light. Don't make light. They is three dead men that makes it not something to pass over lightly."

"I am not making light", said Tobias. "What happened to those fellows is a shame, a tragedy, but the world *is* full of such tragedies. War, famine, murder, greed, lust, and all manner of ills afflict this world. It's a tragedy to me that Sarah should face such superstitious and mean-spirited talk over any such things that might befall those around her."

"Three men!" replied Mama Ann with surprising intensity and even anger. "They had life snuffed out of 'em. No ways around it. None."

"It's not as if Sarah snuffed those lives", noted Tobias.

Mama Ann leaned forward, wagging a finger again. "Maybe not with her own hands. But what might she have done to bring such evil upon those around her? Who can know?"

"I know that you or me don't know of anything at all", replied Tobias with some iron in his voice.

Amos Asher came through the front door and Mama Ann turned to him. "This here boy is playin' with fire and he don't even knows it. I think maybe he's gone a little sweet for Miss Sarah."

Asher looked a long moment at Tobias, but then he just shrugged and walked on back toward the office.

"I don't hold with superstition", he said as he was leaving. "But I believe in playing the odds."

At dinner, Ace Redbone's warmth and congeniality was sore pressed to provide its usual lubricating effect. Tobias could only wonder what was at work behind the scenes. Sarah seemed sadder than ever. Jubal looked despairing. Rose had the fear-haunted eyes of a trapped creature. Mama Ann was tight-lipped and most unusually subdued.

Amos Asher was grim. Always stoically grim, now he seemed to radiate a brooding presence through the entire room. Even Ace seemed subdued by this presence, but his eyes were calculating as his gaze moved across the assembled diners.

Tobias ate slowly and deliberately. The food had little taste to him, and he felt as if he were suffocating. Finally, Jubal Tomkins stopped eating, cleared his throat, and placed both his hands on the table.

"Tobias."

"Sir?"

"It has been brought to my attention that you have said some unkind things about Mister Asher."

Tobias frowned, confused. He tilted his head as he considered this. "What sort of things, sir?"

"We don't need to compound the offense by repeating it", Jubal lectured. "Amos has served this family well during its tribulation. I am troubled that a guest in this house would speak ill of him, all for the sake of impressing my daughter."

Tobias' frown deepened; he looked at Sarah just as she looked up from the tabletop. Her eyes were pleading, and she shook her head nearly imperceptibly to indicate to him that it was not from her that such an accusation came.

"I'm sure you're a fine boy", began Rose, but the words trailed off.

Mama Ann rushed to fill in the silence. "It ain't all your fault. Miss Sarah is desperate lonely, and full of guilt, no doubt. You is a fine lookin' young man, but you got to think about this. Think about what has befallen this family."

Tobias' expression turned incredulous. He looked at Ace, but his cousin seemed withdrawn. Only those calculating eyes were engaging the room. With the absence of Ace, Amos Asher's presence became all the more oppressive.

The stony face fixed its gaze on Tobias. "I don't much care what you think of me, boy. But Miss Sarah deserves more than you have to offer. You, the son of a broken man. You come around here beggin' and then trying to wheedle up to Mister Jubal's daughter—"

"Stop it."

Sarah's whisper had the effect of a shout. Everyone turned to look at her. She closed her tear-filled eyes for a moment. When she opened them there was a hint of defiance. "Tobias didn't really say much of anything about Amos. If anything truly disrespectful was said, it was by me. I have told you already that what you have been told is just not true."

"Child," protested Mama Ann, "I overheard the two of you. Mister Asher has worked hisself to the bone for this here family. He deserves better. You should be ashamed of yourself. Ain't you done brought enough shame—"

There came the click of toenails on the hardwood floor as Okra trotted into the room. Nobody even really knew he was in the house, but the sound of voiced tension had brought him into the dining room. He was drawn immediately to Sarah. He went to her and rose so that his forelegs were resting in her thigh. His tail and hindquarters wagged for appeasement. He laid his head on her lap, but his eyes found those of his young master.

Those eyes.

Now, they seemed to say. *We are looking to you.*

Tobias thought of his father, who had told him that there came a time when every man must be the hero of his own life.

Tobias' chair shot out from underneath him with such force as he stood that it fell back onto the floor with a silence-inducing clatter. He stood rigid, trying to collect himself. As he gazed around the room he saw the eyes of Ace Redbone on him, calculating, calculating.

The young man turned to look at Jubal as he spoke. "Mister Jubal, I don't know what it is I am supposed to have said. I will tell you and I will tell him, that I admire much about Mister Amos. I don't like everything about him, but is anyone all likeable?"

He turned then to Amos Asher. "Sir, we seem to have something in common in that neither of us much cares of the other's opinion. But I care if lies are told about me. It is a lie to say that my father is a broken man. He is more of a man than ever you are likely to be. And I ain't been beggin' for nothing. I came only for what my father is owed, and Mister Jubal has graciously agreed."

His anger was loosed now, and Tobias turned his dark eyes on Mama Ann. "And you, ma'am. My daddy says that old age don't guarantee wisdom, and I thank you for the illustration of his lesson. Old woman, you just talk too much. Just too much nonsense and trouble-stirring talk."

He tried to collect himself now, his breath having become short after the burst of adrenaline. He gazed over at Sarah, who was looking back at him with eyes wide and full of hope. He drew himself erect again and let his gaze sweep over everyone at the table.

"I have this to ask. What fault of hers is any of this? Sarah is as beautiful a person as I have ever met. Oh, there might be girls with more moviestar looks or whatever, but *look* at her. Truly *look* at her. There is something in her that shines, and it should shine on every place she goes, but y'all are snuffing it out. You have turned her into a tragedy, but she ain't. She just ain't, I tell you."

He drew his breath again, and his gaze became all the more firm. "I ask you, what is her fault? I will ask over and over again, what is her fault? Answer me, please, someone, what is her fault?"

He passed his gaze around the table. Jubal Tomkins seemed confused but considering. Amos Asher had a cold, harsh anger. Mama Ann seemed stunned. Rose was looking into some distant place with shame upon her face. Sarah's expression shined with hope she dared not believe.

Ace Redbone was smiling.

Eleven

"Now that right there was something."

The laughter from Ace was nearly as stunning to everyone in the room as had been Tobias' outburst. But so natural and unaffected was it that the room seemed to go softer in its presence. The musician got to his feet, shaking his head in mirth as he clapped Tobias on the back.

"You've got a warrior in you, young man", he said as he picked up the fallen chair and slid it behind Tobias. "I thought you might, but to see it roar to life? That was something. Have a seat, Samson, and give that jawbone a rest."

After Tobias had clumsily reseated himself, Okra left Sarah and came over to his young master. The pointy black nose rooted up Tobias' hand for a reassuring pat. Only, Tobias was not sure who was reassuring whom.

Ace Redbone took his own chair and spun it around so that he could sit upon it with his arms resting on the back and his chin upon his arms. His eyes swept around the room, settling on Amos Asher.

"Amos, you look like you've bitten into a lemon. I reckon if I was playing poker with you, I'd have to be thankful I wasn't holding whatever is in your hand."

Ace sat up straight then, though his wrists still rested on the back of the chair. He tilted his head to look first at Tobias, and then at everyone else.

"I have got to admit that this young man has made a lot of sense. Can any of us say what fault should rest upon Sarah?"

They all looked at him dumbly. He nodded his head in an I-thought-so manner. "Perceptions have a way of sneaking up so that people forget what is real is not always what is perceived."

Jubal was nodding his head in a slow acknowledgment of Ace's words. He turned to look at Tobias. "Son, I don't know where that came from, but Lord knows it cut like lightning through the confusion in my mind.

"Look here, I'm sorry if I misunderstood, or was tol' wrong about anything you said. I am sorry too for what Amos said to you. Your daddy is as strong a man as I ever knew, and you are for sure right that there weren't no bit of beggin' in your coming here. If there was any shame to be had, it is on me for not having looked harder over the years to find your father and repay him."

Then Jubal turned to Amos Asher. "Amos, I think maybe you owe young Tobias something of an apology."

There was only a hardening in Amos Asher's countenance. After a long moment of severe silence, the man's eyes turned to his boss. "No. I stand by what I have said, and if you are too blind or stupid to see the truth of it, then it won't be me who's to blame."

Whatever pleading there had been bled from Jubal's expression and was replaced with cold determination. "Watch how you speak to me, Amos. This is my house, and while I appreciate your hard work, I would note that you have been well rewarded all these years. And, it is *still* my business."

A sneer broke like cracking black ice onto Asher's face. "There wouldn't be any business if it depended on you. I am the one who has kept this place together while you and your family wallow in self-pity.

"I had thought maybe I would marry that girl to save the lot of you like I have the business. The business I deserve, but ain't nobody should be stuck with that cursed bit of tart. You can make her put on airs and talk like some kind of white princess, but she ain't nothing but the daughter of a worn-out old man and his too proud wife."

With that Amos Asher rose from the table and stalked out of the door. Tears slid along Sarah's smooth cheeks. Tobias had begun to rise as the words came from Asher's mouth, but Ace's hand on his arm stayed him. Jubal and Rose sat in stunned silence. Mama Ann looked as if she wanted to be somewhere else.

"Is it just me," began Ace, "or does this room seem more comfortable now than it did with Amos Asher sitting over there glowering the way he does?"

Nobody laughed, or even smiled, but some of the tension eased away. Finally Jubal just shook his head in wonder of it all. "Looks like I'll be needing another foreman."

"If I were you, I'd give the books a good looking over", suggested Ace, and then he turned his head to glance at the cook. "Wouldn't you agree, Mama Ann?"

She said nothing. Ace stood up, turned his chair around, and sat back down with his hands clasped together resting on the tabletop. He was smiling, looking at the empty place where Asher had been sitting.

"Tobias, I am guessing that you might have something more to say."

Tobias winced, but then took a deep breath and released a long sigh. "Well, I think maybe I have already said more than I should. But, as my daddy sometimes says, there ain't much use draggin' with half a net."

He looked then at Sarah, but he spoke to Jubal. "Sir, I meant every word I said about your daughter. I know we ain't known each other all that long, but every minute spent with her is a timeless joy to me. I can't say that I am deserving, but if she'll have me, sir, I would ask you to let me marry your daughter."

Hope rose like the sun in Sarah's eyes; her head nodded childlike in restrained enthusiasm. Tobias pulled his eyes from her and looked to her father.

"Mister Jubal, in this day and age, a father can't really give away his daughter without her consent, I reckon. But it seems that I have her consent. I ain't afraid of such nonsense as has been talked about her, but I would ask your blessing. It seems only right to ask for it, to hope for it."

Jubal took his own deep breath and released it as a long sigh. His head nodded. "You are correct that you have known one another such a short time, but in my life, I have found that there are times when time itself is richer than usual. I give my conditional blessing. We can all sleep on this. Ponder on it. I can't think of any reason to say no that my gut feeling doesn't dismiss."

He looked to his wife, whose expression was nearly as hopeful as Sarah's. Rose nodded her consent. Jubal turned his gaze back to Tobias. "So, there it is, but we have to ask Sarah, don't you reckon?"

Tobias nodded and looked over to her.

"Sarah, would you marry me?"

The young lady glowed. She cast a teasing glance at Ace and nodded toward Tobias. "That right there, that would be something."

As Ace laughed, Sarah turned back to Tobias. "I wouldn't want to be the man or woman who tried to stop me marrying you, Tobias Freeman Messager."

"Providential", said Ace Redbone.

In the predawn morning, Mama Ann was walking to the store to begin preparing her famous biscuits. Her face was full of angry consternation, and she was so intent upon what was on her mind that she at first failed to see Ace Redbone sitting on the low step that led to the porch of the store. It caused her a momentary start.

Ace looked up at her. He was not smiling, but his face was placid. He tilted his head as he considered her before speaking.

"Have you actually believed that I do not know you?"

"Come on in, Ace."

Jubal looked beleaguered sitting behind the desk in his office. He shook his head ruefully as he looked at the ledgers spread across the surface.

"I jus' don't know how I missed this. I'm almost afraid to look further into it. I feel the fool. Worse, I'm not sure I can prove anything, because he was sho'nuff clever in the doing, but I know my business, and I can see the holes in inventory, irregularities, and such like."

He leaned back, rubbing his eyes. "Now, if it weren't bad enough, Mama Ann hasn't showed up for work. I sent someone over to the little house I let her use, and they say it looks as if she has done cleared out altogether."

"Maybe she was in on it with Amos", suggested Ace as he gazed out the window.

"Could be", admitted Jubal. "Thing is, he had me hire her, but looking back on it, and lookin' at these here books, I think maybe she was a bad influence on him. Looks like it goes back before her hiring, but it sure gets worser about the time she started working in the store."

Jubal closed the two ledgers opened on his desk and placed them on the stack piled to one side. "Well, now I ain't got a cook and I ain't got no foreman."

"I know somebody who might be interested", said Ace, still looking out the window. "This fellow Tobias and I met on the way here. His name is Davis Johnson, but a lot of folk call him Beetle."

Jubal shrugged. "Doesn't ring a bell."

"He works for the Mastersons at their depot. You know that warehouse fire day before yesterday?"

"I heard."

"Well, he was the fellow that saved all those men by holding up a beam on his shoulders so it wouldn't cut off their escape."

"He's the one? Well imagine that!"

"I talked with him, and I had a sense that he is smart, honest, and very hardworking. He's got a reputation for being good with numbers and organization. He ain't had much opportunity to use it with the Mastersons. You know some white folk are slow to trust a Negro's brain."

"Some?" snorted Jubal. "Well, if you are vouching for him. I don't hardly know you, but there's something about you makes me trust you."

"I think you can trust Davis Johnson. Okra liked him."

Jubal let go a full laugh.

"That seals it then!"

The merchant's gaze followed Ace Redbone's out the window into the backyard. Tobias and Sarah were walking near the creek bank. Okra was weaving around them investigating every scent that caught his fancy, or running up to them to receive some head scratching.

"I have more hope right there with them two than I ever thought I would again", sighed Jubal. "But, I have to admit to frettin' over how quickly all this has come about. I know it sounds strange, given the way I've acted the last year or two about gettin' that girl married, but I feel as if a veil has been lifted from my eyes."

"Accept the possibility as you have, but tell them to wait awhile to actually set a date", suggested Ace. "See how they feel after three or four months."

"That's sensible."

"I doubt it changes much, though."

"Me neither", replied Jubal as he watched his daughter walking with Tobias Freeman Messager.

Tobias and Sarah sat side by side on a cypress log overlooking Cut Creek. Okra looked at them with disapproval that they should have stopped the walk, but finally curled back around to plop at their feet with an exaggerated sigh.

"He just goes and goes", Sarah marveled.

"Back home he don't ever seem to stop, except when my father tells him to. He's a hardheaded thing, but he seems always eager to please Daddy. My mother says that's because my father is the only critter Okra has ever met that has a head harder than his own."

Sarah laughed, "I can't hardly wait to meet your mother and father. I hope it's not too much of a shock for them. You left to collect on a debt, and you come back with a fiancee."

"Well, I've called to tell them Ace and me will be coming home in a few days, but I haven't told them about you yet. I want to tell them in person. Your father is thinking that y'all will follow down the day after me and Ace head back."

Sarah leaned forward to rub Okra's head, eliciting much tail thumping on the leafy loam.

"I can hardly believe all this. I had given up any hope in this world."

"I can understand that", replied Tobias. "Even if it seems silly now, especially in the light of such a beautiful day, I can still feel the chill of it when I remember Mama Ann going on and on."

"She was a troublemaker, and she seemed to do it for the pure love of trouble. Sneaky too. Thinking back on it, I can see where she could seem to be comforting or even praising a person to their face, but there could be a twist to those words that made you doubt yourself, even the very worth of yourself."

"Well she's hightailed it somewhere else."

Sarah shuddered. "God have mercy on those wherever she lands. I wish Amos had gone off with her. He's still skulking around. Daddy has given him two weeks to get out of the house he lets him use."

She was surprised by Tobias' rueful chuckle. He shook his head at her and waved his hand so she would not misunderstand.

"No, you see, it's just that at first I was kind of admiring the man because he seemed unaffected by that way Ace seems to have with people. Then, last night when Ace seemed so subdued, by his standards, I admit that it actually scared me. Then, after my little outburst, Ace just sprang in like a cat after a mouse!"

"That outburst tore the mask right off of Amos", replied Sarah. "I never thought to know such hope again. It was wonderful. I think for all my days I will be able to close my eyes and see you shooting to your feet and making that stand."

"The chair will probably have nightmares about it."

Sarah laughed, "So might Amos. Then in all that tension and all that dark, suddenly Ace is filling the room the way he does. He was smooth, easy, and even seemed amused. I think Amos was prepared for anything but that. He thought my father would break. He thought Jubal Tomkins was worn down. He was not prepared for Ace Redbone!"

She laid her head on Tobias' shoulder as she looped her arm through his and said, "He didn't stand a chance. Not with Tobias Messager and Ace Redbone in the room."

Nobody remembered exactly who decided they should do it, but after a late dinner, they all went to the little chapel. Jubal lit a fire in the stove to stave off the growing chill of a night that threatened cold rain. They each randomly selected a passage from the Bible to read, and it seemed each verse was some form of thanksgiving or expression of hope.

Then Ace played his guitar, and they sang hymns and spirituals together, lit by candlelight. Then the musician whispered a suggestion into Tobias' ear. The young man left, but returned momentarily with a small box.

From somewhere Ace Redbone produced a small copper bowl that he placed on the altar. Tobias stepped forward, and from the box Ace took some incense and placed it on a bit of charcoal resting on the plate.

"This here is some of the incense given to us by the saintly Sister Charlotte."

"He thinks she's saintly because she just seemed totally enchanted with one Ace Redbone", noted Tobias.

The others laughed, including Ace as he produced a match. "A mere contributing factor. This here incense came from Patmos, the island of Revelation. For sure this has been a week of revelation. Now, let us offer to God this holy incense given to us by a most holy woman."

The scented tendrils began drifting through the chapel. Ace led Tobias and the Tomkins family in a prayer. Then an easy, gentle solemnity settled on them all as they each became lost in thought. As she had by the creek, Sarah looped her arm through that of Tobias' and leaned lightly against him. Silent, joyful tears brimmed in the eyes of her parents.

After a few moments, Ace put a hand each on the shoulders of Jubal and Rose. He motioned with his head toward the door to the chapel. When they had all stepped out into the night, he said to them, "Let's give them some time together. It seems a night for reflection."

"And prayer", offered Rose with a smile as she stood on her toe tips to kiss the cheek of Ace Redbone. "I want to weep for joy every time I see them together. Thank you, Ace Redbone, and God bless you."

"Oh, he has", replied Ace. "Since the moment he created me."

With a contented sigh, Jubal drew his coat tight and turned up the collar. "It's looking to be a chilly, wet night. I think I better get these old bones inside by a fire."

"Go ahead, warm yourselves", Ace said. "I'll stay out here and watch out for the young ones in yonder. Look here, I'll even have some company."

Okra had slipped unnoticed to sit beside Ace. He accepted a head rub from Jubal and Rose before they left for the house. When they disappeared inside, Ace turned his gaze down to Okra.

"This has been a pleasant evening. The kind that warms you inside", he said quietly. The dog thumped its tail.

"But I tell you, Okra, there is only *one* happily ever after. It's just beyond the veil of this world, pending, pending, pending. No man, no angel knows when that time will come. Until then, let us remember these words from Scripture: *On your walls, O Jerusalem, I have set watchmen.*"

He raised his eyes to gaze into the starless night. The hair bristled along Okra's back. Ace shushed him with a hand brushing along his neck. Then the two of them began walking toward the creek.

A dark form moved through the night. It carried a can in one hand, and under its arm two lengths of cut sapling. It set down the can, and tossed the saplings to the leafy ground. Rising then, it stood ramrod straight and looked toward the property of Jubal Tomkins.

First it considered the chapel, staring at the candle-lit windows for a long while. Then its gaze moved deliberately beyond, toward the bunkhouse near the Feed and Grain. Then back again to the chapel.

It bent and began tying the saplings to one another with a length of rope. Then, standing once more, it considered the roughly formed cross before gazing yet again at the warm light from the chapel.

A flash of lightning caused it a momentary start. Not because of the bolt, but because in the flash of illumination it saw a man and a dog standing beside a tree. The man stepped forward, with the dog following.

"Evening, Amos Asher. I do not think you should come any further this way."

Recovering from this unexpected presence, the cold, stern face remained fixed. "Do you think you can stop me?"

Ace laughed lightly. "You are a tree of a man, aren't you? Hard like oak. However, I must answer truthfully, yes.

"Yes. My confidence on that is very high. You might say it soars on the wings of an eagle."

Uncertainty crossed the iron face, and Amos Asher looked suspiciously down at Ace's empty hands. A hard frown formed an angry incredulity. His body leaned as if one force pushed him toward Ace, but another held him at bay.

Ace turned around to look back at the chapel. "You weren't quite sure, were you? You probably saw that Tobias and Sarah are alone in the chapel. But then, you *could* wait until Tobias and I retire to the bunkhouse.

"Stick that cross in the ground, set it afire, and then set fire to the bunkhouse. Tobias Messager burned to death, and maybe people believe this nonsense about the curse once more."

Ace smiled again, holding up his hands. "As you noticed, I am unarmed, but then, so are you. I warn you, you shall not pass here this night."

"I don't need no weapons", growled Amos Asher.

"Do you not?" asked Ace Redbone. "Is there not something missing? Something you need?"

Confusion set itself on the face of Amos Asher. Ace took a step forward, and Amos retreated a step.

"You are alone", said Ace. "She is gone. The other one that spoke in your mind is gone as well. Mammon and Asmodai I have bound and cast out. Does it say that in Scripture? Maybe not, but it should. Greed and Lust have fallen before the wrath of God.

"Now, I know what it *does* say: *I have seen Satan fall like lightning from the sky*. Good stuff, that, don't you think?"

Ace stepped sideways again, with Okra matching his movement with a bristling back and a snarl on his muzzle. Amos Asher reacted as if struck and moved backward.

"I'll break that dog's neck if it comes at me."

"No", replied Ace. "You shall not. He won't come at you, and I would not let you do it anyway. Besides, you are alone now; your companions have left you alone."

"That what you think?" growled Amos Asher as he continued to back away. "You think I can't deal with you? I can wring your last breath from you, music man."

"You sound very defiant", Ace admitted. "But you keep backing away from me. That is why I know you will not be passing by me this night."

"You don't know anything", spat Amos Asher.

"I know you killed each of the previous men who were to marry Sarah Tomkins. You came tonight to kill Tobias Messager.

"As you stood brooding in these woods, you watched as we all went into the chapel. That befuddled you, didn't it? The sound of voices raised in song, praising the Lord! Ah, Amos Asher, what were you to make of that?

"You realized it then, that you are all alone now. How hollow has been your strength all along since first you invited them into your mind, your heart, and even your very soul."

Ace paused in his progression for a moment, tilting his head to consider Amos Asher. "They have been driven away."

Amos Asher issued a crackling laugh and replied, "You think I couldn't handle those suitors, those fools, by myself?"

"It does not matter what you could have done, only what you did, and you needed those voices to fix your resolve", said Ace. "You wanted Sarah and you wanted what Jubal had built. With the death of Bryant you thought surely Jubal would see. You couldn't have asked before, or it might have exposed your twin desires, greed and lust. No, he had to be brought to a state of abysmal despair."

"What Jubal built up? For ten years it has been *me*. My sweat and my labor!"

"Jubal was a successful man before he ever set eyes on you", noted Ace. "But, you? You sold yourself to your own delusion and invited evil into your heart to strengthen your resolve. Then you killed. You murdered. Those murders were what wounded Jubal, Rose, and Sarah. You did not earn anything. You stole it by taking three lives."

"I killed them", howled Amos Asher. "I would have killed seven times seventy! I got that baseball player drunk. I wanted him to look the fool, but when he was killed instead, I knew what waited for any other man who set his eyes on what should be mine. I knocked that young fool senseless and tossed him in the water to drown. I loosened the lug nuts on Bryant's tractor; the fool didn't even notice that I had completely removed two of them. I killed all three of 'em; I got 'em all."

"And then young Tobias rises up and defends Sarah", said Ace. "Worse, his unexpected defiance caused you to expose what you are, an evil, conniving wretch of a man. So now you would kill him and have the blame rest upon the Klan and a nonexistent curse. Deflecting blame from you, and reaffirming the superstition you were depending upon.

"But you are uncertain. They're gone, those worming, serpentine whispers you have used to give you courage. You are alone."

As he backed away, Amos Asher's face was twisted by frustrated anger, and he spat at Ace Redbone.

"Careful, Amos", said Ace. "We are approaching the high bank of the creek."

Amos Asher wrenched himself around to look in the direction he was retreating. He tried to move to one side, but Okra had curled around and awaited him there with teeth bared. The first drops of rain began to fall.

"I'll kill that dog."

"No. You could never get your hands on him. And I have warned you that I would not allow it if you did."

The drops of rain began pelting the ground. Amos Asher backed cautiously, with his eyes darting in search for some path away from this man. Ace Redbone stopped his advance and held up one hand as if to parley.

"The wages of sin is death. The Lord says, 'If I say to the wicked man, *You shall surely die*, and you give him no warning, nor speak to warn the wicked from his wicked way, in order to save his life, that wicked person shall die for his iniquity, but his blood I will require from your hand. But if you warn the wicked, and he does not turn from his wickedness, or from his wicked way, he shall die for his iniquity, but you will have delivered your soul.'"

The rain began pouring down upon them. Okra crept like a predator closer to where Amos Asher stood. The man took a step back. Ace Redbone lowered his hand and tilted his head. Water was pouring from the brim of his hat as he fixed his gaze upon the murderous eyes of Amos Asher.

"I have warned you, Amos Asher. Death is your fate. God gives free will, so you may choose. God is Love, so he forgives. You have done nothing that God will not forgive if you choose to accept that forgiveness."

In the torrent of rain the clay edge of the bank gave way, and Amos Asher slipped down the side, grasping desperately at the last second for the stump of a half-rotten sapling. His eyes lifted to Ace Redbone.

Ace Redbone squatted, with his hand extended to the fallen man. The rain lightened, though it remained steady. With his head, Ace Redbone nodded toward his open hand.

"Take my hand, Amos. I will pull you up. The world will demand a price for your crime, but God will cleanse you of your guilt."

The eyes of Amos Asher widened for a moment, before they began to narrow. A sneer formed on his lips. Then he brought up his legs under him, and letting go of the sapling he pushed off from the bank and plummeted toward the creek.

Ace Redbone hung his head for a moment, as Okra moved up next to him, insinuating himself under the musician's arm. With the same hand he had extended to Amos Asher, Ace reached across to scratch the crown of Okra's head.

He got up and motioned for Okra to stay. He walked to the edge of the bank and looked down. Perhaps Amos Asher had thought to push himself into the middle of the creek. Despite being a shallow and moderately swift current, it might have been deep enough to absorb his fall, but he did not clear the cypress knees thrust up out of the water.

He floated facedown with his head bobbing in the current and his broken body awkwardly askew. Blood spread darker upon dark water.

Ace Redbone turned away from the creek bank and motioned Okra to him. "Let's get you out of the rain, boy. There is nothing more we can do here. Only the mercy of God can help that man now."

"We've got the body up out of the creek and packed into the truck", the sheriff's detective told Jubal. "His house is locked; would you have a key, before we break down a door or a window?"

"Yes, sir", replied Jubal. "Jus' give me a minute to fetch it out of the office."

The detective was really just a senior deputy who sometimes wore street clothes. He was a respectful enough man, but Jubal could tell that he did not see much point in investigating the death of a Negro.

Jubal followed him back to Amos Asher's bungalow. A junior deputy met them outside of it. "Ed, it looks like those poles that formed the cross were from a little garden out behind Asher's place here."

The detective gave a nod as Jubal unlocked the door. "Jubal, stay out here, nearby. Got to consider this a crime scene until we've cleared it."

Jubal just nodded and stepped aside as the detective and the junior deputy entered the house. He waited about twenty minutes before the junior deputy emerged and spoke to him, "Ed wants to see you inside."

It occurred to Jubal that he had not once entered this building since he had lent it to Amos. The interior was well kept and extraordinarily tidy, as he would have expected. He saw the detective standing outside the door of what was the smaller of the two bedrooms.

"Take a look in here and see what you make of this", said the detective.

Jubal went to the door and peered inside. The single window was heavily draped, but enough light came through the doorway to cast an illuminating gloom. The room was spotlessly clean and empty save for a single wooden chair that was set facing a wooden shelf on the wall.

Puzzlement was expressed on Jubal's face, slowly giving way to uncomfortable realization as he surveyed the items on the shelf: a baseball, a pair of spectacles, and two lug nuts.

Jubal hung his head. "I think Amos killed my daughter's suitors."

He explained the significance of each item related to the dead men. The detective listened grimly, before sighing, "I've heard tell that such murderers sometimes keep trophies. This place is like a cold, evil shrine. Best we not even try to think on what he was a pondering when he sat in that there chair."

Tobit opened his eyes into the constant dark. He felt both relief and a depressing disappointment. He reached out his hand, feeling for Anna in the bed beside him. When his hand settled upon the curve of her hip, she stirred and asked in a sleepy voice, "What is it?"

"Nothing, really", replied Tobit. "Just a dream."

Jubal watched the sheriff's panel truck carry away the body of Amos Asher. When it disappeared he turned to go back into his store, but stopped when he saw Ace Redbone standing there. He climbed onto the porch and leaned against a porch post.

"Is it a sin, do you suppose, cousin Ace, that I am somehow relieved that the man is dead?"

"Not in and of itself; it appears he killed three men and planned on at least four."

Jubal nodded slowly. "The detective thinks he was going to commit arson and blame it on the Klan. They say the saplings he used to form a cross came from his own garden; they matched others used as bean poles, and two poles are missing.

"Looks that he lost his way in the rain and the edge of the creek bank gave way beneath him. I tell you true that I had a cold dread since he left the house that night, fearful of what he might do."

"You don't have to worry about that now", replied Ace. "We can just pray for his tormented soul."

Jubal raised himself from off the porch post. "I got word to that Johnson fellow. He's coming in to talk to me this evening when he's finished at Mastersons."

"I don't think he will disappoint you", offered Ace.

Jubal eyed Ace Redbone for a long moment. "I reckon not, if you are vouching for him."

He turned to go into the store, but paused to look back at Ace. "I don't understand what has happened here, Ace, but I just can't shake the feeling that it is bigger, darker, and yet more hopeful in the long run than it all seems."

"Is that not really the hope of all things?" replied Ace Redbone as he fell in behind Jubal to follow him into the store. "Seeing as the sheriff doesn't seem inclined to further investigation, it's probably time for me and Tobias to head back to Tobit's farm."

"There is a truck dropping off some supplies Monday. It will be going on to Harper Bay with sawmill parts", said Jubal. "I asked, and they said they were fine with two men and a dog riding in the back. Or if you can wait until Tuesday, you could ride down to Tobit's with us. I need to get this place sorted before I leave, especially with Amos no longer around."

"You have a nice car, Jubal, but I don't think it would be all that comfortable with five people and a dog", replied Ace with a chuckle. "Besides, Tobias wants to speak to his parents before they meet Sarah."

"That would be right proper, I 'spose", said Jubal as they exited the main store and made their way into his office. He sat down weary, but relieved, behind his desk.

"I can't tell you what a blessin' this has turned out to be, Ace. Two thieves rooted out, a darkness lifted."

"And a fine future son-in-law", Ace reminded him.

"He is, isn't he? Yes, sir, he truly is."

163

Twelve

Anna was beside herself in preparation for the return of her son. She cleaned and scrubbed the house. Then she scraped together enough victuals for a modest feast. She had been in near constant motion, when not asleep, since Frank Forgeron had come to tell them that Tobias, Ace, and Okra were on their way back and that he would be picking them up at Martin's Sawmill outside of Harper Bay and bringing them back to her.

"He's only been gone a little more than a week", Tobit noted as she bustled around the kitchen.

"It's been nearly two!" she scolded him. "Tobit Messager, you are a calloused man."

"Not at all", he laughed. "But by the time I was Tobias' age I had been to Louisiana and back by myself. Tobias has only gone about seventy miles or so, and he had Ace and Okra with him."

"You rode a train!" replied Anna wagging her finger at him. "And you ain't my son."

"And ol' Crafty Forgeron, he was fighting in the Philippines when he was Tobias' age. You just worry too much, woman."

"You just shush now, before I take a broom to you."

"Well, since I can't see to defend myself, I reckon I'll have to concede the field", said Tobit with a shrug.

They made their way to the porch, seeking as always the autumnal sunlight of late afternoon. They had been seated only a short while when Tobit reached into his shirt pocket so he could put his dark glasses on.

"They're coming. I hear Frank's truck."

In a moment more Anna could hear it as well. As they both stood, they could hear the faint squeal of the brakes as the truck began to turn into the drive. Anna saw three men crowded abreast in the cab. Then she gave a short gasp when she saw a tawny blur leap from the back of the truck and come running down the driveway.

"That fool dog is gonna get himself run over."

Tobit laughed and stepped carefully from the porch. He lowered himself to his knees, with arms wide and welcoming.

"I hear you coming, boy! I hear ya!"

Okra leapt into his master's arms, licking at Tobit's face and knocking his dark glasses askew. Then the dog bolted over to run in circles around Anna, whining in delight but not daring to jump on his mistress.

Then, with tail and hindquarters wagging as one, he was back into his master's arms. The laughing Tobit enveloped the dog, telling him what a good and brave boy he had been.

"It ain't been but a little more than a week", Anna reminded him.

"Some weeks are longer than others, woman", smiled Tobit.

Anna reached down to remove her husband's hat from his head. She cuffed the back of his head lightly before placing the hat back in place. Tobit roared with laughter, which set Okra into an all new frenzy of joy.

Finally Anna relented and squatted beside them as ladylike as squatting allows so that Okra could throw himself against her in a rush of wagging tail and delighted whimpering and short, gleeful barks.

The truck doors opened and closed. Okra ran to the exiting men, then back to Anna and Tobit, and then back, and then back again.

Anna got to her feet and moved quickly, but with composure, to embrace her son. Then she held him off at arms distance, tilting her head to appraise him. "Well, you look to be in one piece. Good thing for a certain Astier Freeman Losrouge."

"It ain't been just over a week, Mama", Tobias laughed.

"Well, your daddy says some weeks are longer than others."

Frank Forgeron had moved around the meeting, going to Tobit. "Come on, ol' man. Take my arm here and let me take you to your son."

"Who you callin' old? You are near 'bout as old as I am."

"Only near 'bout."

"Daddy."

"Tobias, boy, you sound just fine", said Tobit as he extended his hand. Tobias shook the hand, and then Tobit pulled him into an embrace. "Boy, it is good to have you home. Your mama was near 'bout the death of me with all her worrying."

"Your father, he ain't done no worrying at all", said Anna with a roll of her eyes. "Now, y'all come inside and get something to eat. You too, Frank; every family needs its white sheep."

Frank laughed, "I wouldn't miss your cookin' for all the world, Miss Anna. Not for all the tea in China."

"You don't like tea", noted Tobit as they all made their way into the house.

"That jus' makes the trade all the easier."

They settled at the dining table, sipping coffee as Anna brought them a small ham, a pot of mashed potatoes, deviled eggs, biscuits, and collards.

"You do look like you lost some weight, though", she noted, with her eyes embracing her son.

"It's only been a week", intoned Tobias, Tobit, and Ace Redbone at the same time.

Anna pulled the ham bone out of the collards and presented it to Okra. "Here you go, you foolish dog. I'd reckon you've been nothing but a pester and a bother to them while you were away, but take this anyways."

"He has earned that treat", said the smiling Ace Redbone as he watched Okra trot proudly with the bone in his mouth to his place near the screen door. "But now he can just be a regular ol' dog for all the days remaining to him, as regular or mundane as a dog ever truly might be."

While they ate, Tobias and Ace filled them in on the events of their journey, though Ace made no mention of his confrontation with Amos Asher. It was at the table, from Frank Forgeron, that Tobias first learned about the Dunlin boys and Lenny Morris' late-night visit to the logging-shed camp.

"You didn't tell me nothing about that", he said to Ace with an accusing frown.

Ace shrugged. "It was over; no need to worry you none."

"Well, I could have at least shown Okra some appreciation for his part."

"Your mama jus' did", replied Ace with a wink.

They had finished their meal by the time the conversation had taken them to Cut Creek. With Anna's deep-dish apple pie appearing, there was a brief hold on the story as slices were passed around and coffee refilled.

Anna herself barely ate, intrigued by Ace's retelling of the Tomkins family's troubles. She kept a surreptitious eye on her son as Ace spoke of Sarah. He seemed lost within himself.

Finally Ace came to the confrontation at the dining table. He paused, as if to collect the memory. "I wish you could have seen it. You would have to imagine the great archangel rising from amidst the chaos of pride created by Satan and his angels. You would have to imagine that great battle cry, *Who is like God?* The question that can be answered only in one way, and thus brings clarity, reality itself, and casts out the confusion! Who is like God?"

Ace paused again, letting the image sink in before continuing with a smile of wonder and amusement. "You should have seen your boy. He suddenly just rises in his place. His chair goes flying back, and he levels his gaze on each and every one at the table, and he asks, *What fault is hers?*

"It burned through the despair and the confusion like that great cry of the archangel. There could be but one answer, none! She had no fault, no guilt in what had befallen her. With that question young Tobias restored sanity. Reality."

Ace shook his head as if in awe. "You just should have seen it. He just bore down upon the dark with that question, and routed evil at that table."

"I can't see a lick", said Tobit quietly—his eyes staring into nothing, but his ears hearing Okra gnawing at the ham bone in the foyer. "And yet, I *can* see it. Your words paint it in my mind, as if stirring to life a forgotten dream."

Ace told them then of how Amos Asher was found dead in the creek, and how the sheriff had determined that the man planned to commit arson, intending it to seem as if it were an act of the Klan.

Finally he told them of the sheriff's investigation at the house Amos Asher had rented.

"How could any man be so evil?" wondered Tobit aloud. "And to do it in a manner that might cast doubt on the crimes the Klan has been guilty of over the years?"

Anna fixed her gaze first on Tobias and then on Ace Redbone. "My son could have been killed. If that man had burned down where you two were sleeping, he could have been killed."

"Now, ma'am", replied Ace with a soft smile. "I wouldn't have let that happen. Didn't you ask me to bring your boy home safe to you?"

Anna nodded.

"And haven't I done so?"

Anna shook her head as she smiled. "Oh no, you walked off with my boy, but you brought a man back to us."

Ace laughed for a moment, but then grew serious. "Miss Anna, that's more true than you know right now. I'm thinking you have your suspicions. But that is for Tobias to tell."

Ace looked at him, nodding. Tobias nodded in return, and so he began the telling. He talked of Sarah. He talked of his talks with Sarah. He turned back to the confrontation and reconstructed as best he could how it came to be that he asked for her hand.

When he had finished, Tobit and Anna sat quiet and dumbfounded. Frank Forgeron was quiet as well, but he was gazing in marvel at his young assistant.

"So," Tobias finally continued, "I have the blessing of Jubal and Rose, of Ace and Okra, but besides Sarah herself, the blessing I most need is that of my mother and my father."

"Oh, Tobias", began Anna, but she could not continue as tears washed her cheeks. She did manage to nod with velvety brown eyes alight with pride, joy, and a smile upon her lips.

Tobit sat still for a moment, but then he began to nod his head and shrugged. "I think what your mother is trying to say, Tobias, is that if it's okay with Okra ..."

Forgeron laughed then rose to walk around the table and shake Tobias' hand, and then just pulled him to his feet into an embrace, though the size of the younger man nearly engulfed the older.

"I reckon I'm gonna have to work you twice as hard", Forgeron declared. "You're gonna have a wife to support, young man!"

"Oh, I want to meet her", managed Anna.

"You'll see her tomorrow", said Tobias. "Mister Jubal, Miss Rose, and Sarah are coming down tomorrow. I wanted to tell you all this before you meet her."

"I'm going to have to clean this house!" said Anna.

A wistful smile haunted Tobit's face. "She sounds beautiful. I wish I could see her with my own eyes."

The room was silent for a moment, except for the sound of Okra's bone chewing. Then Ace looked at Tobias.

"You are forgetting the gifts of Sister Charlotte", he reminded. Tobias' face lit, and he nodded as he rose from the chair and went outside to the truck. Okra jumped to his feet with the ham bone securely in his mouth and followed his young master.

When they returned, Tobias was carrying his pack. Okra dropped back onto his bed and commenced to chewing the bone again.

Sitting at the table, Tobias brought out of his pack the boxes Sister Charlotte had given him. He frowned; looking in the pack, he brought out the small copper bowl they had used in the chapel. He did not remember packing it. There was also a very small paper sack, with cheese cloth wrapped around it. Inside was a bit of charcoal.

Tobias shrugged then set the bowl on the table and placed charcoal and incense within it. Ace produced a match and lit the contents, but even before the coils of smoke could rise toward Heaven, Tobit inhaled deeply.

"Incense?"

"I had told the sisters how you missed the scent of it since we could so rarely get to Mass these days. So Sister Charlotte gave me some for you.

"She gave me this also. Well, I guess you can't see it. It's a vial of holy water from Lourdes. That's in France. People are sometimes healed by the waters there."

"I know of it", said Tobit after a soft chuckle. "I did attend Xavier Louisiana for over a year."

"She said we should wash your eyes with this holy water."

For a very long moment Tobit was still and silent, but finally his hands went to his face and he removed the dark glasses, placing them carefully into his shirt pocket. His hazy, dark eyes stared into the nothing.

Ace Redbone rose from where he was sitting and took the vial from Tobias' uncertain fingers. He walked over to Tobit. He leaned down and whispered into Tobit's ear. Nobody else could hear him, but as he spoke, Tobit sat more straight in the chair.

Ace opened the vial, and with his hands he leaned Tobit's head back. Using his forefinger and thumb he opened first one of Tobit's eyes and emptied half the vial. Then using his fingertips he closed that eye. Again with forefinger and thumb he opened the other and emptied the vial completely into it. Then the light brush of the fingertips closed that eye as well.

Ace capped the empty vial, handed it to Tobias, and then returned to his own seat. As he did so, he began to softly sing.

There is a balm in Gilead,
To make the wounded whole . . .

169

As Ace sang, Tobit sat with eyes closed, his lips moving as he rocked back and forth like an old Jew praying before the Wailing Wall. The holy water, and then tears, washed down Tobit's cheeks.

When the last words of the song faded from the lips of Ace Redbone, Tobit opened his eyes. More tears came. With them came gray-white bits and specks like crushed scale. His eyes grew wider.

"My sweet Jesus!" exclaimed Tobit. "I love him as if he were my brother, but, Lord, you certainly *do* work in mysterious ways if the first thing I see with my sight restored is the face of Frank Forgeron."

Forgeron burst out in laughter, then tears filled his own eyes. Anna threw herself from her chair to fall on her knees with her arms wrapped around Tobit's legs and her head resting on his lap. Ace reached forward and gave Tobias' shoulders a squeeze.

They heard the ham bone drop, and Okra came trotting into the room, looking uncertain at his master stroking Anna's hair in his lap. Tobit looked at the dog, and winked. Then he reached to brush at his own cheeks, blinking his eyes.

"I feel like I've got grit in my eyes", he complained. "And what is this white stuff on my cheeks?"

"That right there", said Ace. "That's providence."

Tobit lay in bed. He was watching the dark swell of Anna's hips under the covers. He was reflecting on each rise and fall of her body as she breathed in her sleep. It was a wondrous thing to look into the dark and still see.

He smiled, thinking of Frank Forgeron, who had tried to conceive of some reasonable process whereby Tobit's sight was restored. Frank reasoned that maybe it had simply been coincidence that the scale, the damaged tissue of the eye, had finally been shed with the application of the holy water. Like a scab finally being released by new-grown skin, he decided, albeit without much conviction.

He was mollified by the fact that Tobit's vision was not completely restored all at once. Throughout the evening he continued to feel grittiness in his eyes, and each time he washed them out, even with plain well water, he could see a little better. Frank had nodded firmly, each time, and opined that this reenforced his theory.

Finally Ace Redbone had said to him, "You know, Mister Forgeron, it is said that there are none so blind as those who refuse to see."

Frank just smiled sheepishly and spoke of it no more.

Anna said nothing of it. She simply looked at her husband from time to time and tears filled her eyes; then she would busy herself cleaning for the arrival of her future daughter-in-law. Finally Tobit had scolded her. "Woman, you're going to scrub all the paint and finish off this house if you don't cease with this cleaning!"

Tobit smiled at the memory of it. He moved himself closer to her so that he could feel the warmth of her alongside his own body. Then he slipped into sleep, carried by songs and prayers of thanksgiving that filled his thoughts. It was *his* mind, *his* body, *his* eyes, and it would be a miracle to him until the end of his days.

The air had a crisp, cold edge, but it was sunny and clear. Just after noon a car turned into the driveway. Okra raised a joyous alert. Tobit, Anna, and Ace hurried from the house, but Tobias had been faster.

The young man went to the rear door of the sedan and opened it. He gave Sarah his hand to help her from the seat. She was wearing the white dress he liked so much. As they turned to walk toward the rest of the Messager family, he saw his mother's hands go to her mouth in her habitual expression of surprise, and in her eyes he saw joy.

The two families met in the yard. All eyes were on Sarah, but Tobit spared a look at Jubal as they shook hands and then joined in a back-slapping embrace. The merchant's expression bore some confusion though, as Tobit's clear gaze met his.

"I was blind, but now I see. Ace will explain it", laughed Tobit. "He's good at explaining and telling."

He turned then to see his wife embracing Sarah and telling her, "You are most welcome."

"Most welcome, indeed", said Tobit when the girl slipped into his own embrace.

The next morning, Tobit thought he was the first to rise, but he saw that Okra was not on his bed by the door, so he looked outside and saw the dog sitting next to Ace Redbone on the porch steps.

Tobit went out the door, noticing Ace's duffle packed and sitting at the ready with his guitar case on the porch.

"Are you leaving us, cousin?"

Ace looked up from rubbing Okra's back. "I need to get on. I have obligations."

"Surely you weren't going to leave without saying good-bye?"

"Most certainly not", replied Ace with a laugh. "I ain't gonna leave without having some of Miss Anna's breakfast! No, I was just talkin' to Okra here. We've formed quite a partnership this last week or two."

"He's been a blessing", said Tobit. "I guess I have had many."

Ace nodded. "You have had your tribulations, but in the end it looks as if blessings will trump them. A beautiful and charming wife of great inner strength. A brave, determined son. Friends, like the Reverend Walker. And even a man like Francis George Forgeron, who is a mystery even to himself, but has been steadfast at your side."

"And a cousin who appears from nowhere with songs, smiles, and a joyous heart", added Tobit with an Ace-like wink.

They ate breakfast together with the extended family, and Ace even sang a few songs for them. When it was time for Ace to depart, they all gathered to bid him farewell. Reluctant to see him off, they followed him down the drive to the road—Anna and Tobit hand in hand, Rose and Jubal hand in hand, Sarah and Tobias hand in hand, and Okra trotting beside Ace.

At the road, Ace Redbone paused. He embraced each of them, and scooped Okra up for a moment to receive licks to his cheek.

"I wish you'd let me drive you at least to Harper Bay", protested Jubal.

"I like walking", said Ace.

"It's a shame Mister Forgeron won't get to say good-bye", said Tobias with a shrug.

"Oh, I will probably see him again some day", replied Ace with a smile. Then he waved and began walking. They watched him until he disappeared around the curve of the road. Okra did not whine or fret; he seemed to accept the properness of it all and trotted happily back to the house so he could continue with worrying at the ham bone.

As everyone else turned to head back to the house, Jubal chuckled to himself and said, "You know, that's the smilingest man I think ever I've seen."

Anna nodded. "It was an infectious thing too, weren't it?"

"His coming when he did turned out to be a huge blessing", said Tobit.

"Providential", Tobias decided aloud.

The day after the Tomkins returned home, Tobit, Tobias, and Anna were busy about the homestead trying to get caught up on chores that had lapsed in Tobit's blindness and Tobias' absence. They were alerted to a car approaching by Okra's barking.

A black sedan pulled into the drive. Nobody knew the driver, but Frank Forgeron was in the passenger seat. The Messagers gathered at the edge of the drive waiting for the two men to get out of the car.

The man with Forgeron was a white man of medium height, sandy-colored hair, and green eyes. He was well dressed, in a gray suit and a fine, stylish fedora.

"Tobit", said Frank as handshakes were offered and taken. "This here is Oliver Weston. He's the grandson of Judge Oliver."

"I can understand if I'm not welcomed here", said the man plainly. "But Mister Forgeron says you are good folk who won't hold the sins of my cousin Charles against me."

"No, sir, we wouldn't", said Tobit.

"Mister Tobit," began Oliver Weston, "you probably know that with the death of the judge, half of his estate went to my cousin. But now, with my cousin having died without issue, it has passed back to my side of the family.

"Well, we need a foreman in this county. Someone the Negro farmers will trust, and from what I can tell, the white ones too, at least those worth working with.

"Mister Tobit, I'd like you to take your old job back. Same terms as you had with my grandfather. Think about it for a day or two. I'll be back in the county in a week; we can talk then. Do you think you'll be interested?"

"Yessir", said Tobit. "I'll think it over like you said, but right now, well, I think I'd be a fool not to take your generous offer."

"You deserve it, Mister Tobit. The judge always spoke highly of you, as does my mother to this day. Very highly", said Weston. "I'm a lawyer, Mister Tobit. I don't have much time for running the company. I've got some good men that worked for my grandfather that I've promoted to run the outfit. To a man they say you're the one we need in this county.

"But, my being a lawyer brings me to another issue. I've done some research, some prying even. Things are not the same in Harper Bay as they once were. You feel free to go back anytime, Mister Tobit. The old guard is gone, so to speak. I am not suggesting the new guard is without flaw, but your slate is clean now in Harper Bay, as it should have been all along."

Oliver Weston turned then to look at Tobias. "Mister Forgeron tells me that your son is to be married. Congratulations."

"Thank you, sir", replied Tobias.

"You know," said Weston, turning back to Tobit, "there is no reason he can't be married at the Negro parish in Harper Bay."

"It's looking at this time like we'll be having the wedding at the bride's church", said Anna. "That's customary, and they'll have a new colored church early next year."

"But," Tobit added, "we'll certainly be going to Sunday Mass regular now that we can go to Harper Bay. I thank you for that information and whatever part you played in it."

"It was nothing, really, Mister Tobit", said Weston. "I just clarified some issues is all. There is one last thing, Mister Tobit."

Oliver Weston removed his fedora, fretting at the brim of it with his fingers as he looked at the ground and collected himself. "It's about Mabel Farmer, and James. I don't think the whole truth will ever be let out, but *I* know it. I can't bring that boy back, Mister Tobit. I can't take back the pain my uncle and cousin caused Missus Farmer. But, I would like to do something."

He paused, gathering himself. "I would like to help the Farmer family in some way. Help her other children. Mister Forgeron suggested I talk to the Reverend Walker. He'd know of a way to do such a thing without offending Mabel Farmer."

"That is the best way to go about it", agreed Tobit.

"Good. Also, if you take your position back, there might be other ways you and I can help them without them knowing."

"They should know."

"I wouldn't want to bruise their pride, Mister Tobit."

"No, but they can be made aware of some things, Mister Weston. Made aware in a manner that will make them realize that not all your family is like your uncle or your cousin."

"Yes, I suppose so", said Weston, finally returning his hat to his head. "I can see that the first step to whatever healing might be possible could begin with them knowing that as dark and cruel as the world might be, it isn't always as dark as my uncle and cousin made it."

Weston released a deep sigh. "Well, next week then."

"Next week, and thank you, sir", replied Tobit, shaking the man's hand.

With that Oliver Weston and a grinning Frank Forgeron returned to the car. Tobit, Anna, and Tobias watched it motor off along the drive and disappear down the road.

"Well, if that don't beat all", said Anna as they turned back toward the house. Tobit stopped when he saw that while Tobias was smiling, there was an air of confusion to his countenance.

"You're thinking about poor Jamie, aren't you, son?"

Tobias nodded but hesitated before finally speaking, "I can't help it, Daddy. I was just thinking about how Mister Weston wants to help Jamie's family, but he says himself that he can't help Jamie. The boy died. He died in a way I don't think even Sheriff Oliver deserved to die. I dunno; just don't seem fair."

A sad smile touched Tobit's lips as he stepped toward Tobias and placed his hand flat upon his son's chest, over his heart. "That is the great hope of faith, son. Ain't none of us can undo what happened to Jamie. We can only have hope that the Lord in his mercy and grace will undo the hurt and injustice for Jamie.

"I trust that mystery, son. I trust it because it's all we have. I trust it because it seems that every time evil works a darkness upon the world the Lord brings something beautiful from it. Jamie himself was a beautiful thing worked from a great evil."

Tobias replied with a pondering nod. Tobit smiled more broadly, raising his hand to squeeze his son's shoulder as he steered him toward the house. "Just think on it, Tobias. Think on everything that has happened since our own misfortunes came upon us. Jamie's family is going to be helped. Young Lenny saved from a dark road he was following. Sarah saved from a darkness I reckon I don't even want to be thinking 'bout. On top of that, you have brought that girl into our lives."

"I reckon I can't argue with that", replied Tobias.

The first Monday after Sarah had returned with her parents to their home, Tobias returned to work. Frank Forgeron was already there and fidgeting with a carburetor he was rebuilding when Tobias entered the shop.

The older man looked up. "Morning, Tobias. We sure have some work been piling up in your absence. I just don't seem to work as fast as I used to. Guess you've made me lazy."

"You're about the least lazy man I've ever known, excepting my father."

"You and Sarah set a date yet?"

"No, sir. We're going to do that in January. Officially, anyway. We're thinking late spring."

"You have plans for a honeymoon?"

"I don't know. We've talked about it some. Mister Jubal insists on helping to pay for it. He says that he regrets not being able to afford a honeymoon for either of his marriages.

"I've been thinking that I'd like to take Sarah to the seashore. She loves lighthouses, so I was thinking of taking her to see one. I have to check on buses and places that might let colored folk stay. I've heard tell of a boarding house that is run by a colored couple for coloreds."

"It would be a might sight easier if you had a car", mused Forgeron as he set aside the carburetor and began wiping his hands on a rag. "That way you wouldn't have to fret with buses and what not. Shoot, you could just drive along the coast, sight seeing."

Tobias nodded. "I reckon we could. I reckon Mister Jubal might even lend us his car, but that sure would make me a nervous wreck."

Forgeron laughed, "I can see that, son. I surely can. Not the best way to begin a marriage by having some misfortune with your father-in-law's automobile."

Forgeron put his hands on his hips, looking like an hourglass with his elbows thrust out from his hips above, and his bowed legs below. He eyed Tobias with serious intent.

"I've been giving some thought to what kind of wedding present I could give you. Well, you know that ol' Model A you've been working on all these years?"

"The Tudor Deluxe", said Tobias reflexively.

"Son, I know what it is", chided Frank. "Well, it's yours. No, wait, I know what you're gonna say. You're as bad as your father 'bout these things. It's too much, you're gonna say. Well, you would be right.

"So, here is what I propose."

He reached over to a cleared area of the work bench and slapped his hand down on a piece of paper resting there. "This here is a list of all the parts I bought to repair that Model A Tudor Deluxe over the years. As you are able, you pay me back. Maybe a headlight bracket one week, a wheel stud another, and so on.

176

"The labor was almost all your'n. So, my wedding present to you would be only what I paid for the wreck, and that other wreck we scavenged from. What do ya think?"

Tobias nodded his head slowly and with a growing sense of marvel. "I think, sir, that is still most generous. I think too, sir, that I will gladly accept such a present!"

"Good man", laughed Frank Forgeron. Then he grew serious and wagged his finger at Tobias. "You listen here to me, though. Listen good. While you're driving that pretty bride along the seashore, don't be telling her the make, model, and year of every daggum vehicle you see."

With a sheepish smile Tobias replied, "No, sir. I won't. I promise."

Epilogue

Francis George Forgeron felt his joints aching because of the drizzling cold. He had been to London as a sergeant on his way to France during the Great War, but that had been at the height of the summer. He thought then that a warm English summer made for a passable late spring in North Carolina.

Now, based on these past two days, he thought an early English spring made for a passable early winter in North Carolina. He consoled himself that at least the beer was very good.

Not that his doctor would be pleased with that observation. The man had been warning him that his health was in severe shape for many years. That was why Forgeron had finally decided to retire. A bad ticker and high blood pressure had connived with arthritic hands to convince him the time had come.

London still showed signs of the second war, even now, fifteen years after the last air raid had struck the city. The proud English pointed out how much they had rebuilt in those years, and Forgeron was suitably impressed.

Bored with retirement, but no longer up to stopping by Crafty's Repair to give Tobias any worthwhile help, Frank Forgeron had decided he would like to visit Europe again, in a time of peace. He set aside his ancestral Huguenot prejudice and had visited Rome, even touring Vatican City. He had to admit that the Catholics did at least two things admirably: ritual and art.

He had gone through France, happy to see it in peace. He had even, at Tobit's suggestion, visited a few places in Germany that had escaped major damage in the war. Tobit had told him it would be good for his soul to see a former enemy who was an enemy no longer. It was, in a way, painful, but Tobit had been right.

Forgeron had sold his shop to Tobias, a few years after the second war had ended. Tobias had served in the war, though what little action he saw was secondary as a mechanic in the motor pool. Of course, he could tell you anything you wanted to know about every jeep, truck, or tank he had worked on.

The thought of it made Frank smile. The young man had taken his advice though. He had not let it interfere with the romancing of his young bride. They had six children over the years: twin boys, three daughters, and then a final boy. Sadly, there had been a stillborn son between the last two daughters.

Life always had some hardness to it, thought Frank as the taxi let him out next to Trafalgar Square, near the domed amalgamation known as the National Gallery. That hardness, that problem with pain, sorrow, and evil, that was why Frank Forgeron had never quite been able to truly believe in God. Ol' Tobit had told him though that he had managed to become a preacher of the Gospel with deeds rather than words. Frank was not so sure, but he appreciated the compliment, especially from a man like Tobit Messager.

Because of Tobit, Frank kept trying. He attended services at Gaston Walker's church most Sundays until the reverend had retired. He even went to a Mass with Tobit from time to time. He wanted to believe. He tried hard to believe. Tobit told him desire itself was a strand of faith.

Standing in the fine, misty rain, he considered the steps leading to the National Gallery. He wondered if his doctor would consider that mild exercise or strenuous activity. It did not matter; he had not come all this way just to get back into a taxi and return to the hotel.

He wandered the museum, taking in the sights. He had always been fond of art, especially sculpture. That was the tactile sort of art that a mechanic could understand. Yet today, it was a painting that caused him to halt for another look. He would have passed on by these people painted in their frilly clothes, but for his eye catching the small printed sign that read *Tobias and the Angel.*

Frank snorted. "That don't look a bit like Tobias, or Okra."

"Excuse me, sir?" asked a voice with a lingering East End accent.

Frank looked over to see a ruddy-cheeked, uniformed guard addressing him. He just shook his head. "Nothing really; I just knew a boy named Tobias once. He had a dog like the fellow in this here picture. But his dog, Okra, wasn't such a little foo-foo-looking critter as that."

"Ah", replied the guard. "You see what they've done here, sir, is they've got this one you saw. It's an original. Then they have all these reproductions around it, some full size, as examples of how this has been portrayed by artists over the centuries."

"Oh yeah, I see that", mused Forgeron. "Some of them people don't look so frilly, or their dogs so ridiculous as others."

"No, sir", chuckled the guard. "They do not. It's all from the book of Tobit. It's in the Bible, well at least the Catholic and Orthodox Bibles, and maybe some others. I can't make claim to being an expert at the Bible."

"I reckon I've read it in bits and pieces", replied Forgeron.

"I have, however, heard some of the tour guides say that it is the dog itself, in that story, that is one of the reasons the book isn't in many of the Protestant Bibles. Something about Jews, and other Semites, in those days thinking dogs were unclean animals. They say the dog is probably a holdover from a Persian story, or the like. That being the case, and some other factors, they don't consider it to be what they call canonical."

"Well, I can't imagine a silly little dog like that one traipsing across the countryside or helping run off the Dunlin brothers", laughed Frank. "And look at that little fish that young man is aholding onto there. You couldn't feed three men, five nuns, and a dog with that thing."

"No, you could not", replied a voice from where the guard was standing. "It would take a near record-sized catfish from Catfish Creek, I'm reckoning."

Frank felt a twinge in his chest, a tingle down his arm. He frowned, feeling dizzy, as he turned toward the guard. He saw the blue uniform, but the smiling face was not that of a ruddy-cheeked Englishman.

"Ace?"

"I have been called that", replied Ace Redbone with a smile and a wink.

"You haven't changed a bit", said Forgeron with a frown. His mind was cloudy. He was suddenly so very tired.

"They say my kind are changeless", said Ace Redbone as he studied the art work.

It was all just too confusing, too perplexing for Forgeron. He felt his legs going rubbery and another jolt of pain in his chest. Then a thin streak of clarity shot through his mind like lightning. Thinking maybe now he understood, he looked over to Ace Redbone.

"I'm not going home, am I?"

Ace gave him a gentle, admonishingly humorous expression, with one raised eyebrow. "Why, Francis George Forgeron, home is *exactly* where you are going."

Frank felt a hand on his arm, guiding him to a chair. Another shot of pain caused him to wince.

"Are you all right, sir?"

Frank looked up as he was sitting down, and saw that the ruddy-cheeked guard was easing him into the chair. It made Frank smile.

"Don't be concerned, my friend", he managed in a short-breathed reply. "I ain't walkin' out of here, but I think for the first time in my life, I am truly all right."

It was a blustery day. Tobias loved days like this, especially in the spring when they held a kind of ominous promise. Large, sparsely spaced clouds were parading across a sharp azure sky as he puttered around the cemetery, picking out weeds, but mostly just enjoying the warm sunlight.

He smiled at the tombstone standing near where he had just plucked a dandelion. It was that of his old boss. Mister Forgeron—he would always be *mister* to Tobias—had passed away while on vacation some years back.

In accordance with his will, he had been cremated in England and shipped back to the United States. He had always pointed out that this was much less expensive than embalming and burying a body. The thought of Forgeron's frugality even in death made Tobias laugh out loud.

Another part of Mister Forgeron's will had been more problematic. He had asked to be "buried with that old, ass-kicking mule that had belonged to Tobit Messager. That old mule might have been the best kisser I've ever known."

I'm too old to laugh this hard, Tobias thought. Ol' Joe-boy had died fifteen years before Frank Forgeron, just after the war had ended. Tobias' father had buried the old mule on the slope of a low, ridgelike knoll that overlooked Rush-Knott Creek. Nobody at first could imagine how to honor Forgeron's last request.

There was some talk of spreading Frank's ashes around Joe-boy's grave, but this did not set with Tobit's Catholic sensibility. He checked into laws and regulations concerning disposing of the deceased. In the end, he and Tobias had built a low wall of coquina block. The wall bound most of the knoll on three sides, with the fourth side only a quarter walled. If the wall had been connected, the body of Joe-boy would have been to one side of it, and the small wooden casket built by Tobit containing the ashes of Francis George Forgeron would have been just on the other. Frank Forgeron was the first person, and only white person, buried in what would become the Messager Family Cemetery.

Tobias studied the epitaph engraved on the tombstone: *A man with more conscience than even he knew.* It had been suggested by Tobit Messager. Forgeron's brothers had thought it perfect.

Just about four feet beyond that tombstone there was a flat, eight-foot-by-five-foot concrete slab. With his own hands Tobit had engraved an epitaph for Joe-boy not long after the mule had been buried: *He brought down the temple of Dagon, in the city of the Philistines.* Tobias was willing to allow his father a bit of artistic license, remembering that old tar-paper shack. Tobit Messager could often be a stubborn, solemn man, but he was not without a sense of humor.

Ten feet down along the line of the invisible wall was another, smaller slab of concrete near Tobit's grave. Upon it was written *Okra, the eyes of my soul.* Tobias shook his head.

Over the years his father had become convinced that during the journey of Ace, Tobias, and Okra, he had somehow seen much of what was happening in his dreams, by way of Okra's eyes. Tobias had always been perplexed by his father's odd blending of pragmatism and romanticism.

His father had been bothered by dreams at that time. It was not unexpected given the psychological pressures on the man. Tobias had come to suspect that it was his own recalling of how Okra had kept reminding him along the way of his father's presence waiting at home that had fed his father's notions. Sarah had shushed him on occasion, telling him that he was all too willing to talk himself out of miracles.

He had nowhere near the faith his father, mother, or Sarah did. Tobit told him it was because men like himself and Frank Forgeron needed a tangible world. That's why they had become mechanics. They wanted to touch and feel the connectivity of creation. They had an intense distaste, perhaps even fear, of doubt.

Tobit had told him that nobody hated or feared doubt, however, so much as an atheist. He said they were so repulsed by the reality of doubt that they constructed for themselves a small, materialistic reality that even their own philosophies and laws were proof against. No one is so deluded as someone who has no doubt, Tobit often asserted. He scoffed at their pretending that reality could be perfectly measured and tested.

Tobit had much more respect for what he called the *intellectual integrity* of agnostics, men like Frank Forgeron, whom he considered to be more self-aware than atheists, and more so than even many religious folk. Tobias was not really an agnostic, but it streaked his uncertain faith. His faith seemed ironic to most, as he found it easier to believe with his intellect than his emotions. He could understand intellectual arguments for God. He *desired* with his heart, but that same heart was haunted by the existence of evil and sorrow, no matter what theories his mind offered as explanation.

He looked over the cemetery. His father had been among the last to die. He had outlived Jubal, Rose, and even Anna. Tobit had lived to be one hundred and two years old. He had watched on television the speech of Martin Luther King Jr. in Washington.

One of his grandchildren asked Tobit what he thought about all of that. Ancient then, Tobit had smiled and said he felt like Moses on Mount Nebo. He said he wouldn't live to walk in this new Promised Land. Then he had wagged his finger at the younger folk, grandchildren and great-grandchildren, and had admonished them, "Don't y'all squander it. Don't y'all dare."

Tobias looked at all the tombstones, including the little one for his and Sarah's stillborn son. They had named him Astier, because he was an enigma to them. They had known him only in the womb, and only through what they had imagined his life might be like.

They had named him after Ace, because Ace had been an enigma. They had tried to contact him, but it never came to be. The family in Louisiana had conflicting memories of him. The oldest folk said he had disappeared years ago, and they thought he had been killed when a great storm had struck the coast, but that had been even before he had come to visit Tobit and his family. Others reported stories they'd heard of relatives having seen him, though nobody had actually done so themselves. A few insisted that he had gone over to Europe when the second war started.

Tobias had asked his father once, "What was it that Ace said to you, just before he poured the holy water into your eyes?"

Many years had passed, but Tobit smiled as if it had happened only a few days before, and he replied, *"Be strong, fear not! Here is your God, he comes with vindications. With divine recompense he comes to save you. Then will the eyes of the blind be opened."*

Ace had told Tobias once that life had no happily ever after until Heaven was merged completely with the created world around them. Or maybe his father had said that he dreamed of Ace saying some such. Tobias had grown old himself, very old, and alone now with his beloved Sarah's recent passing. There was so much to remember, and increasingly he remembered it poorly.

For sure, though, those words had been true enough. There was his son, Astier. He thought too of Davis Johnson. He had prospered as Jubal's foreman, and yet his life was no happily ever after. One of his sons had died near the end of the second war.

Life was odd. The Dunlin boys had both come back from the war as decorated heroes. The oldest boy had not changed and died when he had crashed his car while driving drunk. Michael Dunlin, however, had been much changed. He had gone to college after the war and become a prosperous, generous, and ethical businessman in the Memphis area.

Then there was Lenny. He had become a lawyer, more specifically a civil-rights lawyer. He was known also for an idiosyncrasy: a patch of green-plaid fabric that he called his lucky charm. He carried it with him always. He said it had changed his life and served as a reminder of a debt he would work to repay all his remaining days.

Of course, the life of Leonard Levi Morris was not entirely happy. His wife had died of cancer when she was only thirty-six years upon the Earth. One of his sons, always an overly sensitive child, had never recovered and had committed suicide when he was only twenty years of age. But Lenny persevered, loved by his three surviving and thriving children.

Tobias felt exhausted all of a sudden. It happened when you got old and creaky. He sat down next to the small slab of concrete covering Okra's grave. The surface of the slab was warm to his hand as he eased himself to the ground. Looking again to the southeast he saw a large flock of birds folding over itself as it twisted and turned in the air, while the blustery winds echoed their movements in the marsh grasses below.

"It's confusing, Okra", he quietly posited. "It weakens my faith, but I won't let go."

He laughed at himself. He was thinking of epitaphs. He knew what his would be. It would come from John 6:68. Anytime he had expressed how the darkness in the world worried at him, his father would quote that passage. For Tobit, it reflected more than just the Catholic teaching of the real presence in the Eucharist; it was a reality a doubting man like his son could cling to. So Tobias had arranged that his own epitaph would read *Lord, to whom would we go?*

He tilted his face to the sun. His hand rested on the warm concrete slab. He imagined that a wet, pointy nose was sniffing at his fingers in greeting.